PUPPET
PEOPLE

Puppet People

Chapter 1

We boarded the eight-thirty bus like a funeral procession–heads bent with death on our minds. At least mine was. I shuffled past the bus driver and took an empty seat with my bag taking up the spot next to me. Tiffany, my adopted mother, took that as a sign and ushered her real daughter, eight-year-old Mora, to a spot near the back. The latter let out a small whine but was shushed by our mother.

"You know what today is, darling," Tiffany said. I heard clattering as she rearranged her purse full of candy, which she would later sneak into the movie theater. "It's your sister's special day. So be nice to Kindle." I tried not to perk up at the sound of my own name and the way she said it. Like this was some kind of fun experience for me.

The bus driver looked back. His eyes swept the crowded seats as he took in the night's final passengers. Nodding, he announced Miami Beach as the next stop into his mic.

Meanwhile, Tiffany was telling Mora more about how the beach was special to my parents. It wasn't really, but I didn't have the energy to say otherwise. My parents had never taken me to the beach. At least I don't think so. Memories were still tricky, still fuzzy, despite four years of amnesic therapy.

It was the fourth anniversary of the car crash. One I could barely remember. It was the accident that killed Mother, Father, Poppy, and Vince.

In my bag, I had four small marionette puppets that resembled them ready for burial. Their bodies were never found, and unmarked graves named simply "Mr. and Mrs. Kerr" with my siblings underneath did some kind of job, so I took it upon myself to bury fragments of them in the tourist-trampled sand of Miami. Good luck and karma were put up there with dragons and unicorns–but I pretended there was some kind of redemption to burying them. Mother was the one who taught me how to make puppets and dolls. Father was a collector. Puppets practically ran through our blood.

I placed my head on the window, breathing in the smell of tourists. Sand, sunscreen, and sea salt. Soon the bus rocked on its wheels, announcing the stop. I stood, the only one, hugging my bag tighter to my chest, my long blond hair grazing across my face. Tiffany gave me a thumbs-up.

"You know, the beach is about to close," the bus driver said as I got closer.

"Yes, but I'll be here next stop."

"Nine-thirty."

"I know." I gave him a small smile, one that certainly didn't reach my eyes, and jostled my way down the steps. With a hiss, the bus pulled away, whisking away Tiffany and Mora who waved from their seats.

As the bus driver had said, there was nobody around. Even beer-laden tourists knew not to scramble for the last bus. Not that I cared. I liked being alone. And one day when I booked it for a medical school far, far away, I wouldn't have to worry about being stuck in a city bearing my story. A story nobody knew—least of all me.

Seagulls called their last cries goodnight as the ocean cradled the shoreline. Under the fuzzy lights of the pathway, I found my way across the boardwalk and to the sand, scanning for a place to bury the puppets.

The water was pitch-black, only gaining a bluish hue under the light of the full moon. I shuffled forward, the tan sand scattering under every step. Despite living in Miami for four years, I never truly got used to the ocean. The vastness, the deepness, the coldness.

I stepped closer to the ocean. It was the only thing that made the right noise. The noise I heard between patches of memory. The whoosh, whoosh, whoosh, ever persistent. My hippocampus somehow knew those were happy memories—the patches. There were medical terms, medical reasons for all of this. I loved how science all made sense. Death didn't.

I crouched down, brushing broken seashells out of the way to make a smooth surface. It didn't matter where I buried the puppets. The famed beach was much too large to have a regular spot. After fifteen minutes of digging, I had four small holes. Hands already shaking from exhaustion, I pulled out a puppet.

Father. A family man. Always there for his kids, making them laugh, reading to them late at night. He went on business trips a lot. I don't remember much else. Just ideas. Scraps of concrete memories. I buried him in the first hole before digging around for Mother's puppet so they could be together.

Mother was a creative woman. She was always inventing new things and giving us whatever we desired. Smart too. She home-schooled the three of us.

I buried her with grace.

Poppy came next from the bag. Jesus. She would be, like, thirteen now. Almost a teenager, but I had made her puppet still a child. If she had had more time, what would she have done with it? She loved the garden Father had dug for her. I couldn't quite remember where. For some reason, it felt like it was in the middle of the house, but Mother was too clean for that.

Next came Vince. He was a year older than me. He'd be eighteen. He'd have graduated. What would he have done next? It hurt too much to look at my best friend, so I buried him swiftly.

I wiped my hands on my sand-stained jeans so I could bat at my eyes, which were wet at the realization that no matter how far I got out of Miami, I'd still carry the same old grief.

That thought ignited fire throughout me. It practically split me in half. I grabbed a fistful of sand and hurled it at the sky. If God could hear me, I wanted to let Him know. I wanted everyone to know. To know this pain and suffering.

"I hate this! I hate it!" My voice sent tremors through my spine and skull. "Every year! I want to go home! I want to get out of here! I want to leave!"

And as if someone had heard, an explosive noise came from behind me, from the sky. It was like the moon had crumbled. Like a firework right behind my brain.

I craned my neck back for a reasonable explanation over the Miami skyline.

The sky was clear, but there seemed to be something…falling? My heart shriveled. It wasn't airplane-shaped, and it was descending straight down like it had been dropped. I kept a hand above my eyes and stepped back.

This couldn't be. It was a giant hook. One as big as a car coming from the sky.

My mind hurt. It pumped nonsense. Words with no meaning. Ideas that shouldn't be real. This shouldn't be real.

It was swooping lower, skimming over beach resorts, picking up speed, my way. I screeched, spinning back to the beach. Nobody was there. Just me. Me and this thing.

My head pounded and my brain trapped me in a cage of words. Run! Run! Where? The ocean. It was the only place.

I stumbled along the sand becoming deaf to everything but a roaring noise like a thundercloud that wouldn't stop rumbling. The freezing and salty water shook as I plunged in.

I tried to abort the mission when the water came up to my hips. The hook was right above me. I gasped as a wave hit my chest and shoulders. My eyes stung. I was going to hyperventilate or maybe even go into shock. The roaring noise got louder. Seashells cut my feet. The waves were up to my ribcage, each one sent me tumbling back like a boxing match. I reached up to wipe my eyes, but another hit me, and I went under. Pressing myself off the ocean floor with frozen limbs, I resurfaced. "Mother!" Another wave hit, getting salt into my mouth and cracked lips. "Father!"

Which way was the shore? The waves seemed to appear out of nowhere and my soaked clothes were weighing me down. The bottom was getting farther away. I couldn't reach it anymore.

Something huge stabbed my shoulder. I screamed as it punched through flesh and tissue.

Then the pain was gone, like the sand and water.

The only part of me I could move were my eyes, but just barely. After many tries, they flickered open to stars–thousands and thousands of stars high above the beach.

Chapter 2

My vision blinked rapidly between blinding light and cold darkness. There were flashes of blond fur or hair so bleached one might mistake it for white. I was lying on a wooden shelf. Something kept pinching my wrists and knees. A constant smell of heat combined with the slow and steady pinching pattern, made me feel like I was being sewn together. Voices boomed from all around, but they were jumbled. Something or someone jerked me into a sitting position. There was only the light, but occasionally a shadow would dip in.

My body strained. I was dangling now, hanging from something attached to my wrists.

Screams and shouts. Something rammed the back of my skull. I pitched forward, falling. Falling forever.

***

Birds called while a chill shocked my nerves. My arms and legs swung like a clock's pendulum as I walked. I forced myself to stop moving, to go back to sleep, but I couldn't. But my body wouldn't listen to its own nervous system.

I shook the grogginess away before opening my eyes.

Color hit me first. Bright greens and browns bathing in natural light. They melded together forming the shapes of a mountainous forest with white clouds above thinning out like thread on a spool. The trees were bunched together, spreading above like a tunnel. The ground was a dirty path with strange blue mushrooms sprouting. The trail was cut oddly like it was in a hurry, but there was nobody around but me.

This wasn't Florida. What had happened? My stomach sank, and I tried to gag. My breathing was shallow.

"Hello?" I squeaked. The birds stopped. "Hey!" My voice shook as it boomed across the forest. "Somebody let me out of here!"

Nobody did.

I coughed out a sob, my eyes welling up. Oh God, where was I? What was wrong with my body? I had to move. I had to. I focused deeply on my right arm, willing it to stop swinging. I stared until my vision shook. Gasping, I closed my eyes. This didn't do anything. It was like I was in someone else's body altogether. I couldn't control anything.

As I rounded a bend, I caught up to a row of people my age. My heart swelled. I wasn't alone. If I could get closer, maybe one could hear me. We all walked in the same formation. When my arms swung, so did theirs. Continuing up the hill we were climbing, everybody had a horizontal brown cross over their head, each with thick skin-colored strands coming down to attach to the wrists and knees.

My stomach hurt like someone had poured acid inside and hit blend.

They were marionette puppets.

No.

Closing my eyes, my knees jerked forward by themselves.

We were marionette puppets.

But this was just a bad dream, right? I just had to wake up. But I couldn't. The harder I tried, the more I realized how wrong I was. My mind blurring, I flashed back to the beach. That hook, the way it came from the sky, this landscape, those weird creatures. I had been abducted...by aliens. But this couldn't be. Aliens weren't real. But how else could I explain it? And whatever was going to happen next, I was going to have to do it with someone else controlling me.

The boy in front of me was carrying a backpack full of pickaxes.

"Hey!" I was just as surprised by my voice as he was. Besides a gasp, he didn't show any other indication he'd heard me. "What's going on?" I tried again, hurried now. "Where are we?"

Still no answer.

I tried twisting my neck and head but could only get my pupils to dart. The clouds were darkening. Not a good sign.

"Listen, I'm new here. I-I don't know what's going on. Who abducted us?" I swallowed, my throat feeling like it had been wiped down with sandpaper. "Who's controlling me?"

This got some attention. His strings jangled and his head twisted backward to almost an inhuman degree. His face sent chills. He looked tired; any spark of life was gone from his eyes. He glanced up at his marionette controller, just like the one I had made a few hours ago. Or had it been days?

"The Puppeteer," he said, voice distant.

"What? Who?" But his head snapped back like a spring. After a few minutes of trying to get his attention again, I gave up.

The forest ended in a mountain range, with the path fading out into the opening of a large cave mouth. I tried to force my body to get away from the lion's mouth we were heading into. But one by one I watched my fellow abductees get swallowed into the damp darkness. As they disappeared, their footsteps faded away. My heartbeat quickened, head lightening. Just by getting close, cold air hit me, but I couldn't even shiver.

The path curved down a ramp, and black took over my vision. Further ahead, wheels squeaked, and metal clashed against metal. My mouth dried. I could be walking right into my grave, and I'd be helpless to stop it. My screams spiraled down into the darkness.

Rounding a corner, I was hit by a strong light. My screams stuttered. A massive mine played out in front of me. I flinched at the dazzling walls zigzagging with veins of a golden sap. Most of the other marionettes swung pickaxes at the walls, not even stepping back when they were showered in mini avalanches of dirt and pebbles. I coughed at the fog of dust which sprayed back from some of the bigger swings. I got a whiff of something familiar as I sputtered, but I couldn't place it. A few marionettes were wheeling minecarts from person to person, collecting the gold. But no matter what they were doing, everyone had the same blank expression.

Moving forward, my controller hovered downward to fit inside the tight chamber. Keeping close to the walls, I was forced to a cart. Leaning over, I could see one last pickaxe, like it was made for me. My hands gripped the gritty handle and swung it back over my shoulder, but not even gravity could make me stumble over as my strings tightened to keep me upright. Was this that Puppeteer's doing? Or had that guy been messing with me? Glancing at the people around me, I doubted anyone had any emotions left to joke.

I ambled over to an empty wall and without any kind of hesitation, swung deep at the gold veins embedded deep inside the rock. Chunks of dusty rocks came off.

Aliens…how did they hide from us for so long?

A girl came up beside me. She had messy black hair that went down to her hips and swung harder than my controller forced me to. I was probably getting the amateur treatment. Despite how close she was, I felt a million miles away. A million miles away from sanity.

I had to try though.

"Hey," I said, but I might as well have been invisible. "Hey!" I shouted, this time making her eyes nervously dart my way before returning to her axe.

"Listen, I just want to know where we are. I mean, obviously, we were abducted…right?"

She didn't answer, but her eyes said yes.

"How long have you been here?" I asked.

No answer.

I sighed. I wanted to fight again, find a way to get out of these strings, but from what I could see they were a part of me. Some kind of skin? Or tissue? Maybe muscles? Or maybe it was some kind of alien substance. Something I would never comprehend. Whatever it was, struggling was useless.

"We don't usually talk."

I would have jumped if I could have. I glanced over at the girl, blurting: "Why not?"

"The Puppeteer doesn't like it."

Again, with this "Puppeteer" person. "Who's that?"

Her eyes flickered upward. "She's our savior."

I laughed, but her piercing eyes told me otherwise.

"But didn't she abduct us?"

She swung against the wall, hard. I could practically hear her teeth rattle. Almost like her controller was angry at her. Or whoever was controlling her was.

"Please. I don't want to talk anymore," she said, her voice watery.

"Uh, okay." My face heated. Already I was making people upset. Maybe I should just shut up.

My axe hit the wall again, revealing a yellow, glittery trail ingrained in the rock. Something changed with my controller and strings. I moved much faster to grab a bucket and fill it with the gold flecks. The rock didn't have any unique properties–it was just dried, yellow glitter glue–and when the bucket was full, I placed them next to other full buckets.

After what must have been hours of hit, gather, repeat–with no psychical strain on my body–I returned the axe and soon we were marching back through the mountains again.

By this time, I was next to brain-dead. My mind had nothing but swing, hit, and gather as a constant replay. I heard it, I saw it, I felt it in every crevice of my mind.

I ended up nowhere near the boy I talked to earlier or the girl in the cave, so I couldn't ask where we were going. Not like they would have answered anyway. Which meant we could be going anywhere. Another cave? Maybe the aliens' spaceship? Which brought up the point if I was even on Earth anymore. A little voice told me that was stupid–of course we were–but the rest of me said to shut up and look around. Look at the buildings we were approaching. They looked almost heart-breakingly like Earth.

There was a main building and a smaller one connected by a silver tunnel. The main building was massive and looked to be made of pure silver with no windows or doors.

This thing, the smaller building…was a literal dollhouse. No other way to explain it. With its gorgeous purple exterior and rose-red roof it was a gothic castle. Golden lights poured from what had to be ten-thousand windows, its warmth illuminated the darkening planet like Christmas lights in a blizzard.

As we marched through into a parlor, my limbs finally loosened and prickled, like all of my muscles had been unlocked. Some of the other abductees fell to the ground gasping. I staggered back against a wall and slid to the ground in a slump. My controller came clattering to the ground beside me. I flexed my arm and sighed when it actually moved when I told it to. My eyes teared up as I tried the rest of me. All accounted for and without any pain. With a watery smile, I took in my surroundings.

The parlor I found myself in had brown, flowery wallpaper, and oil lamps with fake and fluttering flames. The furniture was like something I'd see in an antique store, but oddly, very red. Like fresh drops of blood with chestnut brown touches. Had the aliens been abducting for so long this once looked like normal furniture to the abductees?

I shuddered as ripples of conversation came up from the other puppets–calling them human made me feel ill. I was a fly on the wall, listening to them talk not about the mining for hours, or the controllers, or the aliens, or what the yellow substance was, or the Puppeteer. Just squeaks of noise. Some had their controllers slung over their backs like the picture Tiffany had of Jesus carrying the cross back in the living room…back on Earth. Others held them awkwardly in their arms. While even stranger still, some let them grate across the scratched wood floor as they mindlessly shuffled around.

I tilted my face toward the ceiling. I could see all the way up through staircases to the top floor's ceiling.

"Are you new?"

"What?" I jumped up so fast, my vision was overtaken with spots. "Yes, I am," I said to the voice in the abyss.

Out of nowhere, it felt like people appeared, standing in front of me with controllers cradled in their arms or hooked around their backs.

"What's your name?" Someone chirped.

I never cried easily, but my eyes were watering. Such relief to hear another voice. "Kindle. Kindle Kerr."

"Where do you come from?" I couldn't tell where this voice came from, but there was some warmth to it. Warmth I flocked to like a moth.

"Florida. Err, Earth."

Giggles. My face flushed.

"We're all from Earth," said the first voice. Now I could pinpoint her in the crowd. A dirt-covered girl in a white dress. The braids on her back reminded me of Mora's.

"Where am I? Someone said something about a puppeteer?"

"The Puppeteer," they more or less said simultaneously, spurting words like an open wound. Apparently, she was our capturer. They never saw her. But they said she was a gift, a goddess. She would take care of me like one of her own. But nobody but my dead parents could master that role.

The loudest and most contributed voice ended up belonging to a guy called Lin Martin who had a strong French accent and was apparently the aliens' first abductee, so when the wave of praises about the Puppeteer was abandoned, I turned to him.

"Why are we here? What does she want with us?"

To my surprise, he rolled his eyes. Just because these people were being helpful didn't mean there wasn't one jerk hidden. "Couldn't you tell? We're mining the gold gel."

"Why?" Instantly the atmosphere felt like I ran into a wall.

"The Puppeteer knows," braid-girl whispered.

I frowned. "But nobody here knows? So, the gold gel just disappears?"

"Basically," Lin said. "The Puppeteer is the head alien here. Sometimes people go missing too."

"George," a collective voice grew.

My mouth dropped. Lin had said that so casually, I couldn't speak. My mind couldn't process this. Missing? Some started to trickle away like I wasn't going to say anything else.

"Wait!" I shouted, stopping only a few. "What happened to George?"

But nobody could answer.

"Could you at least tell me why I can move again?"

Lin sighed. "The Puppeteer chooses when we're controlled and when we aren't. As long as the controllers are on the ground, we can move normally. But don't even try to fight it when it's in the air. It's pointless."

I frowned. "But there's got to be a way back home. A way to get out of this."

Everyone looked at each other, their glances conveying thoughts I couldn't begin to decipher.

"It's good," one girl answered like I had asked about her day. "The Puppeteer's here to take care of us. We're safe here."

Everyone nodded and repeated her words. I clutched my stomach at its sharp pains. The group around me peeled away, leaving me slumped on the floor, cradling my head.

What was this place? And what had happened to these people?

I spent the next few hours looking around. Everyone just wandered around like zombies, casting undecipherable glances at their crosses, their controllers. I tried to talk to a few, but nobody paid any attention. Occasionally I'd catch one saying the Puppeteer's name, but that was it. They were practically sheep, only obeying their controllers, and without the aliens' puppeteering, they had nothing to do. No one to be.

Afraid I was going to end up like this, I went to find a way out and hopefully they would follow me.

The first thing I tried was the front door we had come in at. It opened with a large woosh. My mouth dropped. Why was this just open? Had nobody tried this?

I giggled and stepped out, but that's when someone caught my shoulder, but it didn't feel like my strings and controller.

It had to be the Puppeteer. Some kind of hideous, slimy, eight-eyed, six-legged creature. I screamed.

"Hey, stop it!" some guy said. He was ginormous, but no alien. He had one hand on my back and the other awkwardly clutching his controller. Actually, both holds were really awkward.

I spun out of his grip. "Why not?"

"Man, you ask a lot of questions."

"And you guys just want to rot here!" My anger fumed again. I wasn't an angry person, but these people made me want to lose it. "This is our way out. We can leave."

"And go where?" Another girl chimed in. "It's dangerous out there. We get that you're new here, but just listen to us."

"What's going on here?" Lin butted in. He surveyed the two surrounding me before landing on me. "Why are you trying to leave?"

"To escape the Puppeteer! To go back home." The three around me shook their heads in unison. Lin spoke up. "And go where? Do you think you are just going to sprout wings and fly all the way back to Earth?"

I shrunk under his words. I hadn't thought of any of that. How was I going to get home? He was right. If I left the Dollhouse, where was I going to go? Who knew how big this planet was and how far I was going to get. How long before I starved?

"You're right," I said much to Lin's delight. I lowered my head as the girl slammed the door shut behind me. "Running off isn't the right way to get out of here." The girl clucked her tongue.

"I mean," I finished, "I could starve out there."

Now all three of them laughed.

"What?" I said, frowning.

"We can't eat," Lin said. "We don't even need to drink. The Puppeteer had upgraded us beyond that."

My fingers glided along my stomach. "I guess." I sighed and stared out the window. There was still the massive building just to the left of the Dollhouse.

"What about the other building?" I asked the boy beside me who seemed to be the most compassionate. I mean, at least he had stopped me from killing myself outside. I pointed to a door on the wall behind me. "Isn't there a tunnel leading there?"

He shrugged. "I don't know. Abandoned, I guess. We've never been over there and never seen anyone there anyway."

"And I wouldn't try going over there," the girl said. "No windows, no doors. It's basically a metal box."

"How do you know? You can't see the other sides from here."

Lin frowned. "Sometimes we go outside, but there's nothing on the other sides either."

"Really?" the girl said bitterly. "I didn't know you explored over there."

Lin furrowed his brows. "That was a long time ago, all right? Before I realized how great the Puppeteer is."

"And how do you know she's great?" I asked. "How do you even know anything about her if you've never seen her?"

"Because she left me a note after my first few days, explaining all of this."

And by "all of this," he clearly meant nothing, but I didn't say anything. I couldn't stand this conversation much longer. I needed to clear my head. I needed to think. I mumbled a quick sense of gratitude and stumbled out of the group to explore the rest of the Dollhouse. Because there just *had* to be a way out.

The first floor was divided into two rooms: a kitchen and the parlor we had first come through. The rest of the floors were gorgeous bedrooms and bathrooms that felt like they belonged in Buckingham Palace, but nobody was in them. Nobody looked tired or sleepy. That was until I rerouted myself back to the parlor. Four people stood around an old grandfather clock. Clocks were the one thing that seemed to be in use. There were only three tick marks divided like a peace sign, and the only hand was dangerously close to the top.

"What's this?" I said, knowing that puppets in groups were more likely to talk.

"Soon," the boy to my right said, "we'll go to sleep."

"We have a bedtime?" I asked, not even liking myself for that sarcastic crack.

I picked up one of the clocks from a table. It was just a normal clock, but I couldn't find any source of batteries. I rattled it but didn't hear anything.

"So, how come we can sleep but not eat or—" I glanced over at the others, but they were all collapsed on the ground.

I knelt before the first boy, grabbing him by the shoulders and shaking. "Hey. Hey, are you all right?" He flopped like a ragdoll in my arms. I put my fingers on his wrist. A steady pumping brought me to the next boy, but he also had a pulse. They all did.

I snatched the clock I had dropped beside me. It had ticked past the top. Was this what the boy meant about going to sleep? Why wasn't I asleep?

I stumbled into a kitchen to the left. A play kitchen with plastic cooking instruments. I didn't have time to take in everything as only a few puppets were here, collapsed on the floor. One boy yawned as he curled up on the hard tile. I bent down to ask him what was going on, but he grabbed onto my ankle first, eyes so wide I thought they would explode.

"Don't fight the sleep! She's coming."

"Who is? The Puppeteer?"

But it was too late, his eyes closed and his breathing steadied. I shook him, but he didn't respond. When I opened his eyelids, his pupils were swinging from side-to-side. How was he this far asleep already?

Shivering, I curled up on the ground. He said not to fight the sleep, so I wasn't. Who knows what the Puppeteer really wanted. She might come in here and suck the brains of those still awake.

The Dollhouse was so quiet at this point, my thundering heartbeat and breathing felt illegal. I could almost hear the hum of the fake lights above.

Next was the sound of dozens of people getting up. I opened my eyes a bit. Everyone was standing, single file, lining up outside the kitchen and into the parlor. The front door I would like to guess, but I couldn't see through the walls. They weren't carrying their controllers but rather had them hovering over their heads. They were being controlled. Why wasn't I? Was this why the Puppeteer came? To look for defaults?

I scrambled to my feet and held my controller over my head. Nothing happened. I was the only one not sleepwalking. My heart quickened and I held the cross-shaped controller higher. Everyone started moving forward.

I hadn't been in the Dollhouse long enough to mentally map it, but the controller was taking me back through the parlor, but oddly not the front door. Did this mean we were going through the tunnel I had seen from the outside? When we got close enough, the door creaked open. Hot air blew in, opening to a pitch-black room of nothingness.

Neon blue lights began to glow from either side of the room, illuminating a hallway. Either side was covered with metal shelves like a futuristic library. The shelves held glowing glass cylinders.

The puppets in front of me were sleepwalking into the hallway where a hook would come down and put them on smaller hooks in the cylinder. Like we were mint collectibles. A door on the opposite end of the room had a neon sign reading "Storage."

All around, the puppets were picked off one by one until only I remained. I climbed into a container near the floor labeled with strange symbols on the top. I tilted my head back as the small hook dropped close to my eyes. After a few jerks, it pulled me up a few feet, where I dangled like clothes on a hanger by my controller.

Everything was silent for a few seconds as the other puppets adjusted slightly. My eyes were wide open, even if I couldn't see much. But the noises…they kept coming–loud thuds approaching the metal door at my side of the Storage, underneath the sign. A faint pause, then the door opened.

A silhouette of a woman breezed through. But she wasn't human.

My mouth dried.

The Puppeteer.

The farther she walked forward, the more I could see her outline and her shadow flaring along the opposite wall.

What I did know was her shadow stretched out like a tree branch as she lifted a sparkly, golden lantern. It showed rows and rows of cylinders above her on both walls. I shuddered. There was room for thousands of marionettes instead of the thirty or so we were. She set the light on a shelf where a teen girl hung before opening the door and tugging the girl out like she was an actual puppet. No care whatsoever. I closed my eyes as she thudded past again. A creak of the door, however, made me peek. The Puppeteer was leaving, dragging the girl on the floor behind her like a lion dragging its prey. The door nearly took off the girl's foot as it slammed behind them.

I slammed my eyes shut, stifling a lump in my throat.

I waited in the dark—the lantern having been blown out by the door slamming—for something to happen. I waited so long I could feel every inch of my skin tingle. But nothing appeared.

I wanted to rest but didn't feel tired enough. I tried placing my head on my shoulders or against the glass, but my heartbeat was too jumpy. I couldn't close my eyes without seeing the Puppeteer or the girl again.

One thing was clear though. We weren't just puppets. We were sheep following orders until the slaughterhouse opened its doors for business.

Chapter 3

"But that's not possible," Lin shouted from the ring forming around me in the parlor which had become a hangout spot.

That morning, after being returned to the Dollhouse in the same fashion as before, we were forced on another mining trip. I told someone what happened. But then he told everyone when we got back. Like, I told him that in private for a reason, and now I was the center of attention–a place I preferred not to be. Sweat formed along my neck and I couldn't keep my knees from shaking, knocking against the couch I was sitting on.

Lin Martin stepped forward. "Nobody can fight the sleepiness, and believe me, all newbies try."

"I did." My voice came out as a miserable squeak. "I know what I saw in the hallway. I saw the Puppeteer."

"What about Ashley?" another guy asked from the back of the crowd. "She was taken!"

"I'm sorry."

"But why her?"

I tried to shrug, but the controller in my arms was too heavy. "It's just what I saw."

Lin scoffed. "You were probably just dreaming."

I grit my teeth. "But it felt so real."

Someone touched my shoulders. It was the guy who had asked about Ashley. I didn't realize I was standing so close to Lin–practically in his face–or that my fists were clenched so tightly.

I stepped back although my anger still roared. These people were so stupid! Couldn't they see the Puppeteer was not our friend? She abducted us. She took us from our homes and now was doing God-knows-what when we were sleeping. For all I knew she was going to kill us. I was pretty sure that was going to happen.

Days passed after that incident and I spent most of them sitting on the couch in the parlor, sometimes hiding in a corner, hoping I'd blend in with the wallpaper. I was still strong though. I still couldn't sleep like the others. And to be honest, after the fifth day, I didn't want to be weak like them. I just wanted a way out.

But that was the problem. There was literally no way out. No way to get out of the other door in the Storage, no way to break out of the controller once the Puppeteer had me.

I tried to get other puppets to talk to me…sometimes. To tell me about the planet or the Puppeteer or anything really, but nobody knew jack. So I sat there, on my little sofa, watching the days crawl by.

On one of those days, a loud bang made my saliva stick to my throat like lava. Standing in the doorway to the kitchen and parlor was a girl with orange hair down to her shoulders, and her controller by her feet. I had no idea who she was, but apparently, she wasn't the only one on her quest. About five others stood behind her.

The girl stepped forward; eyes set dead on me. Was she going to hit me? I flinched back, but she stopped and held out her hand in a too-big sweatshirt. "Kindle, some of the others would like to talk to you." She said it like I was going to the principal's office.

"Um, okay?" I got up, shaking as she flung the limp sleeve to the staircase. A few questions popped into my mind, but at this point, I had learned to just be quiet and follow the rules. Eventually, I'd find a way out, but not through my brainwashed counterparts.

I followed her and the others up the staircase. The puppets marched behind her. Sometimes they would march single file like the Puppeteer was commanding them. They would notice this and step away, but some didn't even bother.

The second floor led up to a fork. Three rooms, one ahead, and two to the sides. Again with the third floor, but this time sweatshirt-girl led me into a room that looked like a garden had exploded inside. A king-sized, pink bed surrounded by floral drapes on the left side. Various chairs and beanbags created a semi-circle, some of the seats were already taken, but not by other puppets or even people. No. There were mannequins posed like I had just interrupted a very important conversation.

The rest of the puppets took up the remaining seats until I was left standing in the middle. I shrieked as someone pulled me down into the last remaining chair–a gothic red footstool that sagged under my weight. I shrugged the guy's arm off with a splintering frown.

Lin, across from me, cleared his throat. I couldn't tell if his position meant he was the leader or something, but the eerie silence felt even deader.

"Based on what you have told us," he said, "apparently you have some kind of power."

My skin went cold at the word "power." Honestly, the only reason I couldn't sleep was because someone had messed up while turning me into this horrible creature. By no means would I call it a power.

"It's not really a power but go on. What do you want?"

"That's exactly what we want to know," he said. "We want to know what you plan to do with this power."

There was the word "power" again. It felt meaningless now. Like how you say a word over and over until it doesn't make sense. But I had a feeling that's not what they wanted me to say. What, I had no idea.

"I don't know?"

A few shoulders sagged while others tensed up.

"You aren't going to hurt us?" Lin said.

"What?" I shouted, my voice echoing as the walls closed in. There was no air. Where was the air? I needed air! "No!"

"You're going to ruin us," some other guy said.

"What? I'm not some super-villain."

The confidence in Lin's startled me. "You should leave the Dollhouse while everyone else is falling asleep. The Puppeteer won't even have the slightest idea."

"Why? You told me there was nothing out there but certain death! Why should I believe you?"

"Enough!" his voice boomed. "We've come to an agreement that your presence here will just anger the Puppeteer."

"No! I'm not leaving" I shouted. God, was it always this hard to breathe? Stop shouting.

"Then we'll force you to."

Everyone started to chant: "Leave, leave, leave." Like a collective hivemind, they all stood, still chanting. They pushed me back, out of the room, and downstairs. I ran until I was in the parlor. The few people there looked at me strangely.

By then the group had filled into the small parlor, pushing me against the door. I glanced out the window. The stars were out, and a few clouds were scattered across the sky.

Could I leave? What if I couldn't find my way back? What was out there?

"Leave! Leave! Leave!"

I backed up, expecting the door to catch me, but instead, I tripped over the door strip and landed on the dirt path outside, my controller nearly decapitating me.

"Leave! Leave! Leave!"

Before I could even take another breath, the door slammed in my face. "No!" I jumped up to push on the door, but something was blocking it shut. Peeking through the window, I could see one or two puppets stumbling around like drunks before crashing on the ground, dead asleep. And if that wasn't bad enough, they had pushed the couch in front of the door.

I turned around pulling my arms to my shoulders as a cold wind howled through. I clenched my teeth as it ran right through my experimental body. And based on the darkening clouds in the darkening sky, it didn't look like this was just a quick breeze.

Circling the Dollhouse, I banged on the windows. Maybe one would break. Maybe I'd get lucky. But nope. They were solid.

"Please. Please!" I cried out, each plea getting louder. Who I was screaming to was beyond me. Maybe myself, maybe God, maybe even the Puppeteer.

My eyes pricked with hot tears as the wind grew louder. Dark clouds were beginning to form on the horizon and heading this way. I could start going up the mountain. Find a cave. Make a fire—somehow. Then trek back in the morning.

So that's what I did. Or at least tried to do. About twenty minutes later, I dumped my controller on the cold, pale dirt. I was panting, out of breath, and doubled over.

I had been trying to get to the mines but hadn't seen anything familiar for a while. How could I have gotten lost? I had watched every tree, every rock, but there I was. At this point, going in circles would be a welcomed feeling.

I curled up on the ground and traced my controller. I had made marionettes before. Simple wood, screws, and magnets held me prisoner. I ran over the spot where the arm controller met the main stick of wood.

Something stung my knuckle.

Gasping, I pulled my hand back to massage it. No bump, no burn, no bruise. Just cold and wet. Then another bite, this time at the base of my neck.

I gave the sky a quick glance. Above, the stars were gone, instead, there was a mass of dark gray clouds.

Snow.

Or some kind of snow. Something that bit and burned like embers. I flung my controller over my head as an umbrella, but the weight change was too much, and I toppled over. Grunting, I dragged it behind like an anchor to a group of trees, but the canopies had too many gaps for any kind of protection.

The snow pressed down harder. My nose and eyes were running. Why did I leave? Why didn't I stay on the freaking doorstep? I was smarter than that. What hurt the most was the last thing anyone was going to know about me both on Earth and here would be my mysterious disappearance.

I hit a tree root and fell, my bones clattering against my skin. When I hit the ground, my back exploded in pain and my head went for a swim. I tried to roll over, but the ground gave out. The last thing I remembered was sliding into a giant tree.

Chapter 4

A faint buzzing noise. Then popping. Noises were slowly chipping away at my frozen consciousness. Although my mind was dizzy and cloudy, the crackling of a nearby fire stitched my thoughts together. As my body struggled to move, I smelled smoke as warmth licked my sweaty body. I was cocooned in thick, woolly blankets too heavy to move around in.

Groaning, I managed to open my eyes, but only for a few seconds before dizziness made my eyelids drop. Several tries later I could finally focus on the swirling nonsense around me. I was in some kind of barn, renovated to be livable. A fireplace made hastily of mud and bricks crackled with orange flames and purplish wood. The furniture was made of the same wood. Not the cleanest cut nor the smoothest, but it made do for a couch and table in this empty room. The floor was old and rotting, with holes showing scrapes of dirt while dirty rafters held up a roof and several empty bird nests.

There was a door behind me to my left. It was made of the same kind of wood as the floor, but at least this had been taken care of. There was also another doorway, but I couldn't see what was inside.

It was quiet here. The only noise beyond the crackling fire was a rapid clicking noise from behind. Like tap dancing. What was this place? A second Dollhouse lost beyond the trails? Did it belong to another form of alien inhabitants? Other puppets that couldn't sleep?

Heart hammering at my thoughts, I wiggled out of the blankets. My skin wasn't punctured or bruised from my fall, and my clothes were only wet from sweat. From a quick once-over, I appeared to be in good health. Safe from the acidic snow.

I shook the last blanket off and stepped back. With my mind still running with horrible possibilities, I scooped up the blankets carefully. I didn't want to alert anyone that I was awake. I inched toward the front door to the beat of the tapping. Holding my breath, I reached for the door.

"Hey!"

Yelping, I jumped out of my skin.

I spun around to face a marionette my age. He had a short cut of curly black hair and grass-green eyes. Rather lean, the torn clothes on his tall frame shifted as he motioned for me to come back. He was leaning on the shabby table. "I'm sorry, I didn't mean to scare you," he said.

"Uh…" I couldn't figure out how to get the words out as my eyes landed on the controller behind him. It was webbed with cracks and the two crosses were coming apart. His strings, however, looked fine.

To my surprise, he was still staring, so I sputtered something out.

"I–I was just leaving."

He frowned. "Leaving? You want to leave for the place I literally just saved you from?"

My face heated. A glance out the window told me it was still snowing that awful snow. Taking in a deep breath, I pulled my eyes away from his shattered controller and steadied myself. "You're right. That would be foolish."

"Agreed."

"Where am I?"

"Hell." He laughed bitterly like he'd been wanting to say that forever. "No. No. I'm just kidding. You're, uh, currently in the middle of a sinkhole."

"What? A sinkhole?"

"Yeah. More like a crater. I don't know. But you're in a barn down here. So, I guess welcome to my humble adobe."

"So, um, how long have I been here?"

He gave the kind of face that should have gone with a shrug, but his body didn't move. "I don't keep track of time anymore. By the way, I'm Lewis Bryant. Who are you?"

The tapping noise started again, even louder than the first time.

"Kindle Kerr."

"What?"

"Kindle!"

I couldn't even hear my voice over the tapping at this point. He screamed something at me like "One second!" and hobbled back into the room with the tapping.

I could hear him saying something, just not what. Then he was pulling out a white horse by its reins. It stood on a platform that kept bouncing when the horse slapped its tail. I gasped, my brain catching up. This wasn't an alien horse. No, it had been turned into a different kind of puppet–a jig doll. A kind of puppet that danced when a wooden board was slapped with a hand or foot.

"This is Galaxy," Lewis said. "I can't seem to find any more of her kind out here. Not even another horse. What did you say your name was?"

"Kindle." I eyed the horse. It only shook slightly now. "I didn't know there were jig dolls."

"Jig dolls?"

"Yeah, that's what kind of puppet the horse is."

"Oh." Lewis paused for a moment before grinning. "You know, liking puppets isn't a very popular hobby around here, Kindle."

My face heated, and I tried to smile but that felt dumb. He hobbled over to the wooden bench. "I haven't seen anyone since I came here."

"You mean since you got abducted?" I ignored him patting the seat next to him. Just because he looked nice didn't mean he was.

"Nah. I mean when I got lost. I used to be in the Dollhouse…four years ago? But then the knucklehead controlling me went on a rough ice patch. Down I went down into this sinkhole we're in, shattering my controller." He snapped to attention, staring at me. "Oh, I shouldn't ramble like this. I guess I'm just used to one-sided conversations." He laughed.

"No, no," I said, drawn in by his story. "It's all very interesting."

He tilted his head. "Really?" But his eyes were motioning for me to sit.

I did but kept a careful eye on Galaxy. "Where does she come in at?"

"Galaxy found me much like she found you. I believe she was used as a search-and-rescue horse before her abduction."

I bit down a laugh, but apparently, the rest of my face didn't.

"Honestly, it's a real thing, Kindle."

"But a horse?"

"I used to live on a farm. Horses are so much more useful than just pack animals, you know."

I decided not to fight with the cowboy and instead looked out the window where the snow was letting up. Not a lot, but enough to see the sinkhole's walls. They were huge slopes that seemed to wrap around the building at an angle. More like super steep hills than walls. On the hills, or at least the side I could see, were small footpaths that never got very high. Halfway seemed to be the record. Wherever I was, it was a long way from the Dollhouse.

"You came down there," Lewis said, pointing to the path I was studying. He shook his head. "Thankfully, you didn't go all the way down. You were at the right height for Galaxy to get you."

"She can't get all the way to the top?"

"I'm not sure. I think she would be able to, but she never does."

I swallowed, but he didn't catch it, he just kept on talking. "But I'm trying to get around this, you know. Having a bad leg isn't going to stop me from escaping."

Nodding along I managed a quick glance at his controller. So fascinating that it affected his leg. "So, what is this place, Lewis?" I said, adding his name so he'd look at me.

"I believe it was originally going to be a barn. Maybe. But I've adjusted it to what I've seen fit."

"Is there anyone else?"

"Just Galaxy."

"For four years?"

"You sure ask a lot of questions."

I sighed. "Sorry. I just got here a week ago and everything's so confusing."

"That's all right. A lot of it is." Lewis shifted, his smashed controller falling off the couch. Galaxy put it back into place. "Confusing, I mean. Not much is all right here."

"Okay. One more question."

Lewis laughed. "Is that the question or a request?"

I smiled faintly. "Does it hurt?"

His face twisted in confusion. Like at first he was going to ignore the obvious and spit out some lie, but then he took a deep breath and sighed out: "Not anymore. I'm mainly just numb." He sucked in a deep breath again.

I glanced back out the window at the gnarly tree I had come crashing down upon. Four years. Four years of trying to get out of this sinkhole.

"So, you've been making the footpaths?" I prodded.

"Yeah," Lewis said, Galaxy's tapping got louder as if to voice her frustration.

"How close have you gotten?"

"Halfway. Then I come crashing back down."

I winced. That couldn't be good for his condition. "Is there anything I can do?"

For the first time, I saw a smile. A brilliant smile. The kind that broke through the air's gloom. I liked his smile. It was probably the first genuine smile I'd seen in a while.

"I'll need your legs first."

What? Everything came back in a snap. Like a blurry image suddenly getting clear. I jumped off the couch, bumping my knee on the table corner and crashing down. I scrambled up, fighting the jolt of pain. "Stay away from my legs!"

"Wait! Kindle!"

I was halfway to the door. "What are you, another alien? Take my legs? Like hell you will."

He was laughing now. Laughing! "I didn't mean like that. I swear. I'm not going to eat you or anything" He tried to pull himself together but kept chuckling. "Apparently, I didn't make my request come out as smoothly as I should have. Believe me, it sounded better in my head."

I huffed. He didn't look alien. And honestly, without him, I had no other way. But I wasn't getting any farther from the door. "Then what did you want it to sound like?"

"Not like I was going to chop off your legs. I actually have an idea I've been working on to get me out of here. It would really be much easier with two people, and as hard as I might try, I can't get the dimensions right for it to work with Galaxy."

The horse? What kind of invention would work with a horse?

He wasn't done talking though. "I just need you to help me with something real quick."

Crap. Did I have a choice? No, not really. It was awful to think, but I knew I could outrun him if I needed to. "Sure."

Galaxy bent down for Lewis to grab her back and hoist himself back to his feet. He smiled at me like I was supposed to read his mind and went into the second room.

I was stunned so hard I felt like part of the couch. I mean, I wanted to help him. I liked helping people, and I wanted to be a doctor just to prove it, but did I really trust the guy I'd just met in the woods? It was like one of Tiffany's romances. Boom, the lead heroine meets a cute guy in the woods for no reason whatsoever. Or in her Halloween movies, he would turn out to be an axe-wielding nutcase. I shook my head and got up. Again, I could outrun him if I had to, but I was too curious to ignore him.

I walked into the other room of what would have been the main part of the stable, or barn, or whatever. It had long rows with doors leading off into what would have been pens. Lewis, meanwhile, was on his stomach, propped on a cushion with a piece of smooth slab and a sharp rock.

When I stopped walking, he sat up. "Did you get lost on your way over?"

But it wasn't a jab. Not like Lin or Mora would say. It was just to be funny, and I smiled genuinely.

"Your couch was rather comfortable."

He nodded. "Best seat in the house. Okay, now I want you to stand over by that wall." Lewis pointed to a wall that had an outline of what was probably him and then one of Galaxy.

I started to head over. "What for?"

"I need you to be the model."

"Model?"

"Sort of. I just need your measurements."

"Five-eight."

"Right." Lewis scratched something on the slab. It made a horrible noise that made me grit my teeth. "Stand by my outline, would you? I need to see how you compare to me."

"So, you want me like this?" I stood; arms spread out like his outline. From this close, I could see it was done with different rocks. He was also around the same height as me.

Lewis shot me a crooked thumbs-up. "Yeah, that's perfect."

He started off by scribbling. I wasn't sure if he was drawing me or just writing down measurements. Lewis hadn't struck me as an artsy guy. Then again, I didn't strike myself as a model…or a puppet. Or anyone who would get in this kind of situation.

"What are you making?" I smiled so we could start off on the right foot this time. I didn't want him to think of me as flighty. It was clear now he was no threat.

"Basically, I need a way out of this sinkhole. With my controller broken and my leg a mess, I need someone healthier to be my guide. You'll be controlling me with your own controller and strings. When you take a step, a rope connected to me will make me take a step as well. That way if I start to fall you can keep me upright. Together we'll pull Galaxy out and be scot-free!"

I couldn't help but feel the irony filling my mouth like a bloody copper taste. He was remaking himself into a puppet. And I would be his puppeteer.

I thought back to what Lin said about there being nothing out here. "What does 'free' mean? Where will you go?"

"The Dollhouse."

"You mean the one next to the metal building?"

"The very one. I mean, it's not like there are others."

"You're not George, are you?" I said, recalling the first day when they mentioned someone before Ashley had been taken.

Lewis frowned at me. "No. I've never heard of anyone named George."

"Oh." The air crinkled like foil. Something felt off, but I wasn't sure what.

"Maybe my brother knows him."

"Who's your brother?" I asked, hoping it wasn't Lin.

"His name's Dominique. We were abducted together. I haven't seen him since I fell into this sinkhole years ago."

"I'm sorry."

"Yeah." He glanced quickly back up at me. "But it will be one heck of a reunion story."

I smiled back but felt like his grin didn't quite reach his eyes. I tried to see what he was drawing but couldn't. "You know, I make a lot of puppets. As a hobby."

"Must be ironic for you. Now hold your controller above your head."

"Yeah. I guess so." A memory tried to come, but it fizzled out somewhere between neurons. "So, you invent a lot?"

He made a face. "Dominique...he was good at this kind of stuff. Was a freakin' rocket scientist." He looked up at me. "Literally. He was going to go to Mars one day."

My chest burst with the thought of telling him he wasn't alone. That he was just like me. My older brother, Vince, was dead.

Missing.

No body to report. Doesn't mean they're alive. If only you could remember, Kindle.

Taking a deep, chest-puffing breath, he stood. "Well, I think it's done now. I'll start working on this."

I nodded. "I'll help."

But he waved me off. "No, no, I've got this. Get some rest."

"I can't sleep. I've got some kind of..." *power* "...some kind of medical disability that the aliens accidentally gave me when they made me. I can't sleep. Not even when everyone is sent into the Storage."

At first, I thought he was ignoring me, his back facing me. But then he nodded. "Come look over it then. You would be a nice help with your puppet expertise." I liked the way he said it. *Expertise.* Like I could actually help in some way instead of sitting in corners, waiting to become furniture.

My stomach knotted as he began to work. He had this whole collection of screws and nails he'd wrenched from the barn over the years. Although I wasn't a mechanical genius, I did know a thing or two about puppets. I helped him with the anatomy, and what joints connected and where.

After what felt like hours, long after the snow had stopped, and only puddles remained outside, Lewis clapped loudly, and exclaimed: "That should do it."

I flexed my hand, trying to convince feeling to come back. "Now what?"

I sat with cable wires attached to my knees and arms. They wrapped twice around my original strings. I felt the twisting and knotting Lewis did when I moved. He had told me that he suspected the original strings were made of our own skin and muscles. *Muscle tissue*, I had corrected, plucking at the wires like a guitar. It made sense then why the Puppeteer's grip was so unbreakable. Our bodies thought we were moving ourselves.

"Now we get the heck out of here." Lewis stretched back. I mimicked. We had spent almost all night trying to get this thing to work. Lots of rearranging and test runs. Sometimes I caught him nodding off, so I avoided eye contact and let him drift off for ten or fifteen minutes at a time. Or at least I guessed. There were no clocks in his place.

And through this, I think I understood my rescuer more. He wasn't the creep I thought he would be. And I think I only thought that because everyone else was a sheep, and I just wanted him to be *something*. He was really nice. Chatty, but nice. Super smart too. And he made me laugh.

I gathered up the wires. The contraption would work once I was high enough on the slope. Once I was above him, we'd attach my cables to his marionette controller. Secretly though, I wished for some medical equipment. Maybe I could get a good look at his cracked controller. See what was wrong and fix him.

Chapter 5

Outside, the snow had stopped leaving the sinkhole a disgusting mush of soaked grass and mud puddles. We tiptoed around this, me awkwardly holding the cables like giant spaghetti noodles. Because somehow, I was supposed to get anywhere up the hills when shuffling was my main speed. Even Galaxy's tapping was getting impatient as she danced by Lewis who stared up the highest footpath.

Up close it looked even worse. The snow had wiped away all the debris I had previously stirred up with my tumble. Giant rocks and skinny trees were still shining with melted snow. Slippery too, I guessed. Not going to make my ascent any easier.

I kicked a small pebble with my toe. It spun wildly off into the distance. Craning my neck, the hills seemed to grow. "Much bigger up close," I said, but Galaxy's tapping was so loud I could barely hear myself.

"Now what you want to do," Lewis shouted, probably used to his horse's volume by now, "is use those darker rocks for stability."

I looked back at him, his eyes almost shining as he stared at the top. He licked his lips and put a hand upward like he could almost reach the top. That or he was measuring how high I would get before I tumbled back down.

"You see that sapling? That's how far you have to climb before you pull me up."

As if that was nothing.

I nodded. The baby tree. Then he would be pulling his weight. And probably mine too.

I hoisted myself up, still holding my controller and strings.

"Nice! First rock!" echoed below. "Keep going!"

Another step. Then another. Then a lot more. I was four feet up and Lewis had stopped shouting. He was probably holding his breath like me. The slope had gotten a bit steeper. But I chugged on, reminding myself of Lewis' fall. The one that broke him.

Finally, I threw my body weight on a small tree Its flimsiness gave me vertigo, but at least the slope had smoothed out by that point.

Glancing down the side, my heart sank at how little I had accomplished. I mean, I had made it, but it wasn't as high as it felt. Getting on my knees I threw the cables down where he hooked them to his controller. If it hurt, he didn't show it. He just took it like a champ as I controlled him up. Galaxy hopped after him where there was barely enough space for all of us.

All that was left was the final climb.

I started first, clinging to exposed tree roots like an angry cat. "Working?" I shouted, afraid any more words would propel me backward to Lewis and we'd both fall.

"Yeah, I think. Let's go higher."

He jerked on my strings making the world lose gravity for a second. I pinwheeled to grab the roots. I grunted. "Easy with which way you pull."

"Sorry. Left foot then right foot."

"Gotcha." With in-sync callouts, his getting breathier by the step, we slowly shuffled our way up the slope. I tried to make my movements slow so he could keep up.

"Stop doing that, Kindle."

"Do what?"

"I can carry my own weight. My leg isn't as bad as it seems."

"I–" What could I say to that? That I was a doctor? I wasn't even trained. Just some girl with some dream.

Fine.

Gritting my teeth, I put one hand over the other until we reached the top. I awkwardly yanked back like I was doing a dance until he and Galaxy were up too.

Gasping, I rolled over onto my back. I expected Lewis to do the same, but he was unhooking himself, staring blankly off in the opposite direction. Back into the bleak forest I'd emerged from.

I shivered; the air was much cooler than back in the hole.

"Freedom!" Lewis yelled with echoes bouncing back. "I'm free!" With a smile like that, he was going to crack his lips.

I was going to tell him we were still deserted on an alien planet, but he turned to me and flashed such a grin, that the words were knocked out of my head.

"Great climbing there. Where did you say you were from?"

I hadn't, but the slight whoop behind his words made me feel like I'd known him my whole life. Had I? Geez, what had he just said?

I had totally forgotten everything except to stutter out: "Fl-Florida." Nice. Nailed that one, genius.

"Cool. I've never seen the ocean before. I'm from Kansas. Insert every single joke in the book."

"Are there mountains in Kansas?"

"Barely. We have Mt. Sunflower…"

I burst out laughing, thinking he was pulling my leg, but his face looked rather shocked.

"Oh. Sorry. I thought you were kidding," I said at the same time he jabbed a thumb at the stable and said, "Better than Death Valley."

"What?" Lewis's face was slightly red as he ran his hands through his black, curly hair.

"Nothing. You said you grew up on a farm yesterday?"

"Oh, that! Yeah. It was awesome. So crazy and rowdy with my parents and Dominique there." He smirked at me. "Oh, and the animals too."

Galaxy whinnied, her tapping growing louder.

Lewis put a hand on her mane. "We should probably find the Dollhouse and Dominique. But don't worry, Galaxy knows the way back."

Yeah. Sure. But why not follow a horse on an alien planet? Things honestly couldn't get weirder. Plus, I really did trust Lewis.

After a bit of walking, with me slowing down to help Lewis catch up, I wanted to break the silence. It reminded me too much of the puppets at the Dollhouse, and I desperately didn't want Lewis to be just another sheep.

"Tell me more about Dominique."

Lewis sighed, his hand trailing off Galaxy's back. "Best brother I could have. He wanted to go to space, you know? He was working for NASA. Always dreamed of going to the moon or Mars one day. But just like us, he got abducted. He had woken me up really late at night to show me some rare space thing. We were getting the telescope and stuff ready when that hook came down. I–I didn't know what to do...what to think. I couldn't even run. The aliens grabbed Dominique, but I held on too. I can't wait to see him again. After all these years. I bet he's still the leader of the Dollhouse. Have you met him?"

My heart grew to a dull thud in an endless chest cavity. Dominique wasn't there. Or at least not that I knew of. And I think I would remember someone as the leader. Someone besides stupid Lin.

"I don't think so," I said. "I've only been here for a few weeks. It seems like Lin took over."

"Lin?"

"Yeah, Lin Martin."

"Never heard of the guy."

"That's strange. He says he was the first one to be abducted."

"I think I would remember someone with the name Lin. It's my mom's name."

"Well, he's a real jerk to me, anyway."

"Hmm. Maybe the Puppeteer took Dominique to stage two."

Nightmarish flashes of Ashley getting dragged out of the Storage, motionless feet bumping along behind her. Like an innocent bunny in the jaws of a wolf.

"Where's stage two?" I asked.

Lewis spun around so fast; I stumbled back on some leaves.

"What?" he said.

"I've never heard of stage two. Or been there."

I knew I was an idiot by the look he gave me. Like I'd just said aliens weren't real. Way to go, me.

"Stage two…it isn't a place. How could you have not heard of it? The Puppeteer tells everyone about it. And surely the others told you before you get a chance to speak."

I shrugged.

"No, no. This is, like, innate. Like breathing. Like learning to walk."

I knew that walking wasn't innate, but this wasn't a time my brain was functioning. "What happens at stage two? I need to know!"

"You become a stick-and-rod."

My stomach was falling into an endless dark pit. "That's a type of puppet!" I dropped my controller, head spinning. "We're stopping right here, right now. You don't mean to say the aliens make other puppets besides marionettes and jig dolls?"

"Oh boy." Lewis slumped onto a tree stump. His eyes replaying something I couldn't see. Perhaps something I didn't want to see. He only looked up when Galaxy nudged his shoulder. "How much do you know about this? About the aliens and the puppets?"

"That there is one main alien…" Lewis was giving me an "I-can't-believe-you're-that-dumb" look, so I stopped.

"I'm going to have to start from the beginning, aren't I?" Lewis sighed. "You better sit down too."

I barely found a good rock when Lewis began his horrifying tale.

"First off, you're right. There's one main alien—the Puppeteer. She's the head honcho. She oversees everything that's going on, but she's not the one controlling you when you go mining. Those, if I remember correctly, are her children. These aliens control us from somewhere far away to the gold substance that is used as both an energy source and a way to turn humans into marionettes once abducted.

"Now this is where things take a turn. When we've been a marionette for long enough and are displaying certain traits—although nobody knows what those are—they get upgraded to the next type of puppet–a rod-and-stick puppet we nicknamed 'rods.' Basically, they are like us except the only thing they can't control is their arms. The Puppeteer usually sends a rod down to us miners and tells the newcomers what's going on. Although based on what you've told me, they haven't done that in a while."

"No," I said. "I…what happens to the rods? Do they mine?"

"No, the rods clean and attend to the aliens in a different place other than the Dollhouse. That big main building. I have no idea what that is so don't ask."

And the puppets thought I was the danger, but they didn't even know the half of it.

Galaxy burst from a gathering of bushes, rocking violently. She made a high-pitched snort, making Lewis jump from his seat. "She's afraid of something."

A cold sweat broke down my back. "What?" Could it be the Puppeteer?

"I think it's the Dollhouse." Lewis was shoving his way through the bushes Galaxy had come from. "Wow. It's so much bigger than I remembered." He turned toward me with a huge grin. "Come on."

By the time I was fighting the brush, Lewis was halfway down the hill. Galaxy made a high-pitched huff. And when I turned toward the horse, I swear I saw fear in her eyes.

"Lewis," I shouted back, not taking my eyes off Galaxy. "Galaxy's not coming."

"Seriously?" Lewis called back. "Why didn't you tell me that before I got to the bottom?"

Galaxy by now was backing up slowly, shaking her head more so than usual. What could she see that we couldn't?

Lewis squeezed past me, his shoulders bumping mine. "Galaxy?" He put his hand on her head. After a few seconds, he pulled away like this was some kind of fantasy movie. "She'll stay here. She won't wander far."

I smiled. "So, you can talk to animals, now?"

He rolled his eyes. "You just get to know them after a while. You never had any pets?"

"A dog," I blurted. But I never had a dog. Why would I even…? God, I couldn't look at this guy and talk, could I? "I mean, I almost got a dog, but my parents said no. They're dead." Aw, geez. Just shut up.

"Oh." Lewis rubbed his neck. "Sorry."

"No, it's okay. I have a good home now." Liar, liar, pants on fire. "Plus, with every passing day, I remember more and more about them. Let's forget this came up."

"All right." Lewis waved to Galaxy before parting the bushes. "Ladies first."

I slipped through the slit and reentered the dark, gothic presence of the Dollhouse. Here I was, back to safety. No. Safety wasn't the right word. It was a prison governed by a diabolic "savior."

Since it was still so early in the day, the rest of the marionettes would be asleep. Which left me time to think of an excuse for why I was back after my witch trial. Together we rammed into the door until the couch moved enough to creep past.

Re-entering the empty Dollhouse felt like I'd just walked into a haunted house. It was pitch dark, the only light coming from the second and last setting sun. I fumbled my way through the parlor and into the kitchen where at least the fake stove and fridge had tiny lights. Here I could see my dirt-caked palms from dragging Lewis up the slopes.

Behind me, Lewis was stroking the furniture like we were back on Earth and not some brain-hungry planet.

"It's exactly how I remember it," he said, facing me. He looked even worse with mud smeared over his clothes and face.

"Do you remember the showers upstairs?"

Lewis grinned. "Don't want me to stain the furniture?"

"I honestly couldn't care less about this place."

"Me neither. It can burn in Hell."

"I think this is Hell."

Chapter 6

Under the sound of the second-floor shower screeching away, I scurried to find a clock to see how long I had before the others awoke. It wasn't the problem of finding a clock–the place was chock-full of them. No, the problem was finding a clock I hadn't destroyed or messed with. A few days ago, I had decided that the clocks had something to do with when the other puppets fell asleep. But after spending a whole afternoon smashing clocks and whipping back hour hands, I had to admit defeat. That was also when the non-existent glances at me became scared glances.

I padded up the stairs to the third floor to a clock hanging just out of my reach. I hadn't even been able to shatter the face by chucking my controller at it.

Squinting in the dark, I saw it was almost to the second mark which would release the others from their comatose states.

No time for a shower then.

Speaking of which, I heard a door open and close on the second floor. I tiptoed down to meet him on the staircase going upwards.

"What time is it?" He rubbed his eyes.

"About time for everyone to come back." I bounced on my heels. "Are you ready to see Dominique?"

"Of course I am." He glanced at a mirror hanging crooked against the wall. "I wonder if he'll recognize me."

"I'm sure he will."

A metal screech made us both jump. Lewis wrapped his controller and strings around his back like most puppets did and hobbled down the stairs. I sucked in my breath, hoping he wouldn't fall.

Would Dominique remember him? Jealousy spiked in my stomach. No. I should be happy for him. I *was* happy for him. He got a second chance at seeing his brother again whereas I would never. From my spot still on the second floor, I saw Lewis disappear into the parlor, shouting his brother's name. I pressed my palm against my temples. I would give him some space to sort things out. He hadn't seen his brother in years, but together they had been in this horrible place for four years. How much must have changed. Their parents must be worried sick. Tiffany was probably worried sick. What did she think happened to me? She was probably at church every Sunday praying for my body to wash ashore to kill the suspense. No. Knowing her, she probably thought I was still out there. Like I'd run away. But she could literally search every corner of the Earth without finding me.

From downstairs, I could hear shouts arrive as the puppets woke up. The puppets had no idea they slept in what I had nicknamed the "Storage." At least they didn't until I told them what they were missing. For all they knew, they fell asleep wherever and woke up in the parlor the next morning.

"Dominique?" Lewis' voice rose. "It's me, Lewis."

"Who are you?" someone said. "Are you new?"

"No. I'm looking for my brother."

I hurried downstairs. Everyone was mashed inside the tiny parlor, taking up the antique sofas and creaky chairs. Everyone was staring at Lewis who was standing closest to the bottom of the staircase. I looped around until I was beside him.

"Hey!" Lin said. "What are you doing here? We exiled you. How'd you even get in?"

In the week I'd been here, I'd learned ignoring Lin Martin was the best option. "Hey, everyone. This is Lewis Bryant." Nobody perked up at this news. "I found him while I was outside."

"Why's his controller broken?" Some girl who'd played a part in my exile said.

"I fell." Lewis managed before Lin had another brilliant insight.

"That's impossible. We would have noticed if that happened."

"But that's the thing," I said. "Lewis was abducted–"

"With my brother!" Lewis interjected. "His name's Dominique."

Everyone glanced at each other. Were these people so devoted to the Puppeteer that they had forgotten their own names? Where was Dominique?

"Nobody's been abducted with another person," Lin had to say.

"But he was abducted before you, Lin," I said, realizing Lewis had no idea who was yelling at him. "He was abducted four years ago."

That stopped the mumbling in the room. Even Lin had nothing to say for a solid ten seconds.

"Impossible!" he finally said. "I was the first one abducted and that was two years ago."

"How do you know?" Lewis said, stepping closer to him.

"Because the Puppeteer left me a note saying so! This place was empty when I came to it. I had never heard of you or your brother before."

"Dominique," Lewis corrected, his eyes darting over the parlor.

"Do you have proof of this abduction?" some girl in the back said.

"Yeah. My number."

"Number?" I asked as Lewis flipped over his controller, and gently pointed out a stamped number on the middle of the cross.

"Q33," he read.

Lin crossed his arms. "So? Those numbers are random."

"But look at your own number. It doesn't have a letter in front."

"Fine," Lin said. He sighed and looked around "So what? Where's your brother?"

"I..." Lewis scanned the crowd as if begging for someone to volunteer to be Dominique. "I don't know. He's not here. And I don't recognize anyone either." He spun toward me, face reddening. "He must have become a rod."

I wanted to cry. All he wanted was his brother. All he wanted was some sense of familiarity. He had trusted in me, and I couldn't even comfort him. "I'm so sorry," I started.

"What's a rod?" someone asked.

Lewis looked at me, his body deflated and the light sapping out of his eyes.

I nodded at him. "I'll take care of it."

Without a word, he went back upstairs.

As I explained what both the puppet rod and the alien experiment rod were, I couldn't help glancing back at the staircase. It felt like I had slapped Lewis across the face.

"Any questions?" I wrapped up my talk with.

Again, everyone was stunned. I couldn't tell if they understood what I was saying. If they could even comprehend it. Finally, Lin spoke.

"How can we believe you?" For once it wasn't angry. He sounded scared.

I threw one last look back at the crowd. "You'll just have to."

Then I bolted upstairs to find Lewis.

I eventually found him in the creepy mannequin room I'd had been confronted in before my exile. He was swinging a pillow around, knocking the angry mannequins over.

"Lewis," I said gently from inside the door frame. Something I had always hated when Tiffany did, but now I had no other choice.

He spun to me, dropping the pillow. "How could she do this? I just don't get it. Where is everyone? Did the Puppeteer just turn everyone into rods? But why would she do that? She needs the miners; they're the whole point of abducting us. Why would she start fresh?"

"Because she's an insane alien overlord who enslaves teenagers?"

"But *why?* Why ruin her whole operation?" he sighed and sat in a chair previously occupied by a mannequin. "I don't get it."

I sat next to him. "I don't either, but we're going to find out."

He cupped his chin in his hands. "How?"

"If we can't escape this planet, then we have to get straight to the source. The Puppeteer."

His face twisted. "You're insane. How?"

"We're going to become rods. I mean, you said if we had good behavior, we'd become one, right?"

"I mean, yeah. But clearly, things have changed. When I was first abducted nobody worshipped the Puppeteer, everyone knew about the rods."

"But we're going to find a way. I promise."

"Why?" he blurted.

"Because I'm getting off this stupid planet. And the only way to do that is to get closer to the Puppeteer."

Chapter 7

Understandably, for the next few days Lewis got used to being back in the Dollhouse. He marveled at mundane things like a bookcase full of unreadable text and a few crossword puzzles that had been used half a dozen times already. Although I could tell he mourned Dominique, it was nice to see a face of marvel and awe in the Dollhouse for once instead of the blank stare I was usually greeted with.

For the most part, people stayed away from Lewis and I the two defects. Lewis, like me, was immune to the forced sleeping, but he still had to nap occasionally. However, he could also resist the Puppeteer's controls. Whenever the rest of us went out mining, he would stay in the Dollhouse. Most of those times he spent riding on Galaxy or trying to decipher the alien books.

However, when we were together, we plotted how to become rods. It was slow at first because Lewis had only seen a few rods that had come to the Dollhouse years ago, and he never gave them much thought as they were just messengers from the Puppeteer when they weren't being her maids.

It was on day whatever during one of these plotting sessions that a high screeching noise sounded throughout the Dollhouse.

Screaming rattled the Dollhouse by the bones. Everyone was running, flying up the stairs only to scurry back down. Lewis ran out of the mannequin room and onto the main stairwell, screaming that it was "normal." But that was like trying to control dogs during fireworks.

I was right behind him, clutching my controller and hitting the stairs two at a time. By the time I got to the second floor, sweaty bodies were slamming into me. I swung my controller out front, using it as a shield. Nobody seemed to know which direction they should be going. Up and down, I was being smacked around like a tennis ball.

A hand folded itself into mine. Lewis was next to me.

"What's going on?" I shouted over the blare.

"Arrod!"

Lewis took the next two steps in a flying leap, nearly slamming me against the handrail. My head was pulsing faster than my heart. Arrod? What was that?

"Lewis, what?" I yelled.

He tried saying it slower like I was a child.

"Ar-rod."

"Arrod?"

I stumbled over the last step and out of his slick, sweaty grasp. Most of the puppets were here, spilling into the kitchen and main parlor. The steps managed to come out at the perfect spot, so I was in the front row to the giant door to the Storage. Here, the arrod was coming. Whatever that was.

The doors were partially open with chains stretching across like a web and we were the flies.

Hissing, the door opened wider, making the chains stretch. A keylock sagged in the middle of the links.

My heart absorbed my breath like a sponge. A pale hand with a key poked out of the darkness and unlocked it. The chain sounded like rain as it hit the floor. With a scream of creaking wood, the arrod slunk in. I gasped amidst the screams.

Ashley. The girl the Puppeteer had stolen.

Or at least a creature that resembled Ashley because two wooden rods were attached to her arms that drooped like they had no bones.

Oh my God.

She was a stick-and-rod puppet. I kicked myself. This was the second form. A rod. Not arrod.

The Dollhouse was dead quiet. I stepped forward. "Ashley?"

A thin smile formed on her lips even though it was clear she had no idea who I was. "Hey."

One by one, Ashley's name whirled through the bottom floor like the plague. Like a forgotten chant from a long-dead religion.

"Ashley. Ashley. Ashley."

Lin stepped forward. "Are you okay? You're a…" No doubt he was forcing himself from looking at Lewis. "A rod."

Ashley's arms moved into the pockets of her black sweatshirt. She stared at her arms the same way we marionettes stared at our limbs when the Puppeteer controlled them.

"Good," Ashley said. "You know what a rod is. I would love to be able to talk more but the Puppeteer wants me to read this message. I would hate to see what happens if I don't."

As Ashley cleared her throat, I glanced around. The name of the Puppeteer had everyone staring wide-eyed. Some in horror, but some like they were nothing without her.

"Ahem," Ashley began, "I am the Puppeteer. My children and I control you. That is all you need to know about me.

"What I need is more rods. But things have changed. I need one willing to be a personal servant, and I can't just choose anyone randomly. Therefore, I need a good number of you to participate in a series of challenges.

Tomorrow morning you will be marched up to a different mine, but that will be all the controlling done. You will spend the rest of the day collecting the gold on your own. If you dare take any for yourself, there will be consequences. The one with the most will win.

"All participating puppets will need to tell this rod their numbers which are located on the underside of your controller. And again, the winner will become one of my personal servants. My new right-hand man.

"That is all."

Ashley looked at us, face pale. A mummer rippled through the Dollhouse.

I glanced over at Lewis whose jaw was practically on the floor. Mine would have been too if I wasn't trying to come up with something to say. "This…" I sputtered out, "This is our chance."

"I know," he said, voice squeaking in amazement. Then he shook his head. "It's your chance."

"What?"

Lewis mentioned toward the controller slung around his shoulders. "I can't be controlled by the Puppeteer. There's no way I would be able to keep up with the other puppets when she marches us to the cave. Plus, she'll know if I enter my number. I'm not one of you guys. I have a letter in front of my number. You don't."

I opened my mouth to argue, but there was really nothing I could say. This was all up to me.

He hesitantly put a hand on my shoulder. It was gentle and made me shiver slightly. "I know you can do it, Kindle. Besides, the line doesn't look that long." I took all my focus off his touch to stare at the growing crowd around Ashley as they happily shouted off numbers like a group of preschoolers. There had to be at least fifteen other people there including Lin.

"Go on up there," Lewis said, having to speak louder over the screaming puppets. "And ask if she's seen Dominique."

With his hand off my shoulder, I stumbled forward. I swung my control off my shoulder to find the number.

"Are you Kindle?" Ashley asked when I got to her.

I nodded. I couldn't stop staring at her broken arms.

"I've heard so much about you. Apparently, you're the black sheep around here," she laughed, but it sounded filtered, like speakers with sand in them. How long has it been since I heard a puppet besides Lewis and me laugh?

I faked a laugh too. She had no idea. "Yeah. I guess I better win then. Right?"

Her body movements grew stiff. "Right."

"So, how did you do it? Become a rod, I mean. What's the secret?"

Ashley shrugged. "Maybe I did something. Maybe I didn't. It's a mystery to me." She glanced around the room. "Actually, can I tell you something?" I nodded and she leaned in closer, her voice a whisper. "I'm glad I did. I prefer being a rod." She jerked back like I had slapped her.

But I felt like the one being slapped. Could an abductee even have favorites? Wasn't that Stockholm syndrome? Where you grow attached to your captors? God. She was a sheep too. How could I have been this stupid? She thought this was normal. Like her parents had moved and she liked her new school better.

I quickly rattled off my number as the crowds pressed in like we were at a freak show with the Amazing Stick-And-Rod Girl. Only time for one last question as I was being pushed away like the tide.

"Ashley!" I saw her head jerk up among the sea of puppets. "Do you know a rod named Dominique?"

"No!" And just like that she was lost to the crowd.

Dang. My body numbed like I was being controlled as I made my way back to Lewis. I hated how his face fell when he saw me.

"He's not there, is he?"

"No. But think about it. Ashley just got there. I don't even know all the puppets here, so why would she know all the rods?"

Lewis took a deep breath. "You're right. I've got to stay positive. Dominique's got to be there."

"Yeah." I whispered the motto Lewis came up with: "Stay positive. Stay sharp. Stay smart. Don't let the Puppeteer control more than your limbs."

The rest of the day trudged by worse than the last day of school. I spent most of it with Ashley and Lewis. Turns out Ashley lives in Florida's panhandle. No matter how hard I tried changing the subject, she wouldn't talk about being a rod.

"Listen," she said at one point, "it's not that I think you're being buddy-buddy with me to get information. I just don't want to talk about it."

Odd. I thought being a rod was her new favorite thing. But as she stood up to go back through the Storage, I saw her bruised and scarred arms. She didn't tell me because she was afraid. Afraid of the aliens. Afraid of the Puppeteer. Afraid she had said too much. And it scared me too. Lewis came in right after her. He smiled faintly at me, and I smiled back. I scooted across the couch so he could sit with me.

Instead, he glanced at the window behind me. "Looks like it's getting dark out."

"Yeah. Ashley just left."

Nighttime was my favorite part when all the other puppets were gone except for me and Lewis. He still needed to sleep so this time alone wasn't very long. I secretly looked forward to it, especially after a day like today. We usually talked and watched television. We hadn't shown any of the puppets the TV power cord because we were afraid it would blow their minds.

Lewis and I had a few theories on where the previous puppets went. That they all moved on to the next tier. Why? We didn't know. Maybe the Puppeteer just got sick of them like parents did after summer vacation.

Or maybe they died. But I didn't share this theory with Lewis.

As I thought about this, he turned on the television which showed black and white puppet shows. Like the Puppeteer had filmed them on a family trip. But I could see his eyes flicker to me.

I wrapped my arms around my legs that were tucked into my chest and smiled. "What?"

"I'm worried for you. I should have never forced you to sign up."

My heart dropped as I looked at him. Slightly curly black hair that formed around his face like two parentheses. His lips were turned down, erasing his dimples.

"No. Don't be. Please."

Lewis sucked in a deep breath and smiled at me. And it wasn't all that fake.

"You sound like me."

I laughed. "You sound like me."

He laughed too, and our eyes caught for a second.

"I like you, Kindle. Is it wrong that I'm glad you were abducted?"

"Yes, it is. But I'm glad we still met. You're the only one I can trust around here."

"Yeah," Lewis said. He clicked to another channel, but neither of us were paying attention to it. "I'll stay up with you. All night. Watching…whatever this is." He made a face as one puppet started flying through the air.

"I'll be fine. No need to protect me." I punched his arm.

"Hey." Lewis rubbed the spot. "Can't I spend time with you without you thinking I'm obsessing over you?"

"Nope."

"I just worry about tomorrow."

"You think I'll die?" At this point, it was getting harder to keep a wit going.

He focused on the tv. "Worse. I'm afraid you'll end up like the rest of us."

"You're not a sheep," I told him.

He tried to play it cool. "What?"

I bit my lip. "I'm not sure how hard it is to become one…but…sometimes…when I'm alone…I feel the Puppeteer calling to me. That if I just shut my eyes, I'll be safe and warm."

He gripped both of my arms fast.

"You're not going to be like that. I won't let you. This is why you're joining that competition. Get out of here before she catches you."

"What about you?"

"You keep me strong."

And that's how we spent the night—side-by-side but only focused on the television.

Chapter 8

When Lewis finally went to bed, I spent the rest of the night thinking. Thinking horrible thoughts about tomorrow.

When it was time to meet the other puppets, I went down to the parlor where Ashley stood guard by the front door like a bouncer, limp arms crossed. She was screaming at the volunteers that the Puppeteer wasn't coming to send them off, but for them just to get in line. The line of puppets in front of her was groaning and complaining. One shouted that they deserved to see her.

"Wow," I said to Lewis standing next to me. "Looks like I might actually have competition."

"But you can't let these guys win."

I was a bit taken aback by his seriousness. I was beginning to think Lewis Bryant was anything but serious, so his steady, heavily chosen words made me falter.

"Obviously," I squeaked, eyeing Puppeteer fanboy Lin at the front of the line.

"I wish I could go too," Lewis said. "Maybe I could sneak in. Pretend I'm a wild animal or something."

"No." Ah, there was the Lewis I knew. "The Puppeteer doesn't know you exist and let's keep it this way."

Lewis' chin dropped to his chest. "I hate it when you're rational." But I knew he was just teasing.

Ashley raised her arms—or I suspected the Puppeteer did by the look of surprise on her face.

"All right, marionettes, you'll be heading off now. What lies ahead of you will probably be dangerous. But remember, the Puppeteer is always watching over you. She won't let anything happen to you."

I rolled my eyes while Lewis, who I had left to get in line, made a strangled grunt. We were the only two noises in the silence.

Our controllers raised and in a single file, we were all marched out the door with Lin in the lead and me in the back.

Same mountains, same planet. Over the same dirt paths, across the same rivers. I nearly knew the whole way by heart. Was I growing numb to it? No, I wasn't going to be like everyone else.

At the halfway point, however, we took a different, secluded path. The ground was mulch with wet pine needles compared to our usual route. Curly red moss hung from tilted trees and mushrooms littered the ground. Up ahead, the path was cleared in a zig-zag pattern. Almost like a snake made of axes had cut through. The soft dirt even had a strange pattern to it. Like the kind a sock leaves on your skin after wearing it too long.

All of that was forgotten when we got to the cave. It was made of a light-colored rock, and we had to duck to get in. Like the planet was stifling a yawn. Straight from the get-go was a steep decline. I wanted to grab a wall to keep from falling, but the alien controlling me was more confident. That or it didn't care at all.

This led into a small tunnel, and we began creeping away from the natural light. I choked on the stench of dirty laundry and sweat. My eyes watered as I pressed on, but it only seemed to get stronger. When I stumbled out into a new chamber, I could breathe again. If the room left me with any breath left, that was.

Emeralds and rubies poked out of the walls like sequins. Diamonds and gold stuck out of rock clusters in the corners. My eyes were ready to explode.

My controller clattered to the ground, making me shout. Slinging my controller over my back, I turned around. The other marionettes were still standing there, single file, with their controllers in their arms, waiting for it to move. It was like watching a child hold a dead bird. They didn't understand it wouldn't move again.

Ashely clapped in a few people's faces. "Come on. You've got to get those gems. You signed up for this, didn't you?"

I turned so I couldn't see their reactions, but I imagined it was like yelling at someone half-asleep. They understood you wanted them to do something, but not what.

At least this meant I got a head start. I grabbed an axe from the mining cart with my number–forty-five–on it. Then proceeded to slam it into the wall hard. Dirt and shiny slivers rained down. Lin was quick to follow lead with the others shuffling behind. With axes in their hands, they looked less depressed doing something they were used to. Like industrial zombies, they got to work.

Lin, I realized, was going to be a huge problem. Not only was he way more motivated than the other marionettes but was faster and stronger with an axe than me. He worked like a natural.

Time went by a lot slower now that the Puppeteer wasn't controlling us. It must have taken me an hour to fill the cart until I couldn't see the bottom anymore. Cursing slightly at Lin dumping another bucket in, I wiped my sweaty, dirty face.

I wasn't built for this. Lewis was. Lin was. I was just some girl from Magic City, Miami. I grabbed the cart's rim and slumped my shoulders which were rubbed raw as well as my knees from the strings.

"Just a small break," I whispered.

The ground rumbled. I toppled over landing on my hip. Tears welled, but I blinked rapidly to keep the dust out of my eyes. A loud bang and more shaking. I held onto my controller like a floatation device as my vision blurred. Everyone was screaming. Buckets of gems fell like glass rain. I shouted as the rumbling grew louder. I couldn't hear a single thing. My head could barely function. I must have hit more than just my hip.

All I knew was I had to get out of the mine.

I used a mining cart as a crutch to stand. I only managed a glance at the exit before something barreled out of it. A thing so childish it would only be time before it became a monster to a wicked imagination.

A giant sock puppet snake.

Its once-white body had the same markings as the dirt on the walking trail. An almost human anger blinked through its slit eyes as it unfurled, taking up almost the whole mine. Its head bobbed and weaved, tasting the air with an elastic tongue. The other puppets were calling for the Puppeteer. The snake, meanwhile, had frozen. Then with a burst, it swung its head at a girl trying to sneak past.

The snake grabbed her in its mouth and tossed her like a ragdoll. She hit the ground and rolled.

"Oh, my God!" Ducking, I scrambled to her.

The mine had become a war zone. People running, the walls crumbling, the snake hissing. I gagged on a sweaty smell.

"Get out of my way!" I pushed someone aside to get to her. She was on her back, hand on her head. Her hair covered her forehead, but her fingernails were shiny with blood.

"I'm getting you out of here. Can you stand?"

She stretched her leg a tiny bit, winced, but nodded. "Hold on to me." Grunting, I grabbed her arm and pulled. She stumbled forward like a jig doll. With her head facing the ground, and the light fading, there was no way to tell if she had a concussion.

"I'm too tired, Kindle," she said. I didn't even know she knew my name, never mind what her name was.

The girl whimpered, so I lowered her back down. "Tired? You mean hurt?"

"No." She yawned.

Oh. She meant that kind of tired. The tiredness you don't wake up from. Did she even know it? Or did she think this was the Puppeteer making her sleepy?

For God's sake, don't think. Move!

I laid my controller on the ground. "Hey," I said hard and urgently like my heartbeat. Over my shoulder, the snake had a puppet by his controller swinging him around. His screams made me want to curl into a ball. "Listen, get on my controller. I can't carry you out, but I can pull you like a sled."

The girl didn't answer. She was breathing, but slowly.

Hands shiny with dirt and sweat, I flipped her onto my controller. As I stood, it felt like someone was pulling at a leash around my wrists and knees. Since the strings pulled on the front side of my knees, I would have to drag her by walking backward out of the cave. Three steps, and she rolled off. I bit back a howl.

With a loud bang, three puppets hit the wall thirty feet to my left. This time, they didn't get up like the girl had. I cried out, my chest giving in. Most of the puppets were on the ground, covered in sock puppet saliva. Were they all dead? No, calm down. I steadied my breathing to focus on theirs. But it was too ragged to match. The snake swiped again, this time making a pickaxe rattle across the ground. It was only five feet away. I eyed the snake who was facing the other way. A quick prayer and I jumped for the axe. I slung it over my shoulder only to stumble back at the weight. When I regained myself, the snake was flickering its tongue at me.

Heart pounding and head aching, I stared it back in the eyes. The snake was made of wool. Maybe I could unravel it. No. That was crazy. I wasn't a sword-slinging hero. I raised the axe as its tongue poked out.

My body screamed with anger, every bone rattling with a fiery-red hate as I turned away. The Puppeteer knew this was going to happen all along. I spun back.

"Go away! Leave!" I swung the axe, but missed, nearly taking myself to the floor.

My muscles were so tight that shifting slightly hurt. The axe fell from my hands and clattered on the floor. As the snake pulled back to lunge, I flung my hands out in front of me, hoping to protect my face.

I waited in the darkness of my eyelids. One second passed, then another. It was too long. Like an awkward silence. One by one, I dared my eyes open.

The snake was still there. Breathing in and out in a way that made me sway. It wanted me. I dared it to leave. To slither away, to use those contracting muscles to forget about us.

The snake looked down at me. I had blisters from holding the axe too tight. Just let it be quick.

With a strangled hiss, the snake fled back down the tunnel. With a whisper of breath left, I stumbled to my kneecaps. I was empty, but so, so heavy. What the hell was that?

Blinking back tears, I sat on my legs. I let time pass like that. I wanted to let everything pass sitting there with salty tears biting my dusty skin, but I got up instead. Sniffing, I wiped my face. My face was hot. Lin was somehow beside me, not saying anything for once, just gaping at the minecarts. They were turned over, with gems bleeding over the cavern.

We both turned our heads in sync. There, on the opposite side of the cavern were the three puppets I had seen the snake whip into the air.

Without a single word, Lin jogged forward with me at his heels.

The first one was a girl with long brown hair. She was lying face down in the dirt.

Lin shook her, calling a name I couldn't make out.

She didn't move. The others–two boys younger than me–didn't either.

One of the boys–a Latino–was lying awkwardly with his feet pushed up against the wall. His controller was missing a side of the cross. I could see a small section of his face that wasn't pressed against the wall. His lips were pale and terrified. I grabbed his wrist. Nothing. No. I was just in the wrong place, that's all. I tried the carotid artery in his neck, but there was still no pulse.

The boy I was next to–with a brown buzzcut–was facing up. He looked alive except there was nothing in his eyes. Instead of a window, they were shuttered and battered closed. Somebody over my shoulder shut the eyelids, and I closed my eyes too, feeling nothing. I might as well have been a real puppet.

Someone make this end.

And someone did. The Puppeteer. A bell rang out, and our controllers wobbled slightly. But this was the five-minute warning.

"Quick!" Lin shouted. "We've got to get the injured in some carts!"

He meant the dead.

Puppets exploded, running around like crazy. Puppets…actually doing things that weren't a direct order from the Puppeteer herself. I stumbled to the right, then turned around and drifted to the left. Everyone was running around trying to fix things. It was so bizarre. The three biggest guys, including Lin, had thrown the injured puppets into mine carts.

"My foot!" someone shouted. "Help! I'm stuck!"

I whirled around to find a guy stuck between a mine cart and a wall. I ran over, my pulse counting down the time. How many minutes had passed since the warning? One? Four?

Lin reached the guy at the same time I did. The guy was stuck with his foot wedged behind the left back wheel of the cart and the wall. He was tugging on his pant leg, trying to get his foot to lift. He grunted with each attempt, sweat breaking over his forehead.

"Stay still," I said, holding my hands out. "You're hurting yourself." I knelt, pressing my face against the cart to see better.

"Hurry!" the guy shouted.

"I'm trying," I grunted. His shoe was the problem. If he could remove it, maybe then. But would we have time? All I knew was that if he kept pulling, he was going to sprain himself. "Your shoe. You have to—"

"Move it." Lin pinned me against the cart with his knees before reaching around and grabbing the guy by his leg.

"Wait!" I shouted, but Lin already pulled hard and up.

The guy screeched in pain before stumbling backward and ending up on his rear.

"There," Lin said like some kind of freakin' hero. "Now come on, Kindle. Stop gaping. We're wasting time."

The guy on the ground nodded, his eyes wet. "Thanks, bro." I got up to help him, but he was already on his feet, favoring his left.

My strings tightened and my controller began to hover. It was over. As I scanned the faces around me, I saw weary glances at the controllers. Maybe they understood now. They understood that the Puppeteer was not interested in saving them. She wouldn't have saved that guy; she didn't swoop in to stop the sock snake. She led us to this cave, most likely knowing what we were walking into.

Chapter 9

Securing my controller around my back, I pushed out the Dollhouse's front door to a warm breeze. However, there was nothing else. No birdcalls, no bugs. Outside had been deadly quiet since we'd gotten back from the mines two days ago. The only sound was the wispy grass rustling under my feet as I headed for the newly constructed graveyard.

It only consisted of one mass grave, although if Lewis could find any bigger rocks, he'd make more than one headstone. From my position, the engravings were just squiggles, but I had been here enough times to know the names of the three victims over the last few days.

The rocky top of the headstone scraped against my controller as I squatted down. Just six feet below were people my age, who never got a chance off this planet. They would stay here forever, not even buried in their home's soil. No, here they were buried in the same mass grave. Like war victims. And this had become war. At least for me.

Three days I sat there and thought the same thoughts, watching the trees shiver and the wind howl. I watched red buds stretch out on thin, papery branches, only for them to fall and rot. I watched strange silver beetles emerge from the ground. I watched everything slowly grow only to die. But out here in the decaying wilderness was better than inside the Dollhouse. For three days nobody had heard a word from the Puppeteer or Ashley, letting a seed of doubt spread throughout the Dollhouse. Was the Puppeteer coming back? What was the purpose of the mining trial? Was there going to be more deadly trials? Who was going to be the Puppeteer's second-hand man?

Hulking shadows, gnarly fingers, Ashley's unconscious body being dragged from the Storage.

I shivered and readjusted myself, so I wasn't directly over the grave itself. With the top of my shoes, I nudged the cold, gray ground, folding over a piece of dead grass.

"Kindle!"

I caught myself from toppling at Lewis' greeting.

"Jesus Christ! You scared me."

"Sorry," he said, panting between words as he slung his controller on his back. For the last few days, he had been angrily riding Galaxy more often, and from his wind-blown black curls and calloused fingers, today was no different. Although today, he seemed relaxed.

"Where have you been?" I asked, noting Galaxy tied up to a tree back near the Dollhouse. Usually, Lewis just let her roam.

He gulped in air. "Wandering." He leaned hard on his good leg. "Any news?"

I had a feeling he was holding something back, but I ignored it. "Nope. It seems like for once, nobody wants to even mention the Puppeteer's name."

"Even Lin?"

"No. He's still worshipping her." I pulled a face.

"Oh." He shifted to his other leg and batted at his hair. "Uh, so you've been here a lot." I started to nod, but he quickly cut me off. "So, I found this cool place I want to show you. To take your mind off…this."

"The Puppeteer? Them?" I motioned to the grave. "Or the second trial that hasn't come yet?"

"All of it, I guess. It's not like this isn't important. But I'm worried seeing you like this."

I shifted my foot, leaving a footprint. Was there a dent in the ground from the last three days of being in the same spot? "I guess…" His face was still stiff. "Okay. Yeah." I smiled to show him I meant it.

He clapped his hands together. "Great! We should head out now."

"Is it that far of a walk?" I said, holding my hand out for him to help me up with, not wanting to touch the headstone.

"We'll have to take Galaxy."

"Oh." My face drained as I gathered up my controller.

"What's wrong?"

"It's just I've never ridden a horse before. That's all." I fastened my controller and its strings around my back.

His face lit up slightly. "Yeah. It's fine. I'll be in charge."

In charge.

Suddenly I was seven, maybe eight, standing outside the living room door, back when we had a door there. My father is inside. Alone. I giggle. He's talking to the toys.

The toys?

"If only I could hear you talk too. I think you'd have such a lovely singing voice. And I'd be in charge of it."

I press open the door. "Boo!"

He jumps back, pressing a hand to his heart, laughing.

"My little puppet," he coos, trying to still look scared, but pride is making its way through. He steps away from the couch, revealing a cabinet of dolls on the wall shelves behind him.

"Kindle?" Lewis was stepping closer. "Are you okay?"

I shook my head. "Can't wait to see this place."

"I saw it and knew I had to show you. It's so you."

Lewis told Galaxy to come, and I followed him around the Dollhouse to a stool. Galaxy lined up with it. I hadn't realized she had a saddle on until now. Or where he'd gotten it.

Lewis easily swung into the saddle before instructing me to do the same. On my first attempt, I put my right foot into what I believed was the "stirrup," but he laughed and told me to start over unless I wanted to ride backward. I frowned but redid it to swing on correctly.

My first instinct was to grab the saddle's sides with my fingers, but Lewis took my hands and wrapped them around his stomach. I was glad I was in the back so he wouldn't see my face heat up.

"You okay?"

I breathed in, memorizing the way his body moved when he breathed. At least *he* was still breathing. "Yeah. Just not too fast."

He nodded then prodded Galaxy into a slow walk. The first lurch was harsh. I probably left nail marks on Lewis trying to regain balance. Galaxy tried to stay steady, but her legs still clapped together, making her muscles lurch. The amount of oxygen I could suck in felt tiny. The world was swaying back and forth, and I had to be eight feet off the ground. I closed my eyes and focused on Lewis who wasn't trying to make me laugh for once.

His stomach felt rock hard, not like abs hard, but like something was wrong. I didn't ask. I mean who knows? It could be abs. Or it could be something under his shirt. It just didn't feel like skin.

I felt sicker than before, but I leaned into him, shoving those thoughts out of my head. A few more minutes passed before I croaked out: "Lewis, are we almost there?"

"Yeah. Just between those rock structures." His head bobbed in the direction of two rocky pillars leaning off the edge of the rocky cliffs we'd been following.

I felt giddy for the first time, wondering what it was. Knowing him, he'd take me somewhere I thought was interesting. Although, I wasn't sure I was that interesting. Unless we were making dolls. But that didn't sound very "Lewis" like.

Then I was hit by a smell that made me smile. Sea salt. We were by an ocean. I took a deep breath which made Lewis turn around with a smile. "Guess that gave it away, huh?"

"An ocean! I mean, of course there would be an ocean for life to exist."

He rolled his eyes before turning back to Galaxy. "You're so cute when you're nerdy."

Oh. That was like being hit in the chest with a ton of ice. Cute. But did he mean that in a teasing buddy-buddy way? Or did he think we were flirting? I couldn't see his face for confirmation. A cold sweat broke out over my shoulders at the thought of not knowing. I mean, he was cute too, but that was different when a girl said it to a boy, right?

Then Galaxy twitched, but harder like she didn't want me to think those thoughts. She whinnied and reared back harshly. Closing my eyes, I flung myself on Lewis.

"Relax," Lewis screamed, his voice full of panic as he shook me off. "Tuck and roll!"

Then I realized he was shouting at me, not the horse. We were going to fall!

He curled himself into a ball and rolled off the side of Galaxy. I tucked my head to my chest, but I brought my bringing my knees up, I realized my shoes had snatched onto the stirrups.

"Stop!" I screamed, my hands flying off the saddle like it was instinct. Everything seemed like a movie in slow motion. I was holding my hands over Galaxy's head. Spit formed at her lips. Like a snap to reality, I became aware that she was a jig doll. Then she stopped. Froze.

Lewis was on her, grabbing the reins, and holding them straight out in front of her head. "No," he said firmly.

For some reason, I found that funny. He was going to scold this freakin' horse like it was some kind of dog.

He stared at me wide-eyed as I laughed. "Are you okay?"

I tried to speak, but his face made me laugh harder. "Are…are you?"

He still looked stunned. "Not a scratch. You're the one who's hit their head."

"I'm sorry." I tried to wipe the smile off my face, but it crept up my cheeks anyway. "What happened?"

"I don't know. Whatever spooked her is gone now but thank God she stopped like that."

Nothing was funny anymore because that wasn't her that stopped, that much I knew. It had to have been the Puppeteer. But that was impossible. She had no eyes on Lewis. Or at least we thought. Had that changed?

"Maybe she was just jealous," I said instead, the adrenaline pumping through making me feel much braver.

He grabbed my wrist to pull me off. "Of what?"

I slid off Galaxy until we were both on the small top step of the stepping stool. Way. Too. Close.

"That you were flirting with me?" I said like some kind of confidence goddess. But he made me feel strong like that. Not like I didn't want to bite off my tongue as soon as it came out.

"Were we?"

"What?"

"Flirting?" He smirked.

"I don't know. You started it."

He pretended to push me but ended up taking my hand and guiding me off the step like a princess out of a carriage.

I frowned. "Are you sure you're okay? You took that fall pretty hard and without a helmet."

He waved at me. "I'm fine." "So, do you like it?"

I scanned the beach for the first time. The sand was a bright white just like back home. The water was the same emerald color, but this time with a mix of orange from the sunsets. The only thing missing were the tourists and gulls.

Especially the tourists.

But it felt nice to be alone, but not for once. I wasn't in the middle of the hivemind puppets, and not alone at night waiting for Lewis to wake.

"Yeah. I love it. It's like home."

"I knew it," he said. Like I would have disagreed.

"How did you find this place?"

"Galaxy never likes being around here. I think she hates sand being in her hooves. Yesterday, though she was so eager for a ride, she didn't even care where we went."

"Strange." I turned to the ocean's horizon which the sun had disappeared around. A slight breeze picked up.

I let my eyes follow along the beach. It was a small place, maybe forty feet of coast before it broke off into tan rocks. I crouched and put my fingers in a wave as it broke against the coast. There weren't any shells or living things to bury back into the sand. There weren't even any fish.

"My father loved fishing," I said pulling out the glass shards I remembered of the past as Lewis sat beside me. "He never brought us along.

Occasionally my mother, but I don't think she liked it. She'd rather be doing something quaint like sewing. She made the most beautiful puppets and dolls, and my father kept every one of them."

Lewis nodded and extended his shoes into the ocean. "Sounds nice."

I nodded. "Sorry. I don't know where that came from."

"No, I like it when you talk about yourself. You can be mysterious at times."

I crossed my arms over my chest. "I try to ignore my past."

"Why?"

I scoffed at his rudeness, but let it slide. "Sometimes…it feels like it's fading. Like I have to try hard to remember. Memories don't come naturally."

Lewis nodded. "Sometimes, when I was still in the sinkhole, I pretended like I didn't have a family. That I was raised by horses instead."

I couldn't help it. I laughed.

Lewis smiled. "I never know what's going to make you laugh."

"I'm sorry. I shouldn't have laughed."

"Oh, it's okay." He put his hand over his eyes like a visor. "How big do you think this place is? Big as Earth? Are there islands out there? If we swim far enough, do we reach something?"

I shook my head. "I think it's a small planet."

"How do you know?"

I shrugged. It was a gut feeling and usually, I didn't blurt those out.

"Science stuff," I merely said instead. "You want to go swimming?"

"Sure." With a grunt, he stood and then took my hand.

The water was freezing as I let it lap up to my knees. Lewis was slower, barely sloshing through, like he was going to float away if I let go. His face was a mixture of surprise–both the kind you like and the kind you don't. I knew he was fighting the instinct to pull his arms together to subconsciously protect himself, but the fact he was still holding (a.k.a crushing) my wrist felt huge. A surge of power went through me, and I guided him close, our controllers being used as buoys. By now the water was up to our hips.

"I take it you've never been to the ocean before."

"Do you even know where Kansas is?"

I giggled, but like one of those giggles girls do when they're with their crush. I didn't even know I was capable of that pitch. "Not really. I never had a good grasp of geography."

Actually, what I wanted to say was that I didn't have a grasp of it *at all*. I think my home-schooling parents just skipped geography. Try being the only high schooler who doesn't know how many states are in the US. But Lewis didn't need to know exactly how weird I was. So, I tucked the memory back into my mind like a woman's ruffled dress, stitching it over and over to hide it forever. My weird brain was good at that. Memories didn't really slip out except for that one by the grave. But I deduced that down to emotional stress. Maybe even existential stress.

"So, this is the ocean? Getting hit with waves?"

By now we had gone a bit farther. I was keeping an eye on the shore so we wouldn't drift too far off.

"Basically." I dipped down to my shoulders and gasped at the sting. "Dang, that's cold."

Lewis puffed up his cheeks in an exaggerated manner and dunked under, head and all. He came out, without even a gasp. Almost flawless. It made me wonder if puppets could even suffocate.

He spat and wiped the water out of his eyes. "Huh. Wasn't as cold as I thought."

"That's because you're from the north." I splashed water at him before retreating my frozen finger-sticks back to the warmth of my armpits. I didn't have goosebumps, but boy was it ever cold.

He chuckled. "Want to go back? To the shore."

We both looked back. Galaxy was looking a bit anxious. "Yeah. Your horse looks freaked."

When we got to the shore, Lewis checked on Galaxy. I watched from the warm sand, shivering. After a bunch of petting her head and soft noises, she calmed down.

He came back, looking tired. He didn't say anything, but I could hear the sigh in his voice.

I started to stand in case he wanted to leave. Although I didn't know much about horses, I trusted Lewis' instincts.

I brushed the sand off me. "So, what do you want to do?"

He glanced back at Galaxy, and I could see his tenseness, but the Lewis I also knew didn't back down like that.

He smiled. "Let's not worry about Galaxy. She'll be fine." He scooped up a piece of sand like a snowball and grinned at me.

Ten minutes later, Lewis was making a pile of sand by my controller, my body already buried.

"Would it offend you terribly if I made you into a centaur instead of a mermaid?"

I opened my eyes and focused on hundreds of stars overhead. "I don't even know what that is."

"It's a human with a horse's body."

"Oh. So, it's fantasy. My brother would have known about it. He loved fantasy." I made sure I said it like I knew more than that about my brother.

Lewis formed a horse leg.

"What's Dominique like?" I regretted it as soon as it came out.

If he felt the same, he didn't say so. He rounded the hoof out. "A lot like me. Except he's super serious at times."

"Then how is he like you?"

Lewis laughed. "What was his name? Your brother's?"

"Vince. I also had a little sister named Poppy."

"I don't think your brother and mine would have gotten along."

I smiled. "Are you almost done?"

"It's a shame you won't be able to see this masterpiece."

I rolled my eyes and leaned my head back. For the first time since my family had died, I was fine. I belonged.

A faint whinny came from behind. When I opened my eyes again, Lewis had a strange look on his face. Like he had sucked on a lemon.

"Where's Galaxy?" he said.

I couldn't see behind me where Lewis had tied her to a tree, but by his face, it wasn't good. Lewis stood, smearing sand against his soaked jeans. With quick movements, he was tugging me out of the sand.

"The tracks go that way." He pointed out toward the rocks at the end of the coastline.

We followed them until we ran into Galaxy, about halfway to the rocks, grazing in a shriveled patch of grass. She had neither her saddle nor reins. Lewis noticed it too, as he patted her back.

"I left the saddle loose, but it shouldn't have come off this easily. Unless something spooked her..." He looked further down the coast. "Come on."

I didn't budge. "And we should go toward it?"

"I have to find that saddle."

With no other explanation, he set off. I scampered after him with Galaxy dancing along behind until she saw where we were heading. With a neigh, she stepped back, shaking her head.

Lewis ignored her, walking faster until he was practically running. With a sinking feeling, I realized what he thought would be ahead.

Dominique.

What we found instead was a cave carved into the cliffs. Definitely man-made…Alien-made? Regardless, he brushed aside my cries to stop and soldiered on in.

"Lewis, stop." I tried again. "There could be another sock puppet snake." I kept calling until he disappeared and kept listening until his footsteps stopped suddenly.

"Lewis?"

"Kindle, get over here!"

He sounded upset, so I threw wet hair out of my face and braced myself for what was inside. It was a straight path into darkness.

The air was cool and damp, making the hair on the back of my neck stand up. With gritted teeth, I started naming bones starting from the bottom of me. Phalange bone. The darkness closed in. Metatarsal bone. Was something following me? Cuneiform bone. Where was Lewis? My controller, which I was using as a white cane grated against the wall. Gripping it tighter, I went around a bend and into a chamber.

A golden light from an unknown source lit up a landfill of burnt marionettes, rod-and-stick puppets, and ventriloquist dummies. But these weren't the alien kind. They were toy dolls.

Bent over, I slowly circled the room. "Whoever made these was the same person. The woodwork on the marionettes is too similar."

I lifted a stick-and-rod puppet. Its arm poles clattered to the ground. Her doll eyes were melted, and tufts of material were missing.

Stomach clenching, I threw it back down.

Meanwhile, Lewis had picked up a ventriloquist dummy only to have the jaw fall off. He gasped at the broken horror.

Turning back to the pile, I chose a marionette–a female with long black hair. Or was it just burnt? I lifted the hair to be greeted with a word inked on the back of her skull.

"Snow," I said.

"What?"

"This marionette has the word 'snow' on the back of her head."

"Really?" Lewis started grabbing puppets in handfuls.

I joined in, carefully picking the most intact ones. The rest, I couldn't stomach.

"Storm," Lewis said a bit later. In his arms was a female marionette. He had lifted back her long red hair. "Are these names?"

"Who names their child Storm?"

"I don't know."

We dug around for a bit more but didn't end up finding anything. Our best bet was still that they were names, but that didn't feel right. I had no idea what they meant. Could be part of a cult for all I knew.

"This is too creepy," I said, hugging my arms. "Let's get out of here."

Lewis looked around the room. "Yeah…I just thought there would be…"

I put my hand on his tense shoulder. "I know."

"You're right though. This is creepy. Let's split."

Together we gathered up Galaxy's saddle which was dumped a few feet outside the cave entrance and rode back. It was dark and quiet, and when we got back to the Dollhouse, Lewis barely said goodnight before heading off to his room, but I doubted he was getting any sleep. As for me, I sat in the parlor, thinking the same thoughts on repeat.

What was that place? And why was Galaxy so afraid? Before I could repeat these for the thousandth time, I was lost in another hidden memory.

"No!" I twist out of Mother's arms. "How could you?"

"Honey, it was only a toy," Mother says, bending down to brush hair out of my face.

"No! You ruined him!" I am standing in the laundry room, staring at the washing machine, tears in my eyes, and anger like I have never felt before. I grab a bottle of bleach and throw it at her.

She shrieks and holds her red nail-polished hands out to block it. "Stop it! You don't know how much I sacrifice for you!"

The memory disappeared sharply, leaving me with a splitting headache. Big tears were streaming down my face. I was such a brat to my parents over a stupid doll. But something didn't feel right. I was broken. I had all these memories flooding me. Ones I didn't remember. Ones that made me feel bad.

I ran across the Dollhouse until I was in an empty bedroom. I threw myself under all the sheets and comforters. All I wanted to do was sleep and forget. But neither of those would happen as long as I was still on this planet.

Chapter 10

Still on the bed hours later, I rubbed my temples, palms going into dried-out eyes. From the first floor, I could hear movement. The others were coming back from their night in the Storage.

"Kindle?"

My heart jumped out of my chest. Lewis from the other side of the door.

"Coming." I got off the bed to let him in.

"Ashley's here," he simply said before turning to go downstairs.

I followed him down to the parlor where I shuddered at the memories that had haunted me last night. But I forgot all about that as Ashley cleared her throat, eyeing Lewis and me. Clearly, we were late.

"Congratulations, puppets," Ashely read words not from her but from the Puppeteer. "I know there was some kind of incident, so I changed the scoring a bit."

I snorted. *Some kind*. Three people died!

"I based it on your actions back in the mine instead of the gems, which you disappointed me in. I have ended up with two winners: Number One–"

Lin jumped off his chair. "Yes! Beat that!"

Ashley glared at him, but he just crossed his arms over his chest, that cocky grin still plastered on his stupid face. Meanwhile, I was shifting back and forth. If someone like Lin could have won, who's telling who's next?

Ashley glanced around the room before continuing. "And number forty-five."

Before I could even remember my number, Lewis was shaking my shoulder. "You did it, Kindle! I knew you would."

All eyes were on me, but Lin's especially bored into my cranium. For the first time, I wondered if anyone had seen my encounter with the snake.

Then some girl put her fingers in her mouth and whistled, making me jump out of my skin. With one quick glance at her face, I recognized her as the girl I had helped in the cave. Out of the corner of my eye, I saw Lewis stick his tongue out at Lin. I ribbed him as Ashley shouted for our attention again, her arms shaking the piece of paper rapidly. Or rather the Puppeteer was shaking it for her. God, when was the Puppeteer going to let her rest?

"No more interruptions, all right?" Ashley cast one last look around the parlor before continuing. If she hadn't, the Puppeteer might have ripped her paper in half. And then probably Ashley. I sunk down.

"These two puppets will continue with a tiebreaker. A game of trivia about this place will start today at noon. That is all." Ashley dropped her head and stepped back like she would disappear. Did she feel guilty for being the messenger?

Lewis spun me around to face him. "This is great, Kindle. I'm an expert at this. I'll quiz you with everything I know."

"So…cheating?" Lin said from over my shoulder. "That's your big plan?"

"It's not cheating," I said. "It's learning. And what are you doing here anyway?"

"You mean right now? Or in the competition?"

"Both."

"Obviously I was the one that saved Joey when he was stuck.

I balked. "That?"

"And what did you do?"

I tried to speak, but my anger was too much.

Lewis put his hands on my shoulders. "You'll never know."

Lin didn't look like he had an answer for that. Lewis probably didn't even know. Heck, I didn't.

"Anyway," Lin said, after composing himself. "I just wanted to congratulate you on tying." He held his hand out.

I shook it, my hand swallowing his. He made a quick face at that and stepped back.

I waited for him to disappear back into the crowd before whispering: "Man, what a jerk."

"But a beatable jerk," Lewis said. "We've got this one in the bag."

"Yeah." I glanced back up the staircase. "Let's get started on studying. I doubt today's a mining day."

Hours passed as we studied upstairs in Lewis' room. Thankfully, he had the same studying methods as me. Take the information and grind it up, stuff it inside my head, and rattle it around so it won't escape. I needed to absorb everything, but instead of spitting it back up on a test later, I had to keep it. The information was crucial, something every puppet should know.

Too bad I couldn't slap the Puppeteer across the face with it.

"Christ," Lewis said, rubbing his eyes, and leaning back on the edge of his bed. We were on the floor sitting crisscross from each other. We didn't have any flashcards or any way to write down the material, so all of it was Lewis shouting out keywords with me repeating as much as I could. "You're basically a computer."

I balled my hands into fists and twisted the hem of my shirt. "But it isn't enough. Who knows where Lin is getting his information from?"

"Not me, and that's all that matters. You basically have a time traveler as a history teacher."

"But memory is flawed. It can be rearranged and disfigured."

Lewis opened his eyes and pulled his knees to his chest. "I know this stuff, Kindle. You have to believe me. And what's Lin doing? Not getting a tour of the Puppeteer's facility which would be the only other thing better than me."

"But you've told him stuff too. And he's bright, he remembered at least some of it."

Lewis shrugged and looked at his feet. His face was off somewhere else.

"Lewis?"

"I didn't tell you everything. I didn't know if it was real or not. It was just a rumor Dominique heard. I mean, I heard it too but–"

"Lewis, what?"

"Rods aren't the only type of puppets around here."

I frowned. Was this another joke? "I know. Galaxy's a jig–"

"No. I mean the rumor goes if you're a good enough rod that this is an even bigger promotion. There's another level beyond the marionettes and the rods."

I covered my mouth, feeling weightless.

"There are rumors that the Puppeteer has another, more powerful alien working for her. One who calls himself the Ventriloquist. He can turn humans into ventriloquist dummies. I heard he can talk through them. Control their voices instead of their bodies."

I threw my arms around the swirly, oak bedpost feeling like if I let go, I'd float away. Everything had been manageable (sort of) until this had to show up. Lin had no idea, and as Lewis wrapped his arms around my shoulders, I realized had to win. I let my body relax in Lewis' awkward embrace.

"Kindle, it's all right," he said in a hushed tone. "It's just a rumor."

"But it's true."

His chin on my shoulder blade flexed into a frown. "How do you know?"

"Because why wouldn't it be?"

He laughed softly and pulled away. "You're such a downer."

A knock came at the door before Ashley shoved it open. "It's time."

I cast one last glance at Lewis before following her out. As we went downstairs, I kept swiping at my eyes, hoping they weren't as puffy and raw as they felt. If Lin saw me crying, he'd throw a party, and right now I couldn't stomach another cocky grin.

In the parlor, Lin was waiting by the metal door Ashley comes from, the one that led to the Storage. He had a blindfold in one hand and Ashley handed me mine like we were fighting to the death instead of taking a history test.

I swallowed, making the fluttering in my stomach grow louder, beating along my organs like a marching band doing taps.

"Put them on," Ashley said. "I can help you if you need."

In what looked like one swift motion, Lin had his tied while I was struggling to fix mine around my ears.

When the blindfold was "snuggly" digging into my eye sockets, Ashley put a hand on my shoulder and my controller in my arms and started to spin me around. She let go and let me spin on my own. Even though it was only the three of us, I felt like everyone was watching. Basically, I felt like an idiot, spinning there, wondering if Lin had to endure this too. Ashley dropped her hand back on my shoulder hard, letting me pitch to the right. My controller tugged, and I let it float out of my hands.

We were controlled through what I thought was a wall, but apparently not. I tried to tune in to my other heightened senses, but my body and mind felt sick. I almost puked, but we kept marching. Marching on and on for what felt like ages until I was stopped. Someone who I could only guess was Lin brushed past me.

My strings went slack, and I reached up to pull my controller to my chest. Then nothing. The silence was deafening as sweat rolled down my neck. I was about to break when a pair of hands whipped off the blindfold.

I flinched back, taking in the blinding white lights illuminating the colors around me. Two red armchairs, two brown pedestals holding two gray orbs, and a giant black television screen that took up almost the whole wall. Three rod puppets stood under the screen, arms crossed, but faces taking in the room like they were just brought here.

Lin stood by one chair, a male rod behind him while I stood by the other. The girl behind me wasn't Ashley, and her squeaky voice told me to sit.

The chair was plusher than I expected, making me dip down a bit. I was stiff as a board though, my controller on my lap and head facing forward. Not like it mattered what I looked at since the back of the chair wrapped around my head like the blinders Lewis used on Galaxy. All I could see was my pedestal and the giant gray orb on it. However, if I craned my neck, I could see Lin perched on the edge of his chair with his head leaning toward a rod. His mouth was open and eyes wide.

"Wow. Is this where the Puppeteer lives?" he said.

I didn't pay attention to what the rod said back, I was going through all the facts so fast, but all I could really think about was what Lewis had said.

I heard he can talk through them. Control their voices instead of their bodies.

How much more of this system was there?

A flicker of blue came from my left. The television had turned on and was now displaying a scoreboard with Lin's and mine's numbers.

A female rod came forward. She had dark skin and long black braids. She had a sheet of paper but wasn't shaking as hard as Ashley usually did. "Welcome, One and Forty-Five, to the next trial. Here you will be doing a trivia test. It is not to see who is the fastest, but rather who has the answer I desire."

What if this was another set-up like the gem collecting? What if any second now the Puppeteer was going to release some bears? I glanced at the five puppets. They wouldn't hurt us. We were all in this together.

I settled deeper into my chair.

The lights went off, making my skin feel electric with fear. Then slowly, the orbs began to glow a soft baby blue before they unfolded into a curved keyboard. All the keys were dark gray except the enter key which was a blinding green. Almost like I was looking down onto an island on Earth's oceans. Is this what the aliens thought would comfort us? A sorry make-shift home?

The number one blinked onto the screen before vanishing just as fast.

A boy's voice came from overhead. "What is the name of this planet?"

Great. First one and I had no clue.

I glanced up at Lin and our eyes met. Face burning, I turned back to the keyboard. At least I wasn't the only one struggling.

Shaking my head, I quickly typed in "It does not have one."

My number on the screen turned from orange to black and five hundred appeared under my name. Lin was quick to follow with the same score.

Did this planet not really have a name? I mean, it must not if I got points for that.

"Second Question. What color is the sand on the beaches?"

I quickly typed in white. My name turned orange, but my numbers went down to zero. My mouth dropped slightly. What the heck? I got it wrong? I tried to type it in again, but my keys flashed red and buzzed.

Lin's name turned orange and he gained three hundred points. I met his eyes. He looked relieved.

For about a second before he flashed me a cocky smirk.

I scrunched my face. Clearly, it was just a mistake. There had to be other beaches. Ones more important than the tiny place Lewis had found. I'd get Lin next time.

Back and forth we bounced through questions with a nonsensical point system. One minute I'd be ahead, score something confidently, and drop. At question fifteen, my clothes were soaked with sweat and my head felt like it'd been sliced in half. I was way behind Lin by a thousand points.

I had my temple twisted up between my fingers, tears on the brim. There was no way I could be losing this badly. Lewis had told me all he knew, and while he didn't know everything, there were questions I *shouldn't* have been missing. Like what kind of puppet were we? Marionette. Why was that wrong? Unless the questions were rigged. Meaning, I was getting points for getting things *wrong*. How could I have not seen it? The Puppeteer wouldn't want someone who knew more than they should about this abduction situation. Then they might revolt. But I'd had to test my theory before I started typing in gibberish.

"Question sixteen. What galaxy are we in?"

I looked up from my lap at the keyboard, but it might have been in another language. Lin's number lit up on the screen. He was getting these so fast. Impossibly fast. I put my fingers on the keys and smashed them. I hit "enter" before I had time to come to my senses. My name lit up. Then my total jumped six hundred as did Lin's.

I was right. The more wrong answers I put in, the more the Puppeteer wanted me. She wanted someone so stupid, they had no idea what was going on. She just wanted someone who would blindly worship her.

"Question seventeen. What kind of wood are the controllers made of?"

I knew this was an alien wood called pow, and I knew Lin knew that too. It was sort of common knowledge, but I decided to push it one more time. I typed in "pine." My name lit up almost at the same time Lin got it wrong. He looked shocked while I reaped in a sweet two hundred points. But my score was still nowhere near Lin's score.

As we finished off the rest of the twenty questions, all I could do was pray I'd catch up. But I didn't.

When the last question went through, I let out a scream and slammed my head back into the chair. Teeth gritted, I stared at the ceiling waiting for the feeling of loss to come and take me prisoner. But at that moment all I could think was what Lewis would say. I had failed.

I took my eyes off the ceiling tiles and to Lin. The other rods were crowding around him. I wanted to become the chair. I should be screaming in rage or crying in grief, but I felt dead. Like an object. Like a real puppet.

I regretted taking my eyes off the ceiling as Lin's met mine. "Don't be a sore sport." He offered me his hand.

"You don't know what you've done, Lin," I croaked. "Don't you know how messed up this place is?"

He rolled his eyes as he pulled me out of my chair but made sure to drop my grip as soon as I was standing. "Just because you lost–"

"Lin, listen to me–"

"Come on, you two," the girl who had been standing behind me said. She handed each of us a blindfold.

I ripped mine away from her and made a poor knot behind my skull. Rage bubbled below, but I couldn't even keep a balled fist as the aliens took over, moving me out the door.

Every cuss word I knew, every threat that crossed my mind was directed at Lin. Although they never passed my closed lips, I wished I was brave enough.

Lin would literally be handed the keys to the Puppeteer. He could talk to her, get to know her. He could free us all if only he had a single brain cell in that pudding skull of his.

Eventually, we stopped moving and my controller lowered, but I didn't give a crap and let it clatter to the ground. If I had been any taller it might have taken me down with it.

I tore away the blindfold in a quick tug. We were in the Dollhouse's parlor. Behind us was the door to the Storage. Nobody was in the parlor, but I could hear movement upstairs. Then a holler. Lewis.

"They're back!"

I stepped close to Lin. "Meet me after this on the third floor, first room on the right."

The rest of the puppets flowed downstairs and into the parlor. Lin tossed his hands up and jumped, shouting his head off. Everyone was yelling and screaming, but I parted my way through, ignoring the few stares directed at me. My face burned as I tugged down on my shirt wishing it was big enough to swallow all of me. Why had Lewis bragged I was going to win?

Because I should have. That's why.

I was beginning to climb the staircase when someone grabbed my upper arm. I shook my arm out knowing it was Lewis without having to look.

"What happened?" he said, voice dripping with disappointment and confusion.

I wanted to speak, but the first floor was so loud, I just motioned for him to follow me because I didn't think I had the strength to do anything but whisper. He followed like I knew he would, finally closing the door behind us on the third floor. He leaned in closer to me, eyes boring into mine, but I just took in a shuddering breath and looked around.

"Kindle, how did Lin win?"

"It was rigged. We were set up. The Puppeteer wanted wrong answers; not right, and Lin got almost all the questions wrong."

Lewis' jaw dropped. "I don't believe it."

I studied the floor, balling my hands into fists. "Well, it's true. Don't worry. I asked Lin to meet me here."

"Good idea." Lewis was pacing the room. "We have to tell him everything though. About Dominique, about my controller, about the other puppets, about the Ventriloquist."

"Can we trust him?"

Lewis' silence made me wince. "There's no choice," he finally said.

"But you don't."

"Of course not."

"I don't either. He's too far gone. Too obsessed with the Puppeteer."

Lewis shook his head. "Christ."

The door opened, and Lin pranced in with a huge grin plastered across his face. I looked away, face heating. I was so below him right now.

"Nice job on the win, man," Lewis said, making the eye contact I would never.

Lin frowned. "So, what did you call me in here for, or can I go now?"

"Lin," Lewis said, approaching him slowly. "While you're at the Puppeteer's side there are a few things we want you to do." Lin was about to say something, but Lewis cut him off. "My brother, Dominique, he's out there somewhere, and we need you to find him."

"Fine. Tell him his little bro said hi. Anything else?"

"Nope!" I quickly blurted, making them both look at me like I had two heads. "That's all."

Lin shook his head. "Weirdos." He stood. "I'll be leaving now."

"Yeah, see ya," I said loudly to drown out anything Lewis was starting to say.

Lin didn't even glance back as he left.

"What was that for?" Lewis hissed when we couldn't hear any more footsteps.

"We can't let Lin know how we really feel about the Puppeteer," I said. "I mean, what if he tells her?"

Lewis shook his head. "But he was our messenger. What now? Ashley?"

"No. I don't trust her either."

"Then who?"

"Me."

Lewis snorted but looked regretful. "Sorry. I know you're smart. I'll shut up now. Just tell me how we're getting out of this."

I paced the room like he had before. "I can disguise myself as a rod. Then, tomorrow, I'll duck out with Lin and Ashley. Or maybe later. I don't know yet."

Lewis stared at the wall for a few seconds. "Are you sure you can pull this off?"

"No. But we have to try. With Lin at the Puppeteer's side, who knows what will happen next."

Lewis rubbed his temple. "You're insane, but–"

"Lewis–"

"*But*! You didn't let me finish, Kindle. It might just work."

Then I could find the Puppeteer and find a way off this awful planet.

Chapter 11

When the next day came, I wasn't there to see Lin and Ashley off. The night before Lewis and I had worked our butts off building a disguise. It wasn't that hard to replicate a rod—all I needed was bunched-up sleeves that looked like my arms were limp and two rods underneath. To accomplish that, I nicked a sewing needle and thread from an abandoned crafts room. For the actual rods, we stitched two long sticks into the sleeves' fabric. The hardest part was figuring out how to hide my controller. Eventually, we decided on strapping it to my back with string and then covering it up with my shirt. It was awkward and bulky, and when I walked, I waddled, but standing in front of the mirror, I didn't make a bad rod. I twisted, trying to see my back, but couldn't.

Downstairs, the cheering and shouting of Ashley and Lin's departure had died down. Lewis would be back any minute. Yesterday I had given him the cruel task of becoming all buddy-buddy with Lin, so it would seem natural as Lewis stood by him when he left. In reality, Lewis was slipping a rock into the doorframe so the door couldn't close all the way. It was small enough so nobody except us would notice.

Butterflies in my stomach, I wondered why no one else had thought of this. Because it was dangerous and stupid? Because the others were brainwashed? Because who knows what would happen if we were caught? We could go missing like Lewis' group.

The door opened and the butterflies fluttered to my throat. I wasn't daring, I wasn't dangerous, I wasn't brave or rebellious. I never got in trouble in school and rarely disobeyed Tiffany. What made me think I could do this?

Lewis came through, meeting my eyes, and I remembered why. The butterflies in my throat turned to ashes and burned on their way down as he stepped closer.

"It looks great," Lewis said.

"Thank you," I felt electrocuted in the silence. "I'll try to see if I can stop back here at night."

"If it's too dangerous then don't."

"I won't." But I would. I couldn't imagine not returning to Lewis. Not after what Dominque did to him.

"Kindle." But it wasn't a scolding. He said it softly, stepping forward until the tips of our shoes touched.

My head emptied, then filled with panic. My face heated. He was so handsome up close with his strong jaw and soft expression. Blindly, I reached up and stroked his cheek. My hands had always felt too big to be girly, but on his face, they felt right.

He closed his eyes. For a wild second, I thought we were going to kiss. I thought about kissing him right there and then. Him, wrapping his arms around my neck and pulling me closer.

"We don't have much time," he whispered, stepping back, leaving me reeling.

"Agreed."

We hurried down to the parlor. Lewis must have done something because there was nobody there, and usually this place was swarming. At first, I didn't see the pebble; it was so small, but Lewis knew what to do. He turned back to me.

"Good luck. When I open the door, it's going to be heavy, so hurry through."

"Thank you, Lewis."

"Wait. Are you sure you want to do this? Nobody's asking for you to be a hero."

"Yes. But they are asking me to sit still, and I can't do that."

He nodded but looked like throwing up.

He quickly switched out the pebble for his hand and wrenched the door open. I helped him pull it open before slipping into the Storage. I turned back to say one last goodbye, but the door slammed shut hard, leaving me in darkness.

Guess I was on my own then.

I stood still, eating my own heartbeat, but no lights came on. I had faint memories of the Storage from my first night. It was basically one long hallway of shelves with human-sized jars on top. Reaching out, I kept my palms along the glass confinements. Sometimes there would be a squeak. At least someone took pride in their puppet collection. A collection of expensive toys? Is that all we were? Of course, the Puppeteer didn't care if we died either so maybe not.

It didn't take long before I could make out a sliver of light on the ground from the exit. The door, like the first one, was gigantic and metal. Like the other one too, there didn't seem to be a doorknob. Panic made my nerves fly. We hadn't thought past this. I had assumed it would be an easy exit since it was not only the single way out of the Dollhouse, but also, we'd gone this way to do the second trial.

Breathe, Kindle. You didn't get this far for nothing.

Scanning the door once again, this time running my fingers along, I found a fingerprint scanner. It reminded me of the one on my phone. But it couldn't be. How would Ashley and Lin have gotten through then? I touched the pad to feel for bumps or a switch, but seconds later the pad turned blue, and the door opened.

Had it really been this easy the entire time? Something had to be wrong. But I could deal with that later.

As soon as I stepped out, dizziness hit me like a bullet to the head. One blink and I was down on the floor with my facial features growing heavier and heavier, like they would drop off my face. Like ice to liquid. Black spots climbed up my eyes until I shut them. Breathing heavy, I felt alone. Like I was at the bottom of the ocean. I realized I couldn't even remember what color the cold tile floor was.

Then slowly, like a song fading out, my face felt real again as did my body. I opened my eyes to an emerald flooring that reminded me of my parents' kitchen tile. Ugly, like a sparkly pickle. When I stood, my controller shifted, but one quick touch confirmed it was still in place. Thank God.

I was in the middle of a long hallway running horizontally. The rest of the tiles were the same shiny green color. On the white walls where thousands of jewels previous puppets must have collected: bejeweled mirrors, framed alien gibberish, ruby clocks. The walls' edges were stacked with ivory statues of strange animals. I bit the inside of my cheek. So, this is what the marionettes died over? Freaking wall décor? Nobody was supposed to be this evil.

As I pivoted to the right, I recognized some of the décor. Like the mirror reminded me of something in my parents' bathroom. And that bust over there looked like something I had seen on a field trip...maybe? It looked like something my father would have made jokes about. He would have changed his voice and pretended to talk as it:

Why only my head? You know, I was pretty ripped in my days? Why is that statue over there made of gold and not me? Outrageous!

He did it for a lot of things. Talked for animals, objects. He loved to read to us. According to my mother, my father was rather shy around other adults, but around us kids, he came to life.

A giant rip formed inside my rib cage. Couldn't anything beautiful stay alive? I glanced at a giant ruby butterfly with a five-foot wingspan on the wall. Not that kind of beautiful. Like…like family beautiful.

I jumped out of my skin as a door ahead shut. It made me sweat. How many closing or opening doors had I missed? How many aliens had seen me so far?

All the rooms had small windows on the doors, and each room was richer than the next. One in particular caught my eye. The doorframe was double-doored and there were chains wrapped around the door. There was a dark cover on the door's window and a sign above reading "Stay out!" in several languages.

I had to know. I pressed my skull against the door and peered through the crack in the blinds into the empty room.

My heart dropped faster than I could hold onto it. *Oh, my God.* On the other side were rows and rows of television screens with arrows on the ground branching out like a compass. This was how they controlled us, the marionettes. I don't know how I knew this. I just did. It was too obvious. The Puppeteer didn't control us, the other aliens did. She watched over us but left our fragile lives in the hands of others.

Holding my shoulders higher so I could at least trick my mind into thinking I was brave, I shouldered off down the hall.

At the very end of the hall, right before a sharp left turn was another door. It didn't have a window, but it was double-doored and silver. Silver cut-outs of shooting stars surrounded it. I jiggled the doorknob which was as big as my hand. Locked. It barely twisted half an inch. I thought about knocking on the door.

On one hand, I could claim an alien had controlled me too. But what if the person on the other side, guessing there was another person, saw right through my lies? I stared at the door, at the four shooting stars.

Screw it.

I knocked.

Nothing. After thirty good seconds, I tried again, but with the same result. I should have been disappointed, but instead, I let out a hitched breath. I don't know what I'd do if there was really an alien on the other side.

I stood there looking like an idiot for a few more seconds before I remembered I was supposed to be working as a rod or at least pretending to be.

I interlocked my fingers like Ashley did if she wasn't being controlled after a while. It reminded me of a computer going to sleep.

I stood there for a few more seconds, double-checking to make sure I looked convincing before I turned to go back down the hallway. As I did so, I realized I had no idea where I was going as I hadn't passed any other rods. I was inside of what felt like a giant hashtag stacked on top of one another. A giant grid. I let my own legs and feet control me this time. Mindlessly, I wandered until I stopped suddenly.

There was nothing around, just a dead-end with a door. No alien was telling me I had to go in, but it just felt it was right.

Tipping the handle back, I went inside.

Dark, but not totally abandoned. It smelled like a hospital, and from the dim viewpoint I had cabinets were open and bottles were on the ground. Without even thinking about it, I turned and flicked a light switch. I shrunk back, squinting at the harsh light, an explosion of energy. Like the lightbulbs were trying to prove themselves. Like they hadn't been used in a while.

When I finally peeled my eyelids off my skull, a gasp shuddered out. This was the room I was in when first abducted. The room they turned me into a puppet in.

But I really had to trust my instincts on that one. When I had first been abducted, I could barely see anything. Something just *felt* right here.

The place was beautiful, but not in the way of gold and gems, but in that way that lit a flame in my stomach. It was a doctor's paradise.

Ten feet in front of me was a large cot hanging from the ceiling by chains. A large wheel, like a spool, sat in the middle of the room. Below it, a metal, square door. Was this where I was pulled up after being abducted? A giant hook, twice the height, was strapped to the ceiling. The counters were full of all kinds of sewing equipment, puppet-making equipment, and doctoring tools. I couldn't pick my jaw up fast enough.

"Hey!"

I screamed, spinning around. Twins, both rods, stood in the doorway, one pushing a vacuum back and forth. The one on the left said something, but it was drowned out by the vacuum's crunch of hitting something hard. The guy reached over and punched the vacuum off.

"I said, who are you? You're not assigned to section five."

"I'm–I'm new here." The looks they gave each other made me stumble over my tongue harder. "Well sort of. Yeah. The Puppeteer picked me and some guy named Lin to become rods."

"Lin?" one said.

"The French dude."

"Oh, yeah. Him."

"He's such a...a jerk." I doubted that was the word he wanted to use.

Also, they'd totally met Lin.

"Well, you can follow us then," said the one with the vacuum. "We're almost done. Just a quick stop at the kitchens."

"Um, no. I'm supposed to be cleaning exits. You know. Doors? Windows?"

They laughed.

One jerked his thumb at me. "This one's funny." I bit my tongue at that. "I haven't seen windows since...Sheesh. Well, since the Dollhouse. No windows here."

"What about doors? Ways to the outside?"

He frowned, his eyes going over me. "You really are new here. There is no way out."

"Then how do the aliens leave? What about abductions?"

They shrugged almost in sync this time. "I don't know. I guess they just don't leave."

"Not to even go outside?"

"Not that I've seen." He looked at his twin who shook his head.

"No spaceships?"

"I don't know. I've never thought to ask anyone. Not like the aliens talk to us."

"You've seen the aliens?" I sputtered out.

"Not in a while. Although one in a cloak has been creeping around."

I shook an image of the Grim Reaper out of my head. "What about the Puppeteer? Have you seen her?"

"No. Only Percy has. He's her right-hand man. He might still be in the kitchen. We're heading there now."

"Then let's go." I motioned for them to lead.

I didn't see anyone else as we worked our way back down the sections. Not like I knew there were sections in the first place. But if I had, I probably would have followed them; therefore, not getting to the puppet-making room. And something about that room was special. I just couldn't put my finger on it. Maybe all puppets felt this way.

I never got to ask because as I was pondering a way to not make it sound creepy, someone cursed really loud and really right in my face.

"Kindle?"

My heart and head jerked back. "Lin!" He was standing by another guy. Both had trays with teacups. Inside was a brown liquid whose smell made me nauseous. I hated tea. Hot tea, iced tea, sweet tea, unsweet tea, all of it. My parents, especially my mother, had a sweet spot for tea, and the smell was making me fall back. Another memory jumping to the surface.

I am holding a tiny bottle in a closet. Something about this bottle, I'm afraid of. Mother is standing behind me, hands on hips, but not interfering.

"It's poison," she says, mad, but with a hint of something else…fright. "You shouldn't be snooping in here."

"Is this what you use on them?"

She frowns. I could see it in the mirror on the other side of the room. The rest of the room is dark, or maybe I just don't remember that much.

"Of course not. Why would I poison anything? You should know better." Accusing. "Why are you so nosy all of a sudden? Something's going on with you. And I'll find out. I am your mother after all."

The memory fled, leaving me feeling empty and cold. Poison? On whom? It had to be rats because why would I suspect my parents of poisoning someone? I tried to remember their occupations, but my past was fading like always.

I looked up to realize I had been staring at Lin for the last...few seconds? His eyes were scrunched.

"You!" Lin said, face red, he trembled all over except for his arms. "How are you here? Percy, she's not supposed to be here." He nodded at the bigger guy beside him.

Percy rolled his eyes. "Nobody can leave the Dollhouse. And even if she did, she wouldn't be able to leave the Storage without a keycard. And she's clearly a rod."

I had to look away as a smug grin bit at my cheeks. Lin thrust out his bottom lip.

"The Puppeteer decided she needed another rod." My gaze flickered between Lin's and Percy's. I didn't know how much I could push it. Could I just say I was joining Lin as the Puppeteer's right-hand man? Percy was nodding at my words, so I decided to hold my jaw in place.

"Sounds like her," Percy said, turning slightly toward Lin.

"No." Lin shook his head. "You're not a rod. Something's going on."

"Oh, shut up," one of my guards said. "She's a rod. Look at her arms that doesn't look right."

I had to look at my own arms. I was holding my hands out in front of me, fingers interlocked.

"Resting phase," Percy said. "Don't worry. You'll learn all the phases soon enough, Lin. Right now, we have to get to the Puppeteer before she starts complaining."

"The Puppeteer?" burst out of my mouth before I could stop it. "Can I come?"

The twins behind me gasped.

Percy acted like I just slapped him. And apparently, nobody slapped a guy like him.

"Nobody's allowed to see the Puppeteer but her helper," Lin said before glancing at Percy. "Helpers."

Color was coming back to Percy's face. "Yeah."

"And if you had won, you would have known that," Lin added.

Fine. Whatever you want, Lin Martin.

"Just testing." I threaded out a weak smile.

One of the twins prodded me with his shoulder. He was still pushing around the vacuum despite it being off. "Come on. We'll take you to section one. They should be dusting in section one, part seven."

***

Section one, part seven turned out to be a human-like living room. I noticed in this section all the doors were locked and not only did the vacuum twins have to swipe a keycard, but also punch in a combination. Although I tried my best to memorize it at their suggestion, they knew it by heart. Maybe it was the only thing they knew by heart.

The living room seemed familiar. A couch on one side faced a huge television, and old, perhaps ancient, dolls and stuffed animals were on cases nailed to the wall. My father would have liked these aliens. "To look at, not to play with," he always said to me and my pouting siblings. Once my mother had taught me to make my own puppets and stuffed animals, I understood. They were artwork.

Around the room were other rods sweeping, dusting, and scrubbing glass with sponges on long wooden rods. The idea of what we were—rod-and-hand puppets—versus the long wooden rod made me feel ill. It was like cleaning the room with a long human arm.

"Who are you?" a girl asked, popping out from behind the couch, wringing a sponge into a bucket. I recognized her as one of the puppets watching me when I was being quizzed.

I looked behind me for the twins so they could fill her in, but they were already gone.

"Hey, uh, things changed at the Dollhouse. They decided to send me up as a rod. Said I knew too much."

Although I tried to stay calm, the color drained from her face. Not that she had much to begin with.

Dang. I really had to stop metaphorically slapping people.

"Wow." She glanced around. "What did you know too much about?"

"Uh…"

"The Ventriloquist?" a girl no more than fourteen piped up.

The first girl, probably an older sibling, looked like she wanted to pummel her sis.

My heart drained. "I…How do you know about that?" *Only Lewis and I should know.*

"Everyone knows," the younger girl continued. "You get briefed on it."

"Well, I wasn't. Guess they thought I knew too much. But honestly, I know very little about the…the Ventriloquist." The word felt dirty this time. Like a secret I shouldn't be sharing.

"It's so sick she leaves the marionettes in the dark," the older sibling said, meaning the Puppeteer. "But you know why." She eyed me like this last part was a question. All I had to do was shake my head slightly before she huffed. "Seriously? They didn't tell you anything?"

I nodded.

Her arms suddenly stopped squeezing the sponge, and instead, she started pushing it in midair like she was dusting something. "Duster!" Someone threw her a duster as she dropped the sponge.

I thought I probably should be doing something similar. I moved my arms up and down like her. She shouted for another, and one sailed through the air into my open palm.

"You see…um," she began.

"Kindle," I said.

"Kindle, when the Puppeteer normally upgrades us, she gives us a briefing on what our new life will be like."

Sounds like the school counselor when my parents died.

"She tells us about the Ventriloquist, her husband." She was talking slowly so I could process this, but really, I couldn't. Her husband? I mean, I knew these aliens weren't some summer blockbuster aliens, but I didn't expect them to be so…so…human. Or are we the aliens? "The Ventriloquist is the next place we go, the next upgrade, but he takes even fewer than the Puppeteer. Usually, two or three every few years."

"Why doesn't the Puppeteer tell us?" I asked.

This time the little sister spoke up. "Because the marionettes are stronger."

The older one nodded in that approving way only an older sibling can do. "That's right. Marionettes have enhanced strength. That's why it was so easy lifting those pickaxes and pushing those minecarts."

Which means I'm still super strong. Sweet.

She didn't appear to have much left to say, so I wandered over to the TV stand and started dusting despite it looking cleaned recently.

"This room looks kind of clean," I said. Better to make allies as I go along. "Should we move somewhere else? I mean this whole place is huge."

"Not as big as you'd think," Lin said, making me cringe.

I wasn't sure if he knew I was a rod or not, but just to make sure, I turned away, careful to keep my arms in dusting motion. "What do you mean?"

"There's a whole cutoff section of this place." Lin joined me in the dusting, getting closer.

I turned to the two girls to prove him wrong. "What's in the cutoff?"

The little one shrugged. "Nobody knows. It's been cut off since we were abducted."

"Oh, " I said.

Lin shook his head like he was disappointed in me. I couldn't blame him. I was too.

I put the cutoff in a mental file of things to do once the rods went to sleep. Which also included visiting Lewis.

Speaking of Lewis…

I moved over to a shelf of toys and started dusting its underside. "Hey, have any of you heard of a rod named Dominique?"

One by one, they shook their heads.

Dang it. He had to be part of the Ventriloquist crew now. Or worse.

"You should ask Ashley," Lin said, making me jump. "She's the head of who goes and comes and whatever."

"I already did, genius."

He grit his teeth and leaned forward. "You think you're really something, don't you? I know what you really are. I asked the Puppeteer if she chose two winners. She said no."

I was grateful my arms were sore, or else the rest of me would have enough energy to shake. I ignored the sweat dripping down my back and onto the control's strings.

I swallowed what felt like sandpaper. "That's because I'm not the winner. We already established that. I'm just a normal rod. Not her right-hand man."

"If you're even a rod at all!" Lin swung his uncontrolled arm around trying to grab the duster out of my hand. I jerked back just in time, but he didn't.

I didn't even see the toy marionette fall. Just a flash of color tumbling downward. But I did hear the loud crack of wood breaking.

Lin swore and dropped to his hands and knees. His right arm was now wrongly dusting the floor.

"What was that?" some guy said, staring at me. I wondered if he could see Lin too. If he could, he'd see Lin at my feet freaking out.

"It's nothing!" Lin blurted, hopping to his feet, his duster nearly batting my face. "Just dropped the duster. Someone alien down the hall really screwed up, huh?"

He had kicked the marionette under the couch, or at least tried to. I could see the back of its head, hair black splayed like peacock feathers. I stepped back to avoid Lin's duster and got a better view. On the back of the puppet's head were big black words:

"Escape Plan"

Just like the puppets in the beach cave. Did the words add up? Were "Storm" and "Snow" part of an escape plan?

The guy was stepping forward now. I shot my hand out, palm outward to stop him. By some miracle, it wasn't the arm being "controlled."

"He's telling the truth," I blurted this time.

The guy dissolved into relief like I was a super trustworthy person. Which I wasn't.

"God…I thought you fricking broke one of the dolls, man," he said.

Lin laughed awkwardly as we started to move out of the room. He tried to hurry out after the sisters, but I grabbed his arm. I ignored the huge glare he gave to my hands.

"Why'd you do that?" Lin said, each word shrouded in disgust.

"You're welcome." I let his arm go. "Listen, I can fix this marionette. It's not that hard."

He glanced around. "What's in it for you?"

"A favor."

Lin wasn't dumb either. "Like what?"

For a quick second, I thought about asking him to let me see the Puppeteer, but then he'd know I wasn't really a rod puppet. I'd have to come up with something else. "I'll tell you later."

"Come on, slowpokes," the little sister shouted.

Lin looked at me, failing to conceal his panic.

"Fine. A favor." He dashed out of the room, leaving me to slip the marionette beside the controller and hope the Puppeteer didn't notice anything missing.

Chapter 12

Unlike the marionettes, the rods were allowed to sleep naturally. We were separated into two rooms–girls and boys–and slept like prisoners on cots. Kind of made me miss the Dollhouse. This room didn't have a name, any decorations, not even wallpaper. Just white glossy walls that caught your reflection if you twisted in the light correctly.

Throughout the night, everyone slept. I would occasionally hear one mumble something or their bed springs creak. Under the cover of a paper-thin sheet, with a small flashlight one of the other girls gave me, I inspected the puppet Lin had given me, twisting and turning it around like a doctor. Female. Caucasian. Blue eyes, long black hair. It was a four-string marionette, just like those back in the Dollhouse. The white strings had turned frizzy and yellow from old age. The controller was held together with what I believed to be magnets. It was the way I made mine too.

The words on the back of her head that I had previously thought were marker or paint, looked embedded into her skull. Like a tattoo on a person. Ouch.

"Escape Plan."

Could it really be? My stomach flipped at the thought of showing Lewis this. We could…escape? Like I was no longer wishing to stumble upon a spaceship, or asking the Puppeteer, but we really had a concrete plan. But where? How? The answers were not here, but back in the beach cave with the other toys.

But first I had to repair the marionette's strings.

Peeking my head out of the sheets, I counted silently to thirty. Not a peep, not a scream, not even a single twitch came from the other cots. It made me wonder if they were actually drugged and if I was immune to it again.

With a quick double-check that my controller was still strapped to my back, I slid off the bed onto the icy floor, and out the door. I started slowly, clutching the puppet to my chest to muffle my heartbeat, but began to speed up when I realized nobody was in the halls. It was a downright miracle the Puppeteer didn't have anyone patrolling the hallways. Maybe she thought more of us. Or maybe less.

I found the puppet-making room I'd been created in with ease, unlocked, and equipment still out. I flicked on the lights, groaning as my eyes burned out of my skull. Slowly, I peeked out the cracks in my fingers like blinds.

With the light still unbelievably harsh, I surveyed the room, making a mental checklist of repair equipment. Ruler? Check. Tweezers? Check. Extra puppet strings? Check. Scissors? Check. Brown coat I hadn't seen before? Check…?

Technically it was a brown hoodie, slumped in the corner like someone was inside. I eyed it to double-check that there wasn't before making a beeline to the counter with the scissors. After gathering all the tools, I set to work.

Measure the strings. Detach the string with tweezers. Measure and cut. Leave extra room to re-tie the knots. Reconnect the string to the wooden controller.

These were things I had known how to do for forever. I couldn't remember a time when I didn't know how to make or repair puppets. My mother must have taught me before I knew my multiplication tables. What she didn't know was how valuable this would end up being. Even my disinterested, bookworm older brother Vince had to learn how to.

I turned around to hold the marionette up to a better light. That's when I noticed the brown hoodie. Or rather I didn't. Someone had taken it. Fight or flight was activated. Maybe I moved it? No, I hadn't given it a second glance since coming in. The room seemed to spin, the lights growing brighter, and thoughts racing.

Calm down, Kindle. There's nothing to worry about. Hoodies don't move. Ghosts don't exist. It's just your sympathetic nervous system doing its job.

I tried to take another step but couldn't. I couldn't move any part of me. I was being controlled. Out of the shadows stepped the brown hoodie. Technically an alien in a hoodie. His hands were out in front like he was holding marionette controllers. His face was shadowed by the hood.

"I knew you'd come." I couldn't tell much by how far away he was standing, but I could tell it was a fake voice. It sounded too rocky to be real.

"Who are you?" I asked.

"You don't recognize me?"

His voice sounded broken-hearted, and I swallowed something like guilt. Even though it was a long shot I asked: "Dominique?"

He shook his head, and my arms jerked around. He was controlling me. "Just get out of here. Stay away from the other aliens. I'm the only one on your side."

My side? What side? The Puppeteer was his mother. How could he be on my side then?

He shook loose his hold on me, walked to the door, then paused. It was dead silent except for a ringing in my head. I couldn't move, but not because of his powers.

"Kindle..." he sighed. It sounded like he wanted to say more, but then he hit the lights, flooding the room with darkness. Blackness was eating my brain matter. How the hell did he know my name?

I waited a few more seconds, replaying our conversation over and over again before peeking outside the door. Nobody. It was like this never happened. But it *had*. That was a fact. Too bad I never saw under the hood.

Getting back to the Dollhouse was harder. Or maybe it only felt that way because this time I was on high alert. If that alien had been waiting for me in the shadows, then who knew how many were out? Was the Puppeteer watching? Was an alien perched at a desk, rubbing their eyes, and chugging coffee, watching me skirt from security camera to security camera?

I was so wrapped in nerves that when I made it to the Dollhouse, the first thing Lewis asked me was what was wrong, and I let all the pressure out in one big gush. All about the strange alien I had met, how he knew my name, how he said he wasn't Dominique. I probably should have backed up and started at the beginning, but the alien's presence stuck to my hippocampus like sand to a swimsuit. He had controlled me without a machine. He had used his own hands like magic. Only magic wasn't real. At least it wasn't supposed to be. I guess with aliens, anything went.

"Are you sure about that?" Lewis said.

"About what?"

"About it not being Dominique."

I was slightly ticked for him calling the alien "it." He had talked to me (in a false voice). He had known my name. He had controlled me.

Sighing, I turned back to Lewis and since I'd got back, got a good look at him. His hair seemed less curly like he'd pulled at it. His nails were bitten to the skin, and his eyes looked bagged. My face numbed. He'd been worrying about me. Or maybe just about Dominique again.

"He shook his head," I told Lewis. "Plus, he knew my name."

Lewis' face melted and he turned back to his nails which had to be stinging by now. "Did anyone else know him?|

"No" felt too harsh, so I began telling him about what I had seen before my alien encounter. He didn't seem to like that Lin owed me a favor as much as I thought he would. All his facial muscles were being used to paint a frown that seemed to stretch down to his sharp chin.

"Don't you think we should be staying away from him?"

I ignored him and pulled out the marionette and handed it to him. "Check out the back of its head. Lin broke it, but I fixed it for him."

Lewis gasped. "More words! Just like back at the beach."

I grinned. "Yep. I was thinking we could ride Galaxy back to the beach cave."

As I was saying this, he was already grabbing the reins off the hook. I loved it when we read each other's minds. He called it "shared genius."

Galaxy hadn't been too far from the Dollhouse, and I was sliding on after him in minutes (with several tries). When the dirt turned to sand, and the sound of water seemed to be a flood in my ears, we left Galaxy tied up to a tree. He let me tie her this time. I made sure to double-knot it and double-check it.

Lewis was already heading for the cave, so I hurried to catch up. He was at the mouth when I finally did. He didn't waste a single second to check if I was there or wanted to catch my breath. Nope. He just plunged into the cave's mouth.

Meanwhile, I shuffled in slowly, testing each step. He was hollering for me to hurry. I expected to turn the last corner to a ticked Lewis, but instead, he practically skipped to me to pluck the marionette out of my hands.

We went around the rest of the cave, trying to find more marionettes with words. But after a few tries, it became clear not every puppet was marked.

An endless time of working passed by before we had all the puppets lined up and ready to go. I wasn't sure about some of the nouns, though.

I'm an alien, your savior. I have a plan to escape. In three weeks, I will break the control system, allowing our invisibility. My parents won't be there but storm the house with pickaxes and snowballs just in case. They can't handle the snow.

Before all of this, I will send down weapons that come from section 4G. There are escape pods ready for launch in that section. You humans call them UFOs. Do not stop. Go for them. It will be hard, but you can do it. Soon you will all be back on Earth.

Open-mouthed, I read it three more times; repeating it until it was as automatic as breathing.

"That sounds great," Lewis mumbled, "but there's one problem." He kicked a marionette head with a tattooed date at me, so it collided with my lineup. The date was almost exactly today four years ago. "That means the alien savior never came. Or they did and succeeded."

"It would explain why you don't recognize anyone here, and why nobody knows of Dominique."

"You don't think that hooded alien was the savior, do you?"

Deep down in my gut, I felt like he just couldn't be. But why? Facts come first. "I don't know. There are not enough facts, and I don't want to jump to a conclusion. If he is, this message is still old. The savior could be dead or off the planet."

"That means it will be us playing the savior. All we have to do is follow the plan…escape plan." Lewis sighed, way off on another planet. "I never thought I'd get out of here."

"What?" Then with a teasing smile: "I thought you were the optimistic one."

"I'm just wondering how we get this whole thing started. Who do we tell? How do we get the weapons?"

My mind staggered for an answer. "I…I don't know."

I didn't even enjoy the way back. I could've had a million things to think about. I had gotten good at it. Thinking, that is. All those nights up made me perfect it. I could be thinking about Lewis' word choices, or Dominique's whereabouts, or Mora and Tiffany, or even my family.

Instead, I rode on in silence, letting the wind scream into my ears. With this plan, everything was going to change, and I was going to be it, ready or not.

It wasn't until we were both back in the Dollhouse's parlor that I got an idea.

"Lin's favor!" I shouted.

"Yeah? What about it?" Lewis said, settling into the couch to look the window. I did this a lot too, ever since my encounter with the burning snow. But enough time must have passed. We must be in this planet's early "springtime." Early enough that we couldn't feel the change yet, but late enough for water not to freeze.

"The favor," I repeated, turning away from the window myself. "I could use it to get you into the Puppeteer's house."

He turned back to me. "Lin has that much power?"

"I'm not sure. But if you came, it would be easier to get those weapons."

Lewis shrugged, but as if he remembered our conversation in the cave, he formed a thin smile that quickly disappeared. "Yeah. I guess I could come."

Like a crazed maniac, I reached out and squeezed his hand just so I could breathe in his smile once again. Absorb its memory in my mind's eye.

God, what happened to me?

Lewis stood. "So, are you heading back now?"

"Do you want me to?" I couldn't believe I actually asked that. What if he said yes? I couldn't imagine going back to the other rods and laying there until it was time to wake up. Over there felt dark, the Dollhouse felt light and beautiful.

"Of course not," Lewis said. "I was just asking."

Well, the rods wake up later than the puppets… I started saying but realized that's not what he wanted. He wanted a big, hearty "Yes!" So that's what I told him.

He looked taken aback by my answer. But also pleased. I was slightly mortified by this spontaneousness, but I couldn't help it around him.

"What do you want to do?" I asked.

"I want to feel human again. I want to climb to the roof and stare at the stars."

I wondered briefly if that was the same thing as being human again. Surely aliens didn't look at stars like we did. As Lewis grunted over the first step to the top floor, I was reminded how inhuman we actually were.

I ran to help him, and for once he didn't argue. He didn't say he was "fine, fine, fine." Something bitter dropped into my stomach. Was he getting worse? Was it even possible to get worse? Once again, he wasn't human.

He continued to hold my hand like he was taking me to prom.

I didn't even know there was a way to access the roof. It made me a bit salty that he never told me about it. When we reached the fifth floor, I knew why. The "entrance" to the roof was a hole in the ceiling the size of our controllers. Lewis only casually said "my brother" with a shoulder gesture. Below the hole was a pullout couch and filing cabinet that led up like stairs. It was too narrow to help Lewis up, so I turned my back and pretended to survey the room so I wouldn't hear his struggle. I was blushing by the time he told me to follow.

Noises came from above as I wobbled across the couch and cabinet. At this point, I had to duck before poking my head out the hole. The roof was flat for a good thirty feet before dropping off steep and deadly like a waterfall. The tiles were less red than they had probably been having been picked apart by snow, hail, and windstorms. But Lewis did end up being right–the stars were gorgeous. Spread out like diamonds embedded into black silk. Like needle-pricks. How many times had I stared back at these same stars, shaking my head at the thought of anything being beyond them? I thought Heaven would be the most distance I would go from Earth.

Lewis called me. With a grunt and tons of wiggling, I snaked through the hole. I grimaced, about to complain about the dirt and cobwebs when he grinned at me.

"Should I have thrown down the ladder?"

I gasped. "There was a ladder?" But then I saw he was just kidding, just laughing.

I turned to the stars instead. "Did you used to do this back in Kansas, er, Earth?" I said quickly so he didn't know I almost blanked on our planet's name.

He leaned his head back, his eyes reflecting off one of the moons. "Is there a Kansas on Mars?" He chuckled. "It doesn't matter. They both look the same." He cleared his throat. "No. Anyway, no. Dominique was the space geek. To me, looking at the stars alone is sort of boring."

A warm belt of amusement spread through my stomach. "I think it's much more interesting with you." We were both on our backs. He rolled over to face me, cupping his hands behind his head like a pillow. I mimicked him. We laid like this for so long I was starting to get dizzy off our carbon dioxide. But I wouldn't dare be the first to sit up.

He eventually rolled back to look at the stars, his breathing fast. "How long have we been out here?"

"Not long enough."

He smiled into the darkness above. "Yeah."

I squirmed. "There's not that much to say, is there?"

"Doesn't matter. I just enjoy being with you."

I didn't know what to say to that, so I just watched him scan the stars, and point at the planet's moon. "Looks familiar, doesn't it? Looks like ours."

I stretched my neck back before being hit with another memory. Or rather a flash of a memory. Like déjà vu.

It left my stomach unsettled. I started thinking about everything that had happened earlier that day. About all the other things I thought were "familiar." Maybe they just looked familiar because it was the first furniture I had seen outside the Dollhouse in who knows how long, but something else etched itself in my gut. I tried to ignore it, but the more I thought, the more sense it made. It made my throat and insides tighten.

"Lewis? Can I say something…strange?"

"I don't know. Being abducted by aliens is going to be hard to top."

"I think…" I blinked back tears. "I think I've been abducted before."

"What?" Lewis laughed. "How? There's no way. I mean, even if it was, even if you escaped with my brother…I would have remembered you."

I shook my head. "It sounds so crazy, but it makes so much sense. When I was in the Dollhouse, things felt so familiar. And I had these memories, these flashbacks that I didn't use to get before. On Earth I mean."

He tried to speak, but nothing came out.

"My amnesia! I mean, it would explain it. Why I didn't die in the crash, but everyone else did. Maybe that's why I'm immune as well to the sleeping gas or whatever kind of chemical the aliens use."

"But it does make sense. Science, Kindle! Why don't I remember you if what you say is true?"

I put my head on my knees. "Maybe you have amnesia too."

"But I don't."

"How would you know? I always felt you seemed familiar."

He was shaking his head. "I don't like this, Kindle."

"It's the Puppeteer. She's gotten to you."

"No. She's gotten to *you*."

He backed up from me on his knees.

My heart fell, the frenzy leaving my heart. "Wait. Don't go." I hung my head. "Maybe you're right. Maybe this *is* crazy." Tears pricked. I didn't want to let go of the abduction idea. It was like I finally had answers, my whole backstory finally made sense, and now I was giving it back up. "Maybe I'm just crazy."

"No, no," Lewis said with you're-totally-crazy eyes. "You're just grieving."

"But that was years ago." My heart squeezed. "It still hurts though."

"It's supposed to."

"I don't want it to. I feel like…they're still alive. It's so wrong."

"No, it's not. I know…I know Dominique could be–"

"Don't say that, Lewis Bryant! You need that optimism."

"And so do you."

With that we both shut up about dead people and let the stars be loud. However, in the end, Lewis whispered to me as we climbed down the hole: "If I had any mind to trust, it would be yours."

Thanks, but I wouldn't.

I went down to the den on the third floor, grabbed a piece of paper and pen, and wrote him a reminder of our plan. Asking him to go inside the Storage at nine o'clock when we took our first break. At least that's when we did according to Ashley.

Not sure why they did it, but they seemed to have similar breaks around noon, three, and six. We were supposed to stand around in the bedroom, but from what I've heard hidden in hushed tones, Lin got to rummage around. I didn't know if Percy was going to be there or not, or if Lin was trustworthy enough to be left alone (I sure wouldn't trust him). Either way, I was going to meet up with Lewis at the door connecting the Storage and the Puppeteer's house. That would be Lin's favor.

Chapter 13

The next day's break time came faster than I thought it would. One second I was dusting, the next a bell was ringing and everyone was heading back to the bedrooms.

The Puppeteer's house was nothing like the Dollhouse. Not in terms of decoration or grandeur but more in the sense of peace. None of the rods constantly praised the Puppeteer or acted like sheep. Everyone seemed alive. More colorful. More personality. I never realized how lonely lonely could be. It felt more like a school day than imprisonment. And when that bell rang signaling the break, we all acted like the seventh-period bell just rang.

Like a real high school, everyone rushed into the hallways. Shoved and pushed, I was bounced around. I kept one hand steady on my marionette controller. I hadn't tied it as securely as the first day, too busy running to the girl's room before the other rods woke up. I made it in with two hours to spare. I should have spent that time thinking about the escape plan–and I did for a bit. I was about eighty percent sure the escape plan came from the mysterious hooded alien. It was easy to think like that. That every four years, an alien savior booked us all out of here. But if that was so, why didn't those on Earth know about it? Why aren't there puppet people from space walking around? Where did I fit in?

"God!" I hissed under my breath. My own voice scared me into pressing a fist into my lips until they felt bruised.

When it got to be six, not a *second* later, everyone flung their covers off. Collective groans rose and cluttered together. By this point, I hadn't been using my covers, so I just sat up and rubbed my eyes, trying not to look too perky. One girl whose name I didn't catch looked at me with one eye open.

"Early bird?"

Caught off guard, I stiffly nodded and stuttered out something about time zones.

"Jesus," some small girl with orange hair longer than her torso muttered now covering half her face, "I don't even know what time zone I'm from. Just know this is crap."

Some of the other girls laughed, but my stomach knotted.

"Hey," I tried to say but got cut off by two younger girls screeching over whose pillow was whose.

"Let the blondie speak!" someone else screamed.

A quick glance confirmed I was the only blond in the room. Creepy. I quickly filed it away for later.

"We're going to spread a secret message to the other puppets," I said, noting the girl who had called for my attention roll her eyes, but I still had most of the eyes on me. "What I'm saying is true. Spread it on, but only to people you trust not to tell the Puppeteer." Everyone froze. "Who's going first?"

Nobody volunteered, so I ended up calling a handful of girls I knew by name to the far side of the room which led to the showers, and told them about the escape plan.

The person I didn't tell was Ashley. Although I didn't particularly think she was a bad apple, she was too close to the Puppeteer.

Someone trusted her for as I pushed past the stream of rods later that day, I saw her looking around and calling my name. I managed to avoid her by slipping behind two football player-buff guys before sprinting down the hall. If she spotted me, I didn't notice.

The one thing I knew for sure was she wasn't going to tell Lin because earlier I had told Lin that I cashed in his favor. At first, he threw a Mora-sized fit before calming down when I produced the fixed puppet. Tight-lipped, he snatched the puppet so hard, I almost burst with his carelessness. He'd be on his freakin' own if he broke it again.

As I headed for the main door leading to the Storage and the Dollhouse, I was only a bit jittery that Lin wouldn't show. But luck have it, he was standing by the door, slightly hidden behind a potted plant that branched out enough to give him shade. I slowed down, half expecting him to jump out and declare "I knew you were a spy!" or "The Puppeteer isn't evil!" (Bless his heart), or "You used me!" Which isn't true. But that would be useless to explain. He'd always be a sheep. Actually, I was surprised he even let me do this.

"You know the code?" I whispered.

"Of course I do!" he not-so-whispered.

"Good." I crossed my arms over my chest as he slid a keycard in. I'm not sure if he hesitated or if it normally took that long, but it felt like hours before the screen glowed blue, and a click unlocked the door. I decided not to tell him that last night this door was unlocked. Or broken. Somehow it had opened for me. Proof of my two-timer alien abduction theory?

He wrenched open the door and gasped.

I flinched back. "What?" Not proud to say, but I ducked behind him.

"This is…" he began but never finished. He sounded sickened and betrayed.

"You've never seen the Storage?" I slid up next to him and realized I was wrong.

He'd seen the Storage before. Ashley had to take him through here to get to the Puppeteer's house. What he was referring to was the dozens of puppets hanging in their jars like fireflies without air holes.

Although I had seen the puppets stored on my first night here, being down on the ground me gave a whole different view. Now that the marionettes were asleep, the darkness was cast in a blue color, like someone had stuck a neon blue light to the deepest part of the ocean, illuminating the strange creatures around. The puppets hung, their heads tilted down and limbs dangling. Craning my head back, I could see puppet jars stacked on puppet jars—most of them being empty.

Shivering, I glanced at Lin who was closing the door behind us like he thought we wouldn't be able to get out again. He stopped with a few inches left, before spinning fast at me, and thrusting the keycard into my arms.

"You know what? You do it. I'm not getting in major trouble just so you can cuddle with your boyfriend during work. He's a freak. Both of you are." He shook his head and slipped back out the door.

"Hey, don't–" I started to say, but he already stuck his head back in.

"I'm not closing it on you. I still owe you this, remember?"

Guess so.

I sprinted down the hallway. I wasn't afraid of the marionettes waking; they still had half an hour. I just couldn't look at them. They, who were so alive, felt so lifeless.

I barely slid the card into the slot when the light turned blue.

Lewis was right in front of me, helping pull the door open. He sprinted in, looking winded and his hair a mess. The door shut behind us with a loud thud that made me wince, and him jump.

He stood there, hand to his chest, panting before meeting my eyes. "Good God."

At least I thought he was meeting my eyes until he pushed past me and stared at one of the other marionettes. "This is…I don't even know."

"A living nightmare," I provided. "Now let's go. Lin's on the other end." But he didn't come. He wandered to a container where a younger boy was displayed.

I couldn't hear entirely what he whispered, but it sounded like a swear.

"Lewis?" I stepped closer, hand outstretched, fingers millimeters from his drooped shoulders.

He spun around. "This is so disgusting! What are we doing here? Everyone needs to see this."

"They already do. Well, sort of."

"Huh?"

"The rods know. They all come through here. They're briefed on things the marionettes don't even know." I licked my dry lips. "But they don't care. They think it's a luxury compared to how we're treated in the Dollhouse. They get real attention from the Puppeteer. They just don't want to be–"

"Forgotten," Lewis finished in a hushed tone. "Like we are on Earth. I get it. But how could they forget all of this?" He was getting angrier now.

I could barely hear myself. "I don't know."

At the other end of the Storage, the door was opening and closing rapidly.

"Come on, Lewis," I said, grabbing his wrist. "We really need to go."

Lewis nodded at the marionette in the glass, face stern, and jaw clenched like he'd made a promise to him. And we had. In a way.

"Let's go," he finally said.

We sprinted to the end where Lin was holding open the door, his face scorched into a frown. "This is where I leave you two. I don't want to get in any more trouble. And certainly not for this crap."

Lin spun on his heels and skirted off.

"Thanks, Lin!" I called louder than I should have but loud enough to make him wince.

I snickered and turned to Lewis, but he wasn't laughing too. He was staring at the hallway, at all the unnecessary splendor, clenching and unclenching his fists.

I tugged his elbow and put a finger to my lips. I didn't think we'd be heard way over here in section one. I just didn't want to hear him voice the disgust I've felt every day since working here.

Together we sped through the halls to where I heard about a suspicious Storage that never unlocks. The place where the weapons from the escape plan would be.

"Thank God Lin didn't check his pockets for that keycard," I said once we were safely in the laundry room, the door closed and double-locked behind us.

"Nice. How much time do you think we have?"

I slid the keycard in until the light turned blue. "A lot. Well, you do." I wrenched open the door. Something resting on the door came toppling down. I had to step back to avoid being hit. Lewis grabbed it.

"A book?" he asked.

I gasped as I recognized the title, thrown into another memory.

I walk into my brother's room where he's reading a fat book. I joke if it's a dictionary. Vince throws me a scowl but in a sibling way. He doesn't mean it.

"It's an adventure book, Kindle. His Honor of Chaos.*"*

I frown. "But why do you care about something made up? Don't you want to know what's out there? Beyond this house? We've never even stepped outside the house."

I come back, the room sharpening. I was aware of everything. The axes were dark and rusted away by what I hoped wasn't blood. Some were worn down, their blades more like a bar of soap than knives. Some were still in boxes labeled in a language that looked familiar, but I couldn't place it. But sharpest of all was the book, *His Honor of Chaos,* still in Lewis' hands. In English. I picked it up.

"This was Vince's–my brother's–favorite." I flipped open the worn pages and my heart stopped. There was writing in the margins. Written in fast scribbles like the writer didn't want to ponder too long before devouring the rest. A space-themed bookmark was pressed between the last two pages. It *was* my brother's book.

I held my stomach. How did it get here? I hadn't seen this book in four years. Last I knew, it was still in an old address, not even the cops could locate in real life or in my memories. Not even my nightmares.

My thoughts ping-ponged against my buzzing skull. Was he still alive?

Could he be here?

No, he was proclaimed dead. But the body...

Never found.

It fell into the river. If he had survived, beating all odds, he would have found me.

Unless he had amnesia too.

No. Impossible. Total amnesia was rare. Look at the stats.

But it's his *book.*

"Kindle," Lewis was pleading. "Let me into this genius conversation I can see going on behind your eyes."

Ping. Pong. Ping. Pong. Pi–

"My brother's here."

"Mine?"

"No!" The realization ripped through me. Completely destroying my cells and rebuilding them in a heartbeat. Those dirtbag aliens. They took him. He's here. "Vince is here! My brother…he's still alive. I was right." I could barely get the words out through a huge grin plastered on my face. I laughed loud enough to make Lewis look at the door.

"How do you know this? The book?"

"Yes. Look at the handwriting. Look at the bookmark. Look at the big 'V' written on the title page. It's his. Vince is alive."

"Wow! This is…I don't even know what to say, Kindle. This is incredible, I guess."

His worries couldn't reach this sparkly, shiny shield that soaked my body in warmth. In giddiness. Was Vince still here? Or had he escaped with the first abductee group?

"I have to ask someone," was spilling out of my smile. "Maybe they know of Vince."

"Maybe Lin?"

Lin. My bubbly shield popped. Like the prick of the "L" in his name was filed to a point. Reality crashed down on me like the ceiling. It was like waking up from a dream and realizing you missed your bus stop.

"The escape! Oh God, how long have I been rambling?"

"No problem." Lewis had been filling a janitor's cart with axes. He was staring at me with a funny look, one hand resting on an axe's hilt like a warrior. "Go ask Lin. I've got this. I swear I do. Just toss me the keycard or whatever you used to open the Storage."

"Right." I slipped the keycard out of my jeans. "Take care of it." The lonely air started spreading like smoke. "And yourself."

"Of course," Lewis said in a serious tone, like he'd really be okay if I left him for a few minutes.

I sprinted out the door.

Usually when the first break ended, Lin delivered the Puppeteer's daily hot tea. Hopefully, Percy wouldn't be there this time.

When I reached the kitchen, Lin was elbows-propped on the counter, head flicking between the clock and the other side of the room. The kitchen was massive. All the appliances were plated in a shiny, golden material. The room stretched on forever with special sections for cakes, seafood, fowl, vegetables, and, well, everything. It smelled like buttery, syrupy batter, and blueberries. I started to remember more, my mind slipping to me sitting at a table eating pancakes Mother claimed to have made, but I knew different. We had servants in this picture. I didn't remember having servants before.

Lin turned to me, and I hated the idea that Lin was waiting for a distraction and that I had to be that distraction.

"What are you doing, Kerr?" He said my last name like he'd suddenly appear threatening.

"Do you happen to know a Vince?"

He looked disappointed. Like he expected a tale of high and mighty adventure instead. "A *Vincent.*"

Vince's name wasn't short for anything. That much I remembered. But if he had any bit of an amnesia-causing brain injury…"What does he look like? Blond? Does he speak English?" Does he stay up past bedtime with a flashlight and book? Does he drink coffee in the morning like he had an actual shot of staying awake? Did he cut his hair with scissors and dye it white? Did he love and protect his two little sisters with everything he had?

"No. Dark skin, even darker hair. But yeah, he speaks English. Strange accent. British, I think. Maybe. Why?"

My heart sank. "Anyone matching the description? White hair? Tall and burly? A reader?"

"No!" Lin sounded aggravated like he just realized he was late for something important. Turns out, I was right. "If you'll get out of my way, I have to make tea for the Puppeteer."

"Is Percy coming?" Going onto Lin right away by asking to come would be an automatic no. But perhaps clogging his mind with questions would make him pause.

"I don't need to be dragged around like a baby anymore." Lin probably meant it like he had chased

Percy away, but it just sounded like a six-year-old complaining he could pour his own juice.

I bit back a snarky "congratulations" and instead settled on asking if I could see how the tea was made.

I guess I made for some kind of companion as he immediately started off for the other side of the kitchen.

The tea machine was easily the size of three fridges, both in width and height. It looked like something out of a sci-fi movie with a million buttons on gold metal and twisty spouts shooting off the top.

Lin opened a cookie jar on the counter, finding packets of what had to be the fanciest tea leaves in space. He ripped it open and poured it down the chute. When he closed the chute, a green button lit up, and he pushed it. All the other buttons turned on, but he just pressed the green button again. I guess the Puppeteer took it black. Or whatever was said in the tea community.

The machine gurgled and steam poured out the top. After thirty seconds a hidden spout spat out a brown, steaming liquid into a cup Lin had positioned.

"Crazy," I mustered, even though watching that was anything but that. However, inflating Lin's ego would probably fill up his headspace. It totally wouldn't prepare him for the one-two I was going to hit him with. "Can I come? Can I meet the Puppeteer?"

"Heck no!"

I winced at how fast that popped out of his mouth. He said something in French, probably a curse word.

I put my head on my chin, pretending to be disappointed, and I was in a way. Time to try plan two. "Can I at least carry the teacup?"

He scratched his face like he was ripping his skin off, leaving faint red marks on his temples. Lin Martin was about to boil over. "Fine. If you'll leave me alone. I can't believe I even let you in here."

He continued muttering in French as we headed back into the grid-like hallways. The bell must have rung for rods were migrating back into the halls, refilling the blood back into this place's arteries while Lin led me straight to its heart.

Two ivory-black doors towered like dominos about to crash down. Thick, golden paint lines crisscrossed the door's center eventually winding down into two spiraling door handles.

Lin and I were still a bit off, on the other end of the hallway. The number of rods had dropped to zero. It sounded eerie just to breathe.

As I stared at the door, something came over me. Normally I would ignore these types of gut feelings, but this one was hard. Like my cells were being replaced by bricks. I had to be in there. But I had to do it alone. I had to talk to the Puppeteer.

Without so much as a thought, I swung around and kicked Lin in the ankle. I took off shuffling down the hallway, so the tea wouldn't slosh. When

I got to the door, I kicked it hard. About four seconds later the door opened, automatically to my disappointment. But why would someone as rich and powerful as the Puppeteer need to open any door?

Clutching the tea tighter, I hurried in while Lin started running down the hall, shouting my name. I made sure the door slammed behind me.

The room was empty except for an electronic board with the alphabet and, in the middle of the room, a surgery table with a silver foil blob on top. Where was the Puppeteer?

The alphabet board blew up with a message scrolling across:

The Puppeteer: *I am suntanning under the foil. What do you want?*

I made my way to the board. A "waiting for reply" message came up. My palms slickened and my mouth dried. After putting the tea on a small table, I pressed "I" and recoiled as it showed up on a screen. I could say anything to the Puppeteer. Anything.

The Rod: *I am here to deliver your tea. You asked for me.*

I sighed. I was safe behind the username.

The Puppeteer: *Ah. I must have forgotten. I've got a terrible headache.*

The Rod: *From what?*

The Puppeteer: *Stress.*

The Rod: *Where would you like me to put the tea?*

The Puppeteer: *No, I couldn't possibly have anything. Just take it back with you.*

The Rod: *Okay.*

The Puppeteer: *But stay for a minute. It gets boring in here.*

I hesitated. Now it was my turn.

The Rod: *Why did you take us? Why kidnap us?*

The tin foil laughed and then groaned.

The Puppeteer: *What a brave puppet you are. I'm guessing my usual puppet isn't here? Anyway, for the record, I did not "kidnap" anyone. I took humans because they wanted to come.*

The Rod: *I don't understand.*

The Puppeteer: *All the humans I have taken wanted to come. There was a pair of brothers–one wanted to see the moon and one hung onto him. Both wanted to go. There was a girl who wanted to see aliens, and I let her. And then there was you. The latest, right? You new ones are always so inquisitive.*

I puffed my cheeks out. I wanted something smart to dance on the tip of my tongue, but nothing would. She had a point. I kind of asked for this.

I was afraid if I waited too long, she'd ask me to leave or stop replying. She'd called me brave, so I let that lead me. Ask something strong.

The Rod: *How would I go about finding a rod in particular?*

The Puppeteer: *I can't help you there. Rods are like your Earth mice to me. Skittering, chattering, too many different looks to keep track of. I don't care about your names, or what you look like. I don't even have a mental picture of you, new one. But that doesn't mean I don't love you all. I care for you. I foster you, no matter how nosy or stupid you are.*

The Rod: *We're not stupid, and you don't care about any of us. You wouldn't let us die if you did.*

The Puppeteer: *Brave one, I like you. Now get out of here before I force you to. I need sleep.*

Chapter 14

Saying Lin was ticked when I came out was the understatement of the year.

"What was that? You think you're some kind of hero?" he exploded.

"No," I said truthfully. "I'm just the one taking action."

"Of this escape? Yeah, don't make that face. I heard from Rabia."

I didn't recognize the name, but my stomach sank all the same. Instead, I pushed my arms back and forth like I was vacuuming. "I guess I've got to go. Where are we vacuuming?"

"The ballroom," Lin spat.

"Thanks," I automatically squeaked before I could take it back. I noticed as I walked past, he stepped way back. Far out of ankle-kicking reach.

The ballroom (which I didn't even know existed until then) was massive. It stretched about a whole block. The walls were pure white with about a hundred painted on windows. They were sunny with painted red curtains in different positions. The ceiling had a tan border that ran down the room, holding onto tiny spots of light. In the middle was a big bronze sun with a chandelier of glittery crystals hanging from the center. The floor was a polished light-brown color. It was so shiny I could see a faint dash of my shirt color.

Although stunning, it would have looked more gorgeous with some kind of furniture. Instead, it was empty. Like a crystalized jewelry box with nothing but velvet dust inside. If they had moved the furniture somewhere else, I couldn't see it. Just a large mass of puppets moving through the heart of the room. One was Lewis, his marionette controller stuffed inside his shirt like mine.

He seemed to be limping more than usual.

"That doesn't hurt?" I asked. He gave me a confused face, so I lightly touched my back, feeling all eyes on me. "Does your back hurt?"

"No," Lewis said quickly. He pointed to the stage on the left-hand side. "I heard rumors that the Puppeteer used to gag and blindfold marionettes and make them dance on stage."

I shivered. "I think I'll work on the opposite end then. We should split up, so it doesn't look like we're together."

We had only been vacuuming for a few minutes when someone knocked on the wall beside me. I was at the very end of the ballroom, alone. It was the alien I'd seen before, wearing the same cloak as before that blocked his face. His posture was relaxed, back slumped against the wall, and head tilted only so slightly. He was watching me with interest.

I shivered. "What do you want?" I said so bitterly my mouth tasted like black coffee.

"I want you to stop snooping around. I want you to forget about any kind of escape for the puppets."

"I'm not planning on escaping. I love it here."

"Don't fool yourself. Nobody does."

"Why are you not hurting me?"

"Because I...I..." He shifted like he was standing on hot sand but trying to pretend it didn't hurt. "You remind me of someone I used to know."

Great. I had the face of an ex. An alien one at that.

"How did you know my name?" I asked.

"It doesn't matter."

"I think it does."

He sighed. "I heard another rod say it. Happy?"

"Where? I didn't think the other aliens communicated with the rods."

"We don't. I mean some do, but not since–" He froze. Suddenly the strong, masculine energy radiating from him vanished. He was like a bunny in the presence of a fox. He grabbed onto my wrist. "Come on! Hurry. With me."

I tried to pull back. "No!"

"Do you want to live or die? Because right now you're running out of options."

"I thought you said you wanted to help me," I cried. Back in the ballroom, the little specks of rods and Lewis were still moving, still vacuuming. Whatever danger this alien could sense wasn't registering on puppet radar.

I was opening my mouth, trying to figure out this when the alien huffed and dropped his grasp on my wrist.

"Fine. Have it your way."

My body stiffened, my arms dropping to my sides. My controller was struggling like a trapped bird to get out of my shirt's neck hole.

I choked and gasped before pulling on the collar where it flew straight up.

The alien circled me, hands outstretched. He growled and raised his hands. I started running out of the ballroom and into the hallways. A few seconds later, puppets started screaming. Including Lewis.

I fell to my knees just outside the ballroom. We were hidden in the hallway like we were about to jump-scare someone. Or we would if we weren't the prey.

I made a strangled noise, and he shushed me.

A garbled woman's voice rang throughout the ballroom. The Puppeteer. I wasn't sure how I knew, but I just did.

"Which one of you took a marionette into here?" she screamed.

No one inside answered. Sweat was breaking through my pores. The alien had said he was saving me. Had he seen me bring Lewis in? Then why not save Lewis as well?

The alien crept forward until he was peeking around the corner and into the ballroom. I scooted about an inch, but still couldn't see the Puppeteer. Only a few puppets I didn't know were in view. They were standing–arms tucked behind their backs in sync–in rows about five wide, three back. Lewis was there in the third row, second puppet.

"Not talking?" the Puppeteer said, still out of sight. "Fine." The puppets I could see fell to their knees. Lewis looked sick, his controller struggling to get out of his shirt.

I turned to the alien beside me. I couldn't see his face, but imagined he watched like a hungry wolf, filled with hatred for his mother.

"Do something," I hissed.

He shook his head and held a quiet finger to his shadow-covered face.

I wanted to speak, but suddenly Lewis screamed from the ballroom.

"You!" The Puppeteer said. "You will be punished for this."

I glanced at the alien. He'd loosened his grip on my arm.

The alien glanced at me, but I was ready. With a jerk, I was out of his grip.

"Kindle!" he shouted.

I didn't stop. I flew back into the ballroom, but Lewis was gone. The puppets were all in a corner because their sheepdog had scared them in. No. Not their sheepdog. The Puppeteer was their wolf.

All at once I wanted to fall on the floor and let this planet suck my energy away. I wobbled. The room felt hotter. I wanted to disappear, run away, and never show myself.

But Lewis.

And, besides, Lin was here. He'd know what happened.

Sucking in a breath I shouldn't have been able to hold, I tucked my controller into my shirt. God help me on the day I actually needed Lin Martin to help me.

He was standing by Ashley, comforting her. It was almost touching.

"Lin!" I barked. "Lin." I reached for his shoulder, but he turned around before I could.

"You," he spat. "That could have been me."

"Listen, Lin, I'm sorry. You're right. I should have never put you in danger. Promises shouldn't include endangering lives."

Ashley stepped forward. "What do you want?"

"I want to know where the Puppeteer took Lewis."

"And why would I tell you that? Karma." Lin stomped off, leaving just me and Ashley.

She put her bottom lip out in sympathy and said meekly, "Lin doesn't know. The Puppeteer made us close our eyes."

"Made you? She *forced* you. Can you at least come with me? To find Lewis?"

She just shrugged. "Sorry."

Something deep inside me cracked. Splintered. Broke. The Puppeteer had taken their humanity away.

I turned away. What was I going to do? I had no idea where he was. And was I really going to confront the Puppeteer? I clutched my chest, and a small squeak came out. He was injured. He wouldn't last a second. I know he kept saying he was fine, but he clearly wasn't. I had to save him. But deep down inside, I knew I was just one girl that could easily be turned around and marched off a cliff.

No. I needed that alien. The hooded one.

I wasn't too surprised to find him still in the hallway in the eavesdropping position. He quickly stood, probably to rival my height (which, surprisingly, wasn't that much taller).

"Can you help me?" I asked. "You have to know where they went."

"I do. But I'd rather die than tell you."

My mind was spiraling out of control. "Please. I must save my friend."

"Why is he so important to you? Wait." His hood raised like eyebrows. "Are they helping you escape?"

"I don't trust you."

"Whatever. I'll help you. On one condition…"

He left an open pause, but I wasn't dumb. I wasn't going to promise him anything or thank him just yet.

He spoke again when he realized I wasn't. "Leave this place. Get out. The escape pods are in section three in a place that looks like a laundry room. I want you and only you to get in and leave. Got it?"

"What? You want me to leave?"

"Only you."

At least that meant he didn't know about the rebellion. "Okay, okay. I'll leave." I waited to see if he saw through my lie. Nope. He was nodding along. "Now where are they?"

"The Trash. It's through the fridge in the kitchen. You know where that is."

The way he said it made me realize he'd been watching me for a long time. He knew I was in the kitchen.

"Who are you?"

"It doesn't matter. Now go before Mother gets there first. And, also, don't let her see you. That's the most important rule."

I was tempted to demand his name again, but he was right. Whatever this Trash was, it didn't sound that amazing.

Running as hard as I could, I was in the kitchen by the time Lewis started screaming. I crouched down in the hallway.

"Don't! Whatever this is, don't! You need me! I'm a marionette!"

My heart broke.

There was a shrug in the Puppeteer's voice. "You are just one of many. I could abduct another human with your exact strength and speed levels by tonight. You mean nothing to me."

I grit my teeth as Lewis' shouts rose. It was a bunch of gargled shouts and hollers. Then words came through. *Don't drop me.*

I started to round the corner but then hesitated. The hoodie alien told me not to. But Lewis.

I strangled down a howl as I pulled on the door handles anyway. Locked. Zip for the keypad as well. I didn't even know this room had a door.

Footsteps with long pauses in between started for my direction. I ducked behind a corner. I couldn't see the Puppeteer, but I could see her shadow. Long hair and wearing a dress. Eerily human. Or were we eerily alien?

That didn't matter now. The kitchen door was swinging shut, and this was my only chance.

Inside, everything was normal, silent, like I had hallucinated the whole thing. I turned to the fridge and wrenched it open. Beyond the fridge door was a slope. A rocky slope leading to a cave entrance. Its slick walls looked moist with humidity. It was a slide to Hell.

"Lewis?" I called, receiving an echo in return. "Lewis?"

No answer. My stomach was cold and empty. I'd have to go down there into the unknown. Surely there was a scientific way of going about this. A way to measure the angle? Rock content? I mean, I wasn't seriously going to plunge myself in without knowing anything.

But then Lewis shouted. He sounded hurt.

I squatted down on the rim of the slide, but gravity took me before I had a second to think. My body bumped and ran down the rock as I shouted. I tried to grab onto the sides, wherever they were, but that just scratched up my palms.

Then the slide curved, and I was flung off. There wasn't enough time to scream before I hit the ground. It was soft like sand and sprayed into my mouth. Blinded, I sputtered and screamed at the pain.

Someone grabbed my shoulders. I recognized the grip's strength, its tenderness. "Kinde," Lewis said, "you shouldn't have come."

I wiped my eyes with my wrist. It still hurt my sore eyes, but it was cleaner than my palms. "It's what you would have done," I squeaked.

I still had my wrists covering my eyes when he leaned near my ear. His breathing was slow like he was holding it back in pain.

"No, that's totally a you thing," he said in a series of sharp breaths through his grin.

"I'm glad you're okay."

"Oh, I'm more durable than you will ever know."

"Durable?" I repeat.

He put a hand on my shoulder and used it to pull himself in front of me. He nodded. "Durable."

I swallowed. I wasn't stupid. He had gotten hurt, just look at him limping. But the air was so heavy, and I could practically feel his hot blush radiating off his face.

"I'm the doctor here," I said, not caring what came out of my mouth. "I'll test how durable you are."

He chuckled. "And how are you going to do that?"

I picked my next words carefully, shaking as I did. This was so bold. But I so wanted it. "Can I kiss you?"

He looked shocked, but not as shocked as I was when he spun me around and kissed me like if he did it long enough everyone in every galaxy would disappear and leave us alone. My being hollowed out with only thoughts of him. I was in control. Not the Puppeteer, not the other aliens.

I fell for his mouth and our lips touched. Again.

The giddiness sent my head rolling and mind spinning. We kissed more. And more. I shuddered as he ran his hands across the back of my neck. So sweet, our hearts pounding so hard it had to be impossible.

I had no time to think, no time to narrate, no time to run this through my skeptical, pessimistic mind because I already knew.

I knew I loved this. I loved being with him. I loved him.

When we finally pushed away, that's when I saw it. A giant hole in his shirt on the shoulder. His skin had a strange coloring.

Thinking he was bleeding, I reached out, but I didn't feel blood. Or skin. I felt wood.

"What?" I shrieked. But somewhere deep down, I knew what. "You're made of wood!"

"No! No! Kindle, please." He had his hands over his chest but not in an apologetic way. He was hiding it.

"You're an actual puppet! Are you even real? Even alive?"

I shot back, shaking. My lips were still tingling, my heart still dancing like a jig doll. It explained so much. How he was able to survive the burning snow. How he was such a great swimmer at the beach. Anger piled in my throat until I couldn't breathe. My sight shimmered. My face burned.

"I'm not wooden!" he shouted louder. "I'm a human. I'm alive. I'm just turning to wood." His head fell with a click of disgust like he couldn't believe himself either. "It's been happening ever since I broke my controller. It used to be just my one leg." His limp! "A few days ago, I woke with it halfway up my chest."

Anger simmered under horror under fading hope. "What does this mean for you?"

"I...I think I'm going to die."

My mouth dried. "You're horrible! How could you do this to me?" I knew it wasn't his choice, but, God, how could he keep this to himself? I could help him. I could *have*.

"You were never supposed to find out," he said like that made a difference. Like it would turn back time.

"So, what, you were going to just wander off like some dying animal?" *You kissed me and then were just going to die?*

"I guess."

By now we were both standing, but blood was still rushing into my head. Only this time it was boiling. "I have to help you. I almost don't want to, I'm so mad."

"But how?"

I looked back up the hole. A sliver of light fell through. "We're going back in. Back to the Puppeteer's and I'm going to remake you." I had no idea if that was even possible, but I made the rest of my speech sound strong just in case. "I can find a way out of here."

"We can help," an old man's voice said. A yellow light pulsed from deeper inside the tunnel.

"What?" Lewis shouted. "Who said that?"

The light grew as if in response. "We did."

Dark brown blobs scooted our way. There had to be at least a dozen. As my eyesight adjusted, I realized they were cardboard hands that were shifting rapidly. Each had a light attached that curiously faced backward, shining on the cardboard.

"Not the hands. Over here."

I turned to the wall which a flashlight was rapidly blinking at.

My breath died out. On the wall were small faces made of shadows. The cardboard hands were twisted to make a human face.

"Shadow puppets!" I exclaimed.

"Says you," said an older woman, her hands on her hips. All the shadow puppets were facing the left wall, so I couldn't tell if she actually saw me or not. "We're real people you know. Wasn't our fault the Puppeteer made us."

"I'm sorry. I didn't know there were shadow puppets here."

"You don't know about us at all?" she gasped. "The shadows?"

"No. But, uh, you said you could help him." I waved in Lewis' direction, not wanting to say his name or even look in his direction.

"Yes," the first man said. "We can show you two a way out. But first I want to know what possessed you to tick off the Puppeteer. Rarely do marionettes get thrown down here."

Before I could tell them, *loose lips sink ships, suckers,* Lewis started to spew our escape plan. Screw him.

I started to tell him to stop, but something was coming down the tunnel. A group of people jerking around, like they were having seizures. The air prickled with a familiar tapping noise. I turned to Lewis whose jaw had dropped.

Jig dolls. They were stiff as they walked, probably from the wooden rod protruding from between their shoulder blades. They each stood on a platform that was repeatedly slapped by an invisible force. It must be miserable.

"What?" Lewis sputtered. "Who are you? How can you be jig dolls?"

"Why did the Puppeteer...?" I started. *Create you?*

One of the jig dolls laughed. She was probably older than Tiffany. As I surveyed the cave, I saw they were all older. The youngest in their early forties if I had to bet on it.

"You'll need to know the whole story for that." A jig doll danced forward. "Us jigs and shadows were the first puppets the Puppeteer made. We did the mining and the cleaning, but ultimately, we were failures. Us jigs couldn't stay still, and the shadows had to work to pick up a feather."

On the wall, shadow puppets were showing the story.

One turned into a bird and flew away.

"Then the Puppeteer met the Ventriloquist."

Two humanoid aliens, a male and female, kissing.

"He taught her new ways. He took her plan to a whole new level. New puppets. And we were cast aside as failures despite our years of service."

A gun, shooting down the bird.

"We were replaced by other puppets. Puppets who could do the dirty work faster and better than we could."

A marionette working in the mines.

"And here we've stayed for twenty-five years, waiting."

A girl with her knees to her chest. A sun circled her multiple times.

"That's horrible!" I said. "So, you're stuck here forever?"

A jig nodded. "Until someone comes and gets us, we're stuck here. With no need to eat or drink, we're invincible. And no thoughts of killing each other when we interact on different planes of reality."

"You can help us though?"

One of the biggest jig dolls, a burly guy who looked ridiculous tap dancing, tried picking up Lewis. Lewis was bouncing, his limbs flying all over.

"St-t-t-op!" Lewis shrieked.

The guy practically slam-dunked Lewis. "Can't help it," he huffed.

I scuttled over to Lewis. His arms were wrapped around his chest. He looked mad enough to spit. I wanted to tell him that I told him so, but instead, I put on my best doctor face and asked: "Are you all right?"

"Yeah. Whatever."

"This place is a maze down here," the big jig doll said. "But just remember: Three rights, two lefts in that order, and you'll come out. There's a bit of climbing to do at the end. Which is why we can't get out of here."

"That's okay," Lewis said. "We'll be fine."

I huffed. "We better hurry then," I said to myself.

Behind us, the jigs and shadows waved us off. I waved back, feeling such sickness for them and anger at myself. I used to love making shadow puppets and jig dolls but look what evil could do with a child's innocence.

Sweat dripped down my forehead and into my eyes. My strangled lungs wheezed out a breath to move my sticky bangs out of my face. My arms and legs were nauseous with overuse as I kicked another jagged pebble out of the way. My heels suffocated in another blister. I was pulling Lewis behind me on my controller.

"Keep all arms and legs in the ride, eh?" Lewis chuckled. "Kindle, I'm fine."

"No," I said for the millionth time.

The controller lost a lot of weight, and Lewis was half-jogging to keep up with me. At this point, I ached so much, I just let him. Besides, the cave was curving to a round dead-end just ahead. Light filtered in through the ceiling in a barcode pattern.

I touched a broken beam about seven inches over my head that formed the base of a jagged ladder. It was made of the same material as the Dollhouse. We were under the Dollhouse. "This is…" I couldn't think of what to say. Disgusting?

Disturbing? It wasn't any human word. "Manipulative," I finally decided. "I'll go first."

Chapter 15

My fists were clenched as we ran down the hallways of the Puppeteer's house. The inferno inside me had given me enough adrenaline to climb through the hole, which had led to a small patch outside the Dollhouse. If I had any sense of calm, I would have wondered who built the hole. Where were they now? All I knew was that they weren't turning to wood. That they hadn't lied to the people they cared about—Did he even care?—and was going to die like a freaking animal. Like he didn't have dignity and grace. Like his life was nothing. But it was something. Something I was going to save no matter how much red I was seeing.

It wasn't going to be a long walk to what I had been calling the Studio–the room where they turned humans into puppets, and the place where I had met the hooded alien. It sure felt like it though with Lewis sniveling like a baby the whole way, breathing down my neck, calling for me to wait up.

God! And I had kissed this guy? Yeah. I had. And I sort of wanted to do it again. To feel a burn that wasn't anger.

In a mumble, Lewis insisted he was fine. And now I knew what "fine" really meant. He could feel nothing. And now we were running like there was a bomb going off behind us.

Technically, there was a bomb. It was the silence that swarmed the air. I felt if one of us spoke, everything would blow apart. I thought I knew him, but apparently not. I couldn't stop thinking about how I accused him of wandering off like a dying animal and he just said, "I guess." Like I meant nothing to him.

Screw that.

He was panting and slowing down behind me. But I ignored it. I clenched my fists and ran faster. If he could leave me in the dust, then so could I. Just watch me. And no, I wasn't being petty, if he so happened to ask. I just wanted him to disappear. I wanted that kiss to never have happened. I wanted to go back and change things. It shouldn't have happened then.

"I know you're mad," he whispered, "but can't you tell me what we're doing here? Because it sure looks like we're giving ourselves to the enemy." He chuckled at that last part gaining him a glare before I gave him the cold shoulder again.

"I think we passed it," Lewis piped up.

"No," I grumbled. "Ahead."

If he asked me why I was mad, I was going to explode. For real this time.

Instead, he stayed silent until we got to the Studio.

I forced all emotion out of my voice and pointed at the operation table hanging from the giant hook in the middle of the room. "Get on the stretcher. And make sure your controller's hanging from those tiny hooks above you."

He glanced at the giant hook that had abducted us before the ones on the ceiling over the operation table. He licked his lips. "Will this hurt?"

"Oh, I hope it does."

His eyes widened and guilt surged through me. I shouldn't be mad; I shouldn't even feel guilty. I had to wipe my slate clean for this operation.

"Sorry," I muttered.

I moved to an IV bag on the counter. Everything had labels in English printed beside the alien ones. "Don't worry. You'll be under some kind of anesthetic. Basically, you'll be asleep the whole time and won't feel any pain. Just like when you were first abducted. Or did you wake up?"

Lewis finished hooking up his controller. "Completely out. Woke up in the Dollhouse on a couch."

"Lucky." I grabbed Lewis's arm. "I woke up in the woods walking and everyone was pretty rude to me."

If I didn't want a conversation, then why talk back?

Thankfully, Lewis didn't say anything as his controller's string lengths forced him into a sitting position, so I continued my work until he was asleep. After double-checking to make sure, I went to work on his marionette controller. I used the carpentry set to fix and glue back the controller like I did with the ones Mora used to break. I guess the brat was useful for something after all. And maybe I did miss her a little bit.

When I was done, Lewis was still out, yet his wooden parts were being replaced with skin. I gently pulled out the IV and turned off the machines. While waiting for him to recover, I put everything back in place and did pocket a few things. As I was shoving a particularly fancy needle in, Lewis was sitting upright watching me. I didn't bother asking how long.

"How are you feeling?"

"Fine," he said. "Like I just woke up from a really great nap."

"Totally normal."

"Can I do it again?"

"What? No, you can't do it again!"

"Relax, I was just kidding."

Silence. The butterflies in the air were on fire and I kept thinking about that kiss.

"Good." I couldn't turn my back to a patient, so I stared at his controller still on the hooks. "Now are you really awake?"

"Huh?"

"I mean, sometimes people wake up, but they're still sleeping. They say crazy stuff."

"Like what?"

Like you like me.

But I knew we were both thinking it. About it. Imagining it. Reviewing it in our stupid little minds.

Screw him.

"Here," I finally said after way too long. "Let me get your controller off those hooks."

"You don't have to. I'll get it."

"Really. You should be careful. I'm no alien." He snorted at that. "I'm not really used to working on this scale."

He tilted his head. "So, you still do care about me? Look. I'm really sorry. I should have told you."

I refused to speak.

"I hate you not talking. Just say something."

I didn't know what to say, and he was already standing to unhook himself. Any stranger would think he'd been normal.

He looked at me and almost said something, but then a bang came from the door. We both jumped. Luckily, I had locked the door when we first came in.

"Why won't this door open?" a familiar voice said. It was the hooded alien.

Lewis was dragging himself under a shelf covered in boxes. When he was fully under, he motioned for me, but it was too late.

The door had burst open, and I saw a flash of the hooded alien with two others behind him. I didn't see any more because one bumped against the light switch, plunging us into darkness. They screamed and scrambled. A crash. They couldn't find the switch. Someone grabbed onto my arm, and I yelled. The hooded alien.

"You shouldn't have been here!" he hissed in a tone just above a whisper. "Now they'll have no choice but to send you to Father."

Their father. The Ventriloquist. The one that controlled voices.

I twisted around so I could kick the alien in the shin, but I couldn't move. The hooded alien was wrapping me in something to cover my head and face, leaving only a small breathing hole. The cloth smelled like dirty laundry and coffee. I couldn't breathe.

"Get out," the hooded alien barked. "I'll take care of this one."

"Good. Now she won't squeal," one said, still hidden in the dark.

"Take the dummy to Father," the other said.

When they left, one hit the lights. I blinked away. The hooded alien glared at me like he could control me that way. Finally, he sighed. "You disappoint me." He fiddled with his hands, and I was on the stretcher. Within seconds he had the IV drip in my vein, and I was getting sleepy. A face. A comforting face.

A familiar face. A face I loved.

A boy with jagged white hair, and gray eyes—so much like me.

The world was slipping, I was either waking up or falling asleep. Time was dizzy just like me. I only had time for one word. The most important word.

"Vince."

Chapter 16

I struggled to open my eyes. My throat was parched and empty. I sat up way too fast and got caught in a web of black stars. I fell back to the warm tile. It felt strange, my back, knees, and arms. Groaning, I reached to feel my wrists. My strings and controller were gone. I sat up, slowly this time, trying to get my heart out of my stomach.

I was in the sky. Or at least in a room painted sky blue. All the walls were this color except the left one. Emptiness just kept going and eventually faded to white. I blinked a few times.

Vince. Why was the name rolling around in my empty head? Who was Vince?

I gasped. My brother. Vince. The book. He was alive. I had celebrated that. Then he was in the Studio. He had been operating on me. No. That wasn't right. He was next to the hooded alien. Right? But why had I said his name?

Grabbing my temples, I pressed down, grunting. "Come on! Remember! Remember! I know this memory is there! It's just dormant."

Then I got one. It wasn't like my usual flashbacks. It was quick. Like a snake flicking its tongue out. Vince was here. Somewhere in the Puppeteer's house. If I could get back, I could find him.

And Lewis. What had happened to him? I was so angry before. Now I'd do anything to know how he was doing, just to have him by my side.

I stood and stretched back to look at the sky-blue ceiling so high I wasn't sure it even existed.

"What have you done with him?" I screamed. "Where's my brother? Where's Lewis? Where am I? Is anyone there? You said you cared about us!"

I swung my head down to my chest so fast, I nearly fell over again. My lungs caved and a sob burst forth.

There was a clicking noise in the distance. I wearily lifted my burning eyes. It wasn't a jig doll but rather a border collie, running at me, tail wagging. It looked almost strange to not see a controller, a jig platform, or even bunched-up arms. Was this even a puppet? Was I hallucinating dogs now? My parents had a dog. I think it was a St. Bernard. Or another collie.

Bending down, I offered it my hand. It snorted before sitting at my feet.

"Hello there, dummy," the dog said. I jumped back. It had a man's voice. It felt familiar, but I couldn't even tease out a flicker of a memory for this one. God, I was going crazy.

"What are you?" I asked.

"A ventriloquist dummy."

I almost laughed at how crazy this was. "Then who are you? Who's your puppet master."

"I am the Ventriloquist. I command this dog to use my words just like I will soon use you, dummy."

"Then how can you hear me?"

"Hmm. She warned me you were a curious one." By "she" he obviously meant the Puppeteer. It made me shiver. I shouldn't be on their radar. I was about to escape, not to be gossiped about. "A special chip in the dog. You have one too. It works better if I'm in range too." The dog itched her ear like nothing was going on. Meanwhile, I was secretly glancing around the room. There was literally nothing here. "Now if you could come with my voice, I'll show you to my private rocket ship where you'll fly to a moon to help me in a conference."

"And what if I don't? Why can't I just walk away? I have all my limbs back."

"And where would you go if I could just make you say…"

My throat closed as a hand-shaped bubble slithered up to my mouth. "I am a dummy," I said. "Please return me to the launch room." I gasped as the hand retreated back to my stomach.

"Don't worry," the Ventriloquist said, as I choked on burning saliva. "It only hurts like that the first few times. Now follow my voice, will you?"

A high-pitched dog whistle sounded. The collie's ears perked up and she bolted into the unseeable. I ran after it, trying to at least keep it in my view. Running was a lot easier without a controller. It felt freeing, but also in a sadistic type of way, it felt weird. It felt alien. Eventually, the room started to fade away into the planet. The white flooring turned into gray cement with ivy growing in the small cracks. The blue walls peeled back to an egg-colored UFO at the end of a runway. Beside it was a teenage girl and boy. They had their hands tucked behind their backs and stone-solid faces.

As I slowed down, the dog circled them before flopping down at the boy's feet.

"Are you *dummies* as well?" I winced at the word.

The girl's seemingly rusted face twitched until she could form a smile. "We're dummies. We've been serving the Ventriloquist for years now." Her voice sounded deep and scratchy like it still had the Ventriloquist's voice somewhere deep down inside.

I swallowed, my own pharynx feeling slimy. "And we're going to another planet?"

"Moon." Her smile was starting to dip. "It's really not that bad. All you do is talk in a room full of aliens instead of the Ventriloquist talking. Although I think he's coming to this one. Not sure what it's about though, so don't ask." She looked at the boy who merely nodded, still focused on the dog.

"Who will be talking? Not me?"

"It's probably going to be you. The Ventriloquist loves new dummies. He's not allowed a lot. He thinks we're toys."

Great.

Strangely the conversation ended there. The girl just spun around, and the boy let his focus leave the dog. I let them climb into the spaceship first.

The spaceship's interior was white with black couches surrounding the back part. A single matching chair up front had a slide-out monitor. It showed a single green dot in a field of yellow dots. One of the yellow dots was double in size and she double-tapped it. An automated female voice said something too fast to make out, but by then the girl was pushing me onto the couch next to the boy.

She was barely in her chair before a rumble hit. I closed my eyes, stomach clenching, teeth clenching. I focused everything on not passing out. My chest was exploding in on itself under the weight of a thousand pounds. The roaring noise outside was outstanding. Like a mechanical hurricane banging on the UFO's sides, threatening to break the windows and peel back its metal shell. Even I was ironed onto the couch.

Then it stopped. I was waiting to collapse, to melt into a puddle now that I clearly had no bones. To my left, the boy was wiping his eyes. The girl was cursing.

"Is it always that bad?" I asked, my stomach still floating somewhere in my jelly insides.

She nodded with big head-bang motions. "Woah, dizzy." She held onto her chair's armrest. "These rides have been getting worse. I heard the aliens have better rides. Feels like being in a car. Screw that."

It occurred to me then that the boy hadn't spoken once. It wouldn't mean anything to me on Earth, but here it felt like the Ventriloquist's fingerprints were all over it. Literally.

The girl turned around as if she had read my mind. "Adam can't speak unless through the Ventriloquist. Happens to all of us dummies at a certain point."

God! Oh, God! My insides crumpled. Just like the real thing, Ventriloquist dummies were called "dummies" not because they were stupid but because they couldn't speak. And now Adam was really one. He had his freedom to move, but he'd paid dearly for it.

"How long has he been here?" I hated talking to the girl about him like this when he was two feet away.

"He's been here the longest." She smiled at me, but then the Ventriloquist's voice came out. "Lottie, leave the new dummy to me."

I wasn't sure if he could hear me, but it was worth a shot. "Ventriloquist? Are there others like you and the Puppeteer, and your children?"

"Sure," he said. "A whole planet of people who can control others."

"What about other aliens?"

The Ventriloquist laughed. "What is with you humans and asking that? Don't get too hopeful. Earth is the only planet we've found alien life on."

"So where are we going?"

"A moon circling our home planet."

"Why?"

"Stop asking questions!" he snapped, and my throat tightened but not by my own accord. I apologized with my own words and sat back down.

As the girl turned to the panel, I put my face on the armrest. I wasn't interested in seeing any more of space. I closed my eyes, imagining my brother. He had to be a dummy too. I imagined he was scared, wishing he had a book to keep him company. How many times had he read *His Honor of Chaos* before he'd lost it? Or had the aliens taken it from him? What about Poppy? Could she be there?

A sudden jerk made my jaw hit the armrest.

The other dummies didn't look phased. Lottie just looked back at us and announced our arrival.

I wanted to shout as Adam opened the door into the vacuum of space. He was going to get sucked out. I was expecting to feel no air and follow him out, but nothing happened. Lottie followed, and I inched out after her. Outside was breathable air. I couldn't even begin to fathom how.

As far as I could see was a rocky gray surface. In the sky, a big blip had to be the sun. How funny it would be if that was Earth's sun. I squinted at the sky again. An orange layer surrounded the sky. Probably keeping in heat and air.

"New dummy," the Ventriloquist said out of Adam, making me jump. "Come on. You're late."

Late? Like I oversaw how fast the UFO went.

I made my way across the moon to where the others were waiting. The surface was rocky, and I tripped more times than I'd like to admit.

Finally, I reached the front of what looked like a boring office. It was cube-shaped with a shiny gray tone, just like the Puppeteer's house. There weren't any windows, just two big doors out front under an awning and a smaller door about fifty feet to the right of it.

"You'll go in that door," the Ventriloquist said from Adam again. He didn't indicate which door until he started making choking noises and flung his arm toward the big front doors.

"Are you okay?" I quickly said. I clamped my lips shut. No. None of us are okay, but we just have to deal with it.

"Just go in that far door," Lottie said in her own voice while rubbing Adam's back. "Once inside, take the first door to the right. The Ventriloquist should be waiting."

"Should?" I said.

Lottie frowned. "Most likely. Better?"

The Ventriloquist spoke up through Adam. "I'll be a bit behind. Trouble with my spaceship Lottie, Adam, meet me at the family spaceship."

They took off fast, and it wasn't until I was outside the far door that I remembered I should have asked them about Vince and Dominique. But they were gone. I thought about running after, but who knew the lengths of the Ventriloquist's powers?

Shaking my head, I pushed through the double doors into a claustrophobic lobby. The walls were covered in a fake wood and the floor was an orange-ish color.

Directly in front of me was a small desk with a plaque reading "receptionist" and a sign strung around a lamp reading "OUT." There was a small supplies closet behind the desk, but that wasn't where I was heading. I was heading for two large black doors to the right of the desk.

I sucked in air to poison the butterflies in my stomach before pushing the doors open.

My first feeling upon entering the conference room was…disappointment? It looked so human. The room was mainly taken by a large crescent table. There was barely enough room for the whiteboard pushed against a closed window and the chairs the aliens sat in. In fact, it was the aliens that made me shuffle back. They looked so human that one might mistake them for it. They all had pale, ashen faces and blond hair ranging from neon to platinum and gray eyes. The men wore suits and the women, dresses. For a second, I wondered if I'd been in a TV and someone sat on the remote, sending me from a sci-fi to some business channel.

Although the way they were looking at me, you'd think I had fallen from the sky. Their mouths were open or covered with their hands. One alien, looking like an older woman, started crying. Nobody moved to comfort her. They were too busy staring at me.

"Kindle Kerr?" The male alien directly across from me rose slowly. "Is that really you?"

I stammered. How the hell did he know my name, my *full* name? Why would the Ventriloquist tell them? Did I speak? Was it my turn? I cleared my throat. "Yes. I am."

"Hey there," a different female alien said like she was approaching a wild animal. Hesitation. Disbelief. Fear. "Are you all right? Do you know where you are?"

I stepped back. And I had thought the Dollhouse was creepy. "I don't understand. Am I supposed to be the Ventriloquist yet?"

Their confused looks reminded me of the doctors when I told them I couldn't remember anything from before the car crash. One male alien bolted out the door behind me. The rest glanced at each other.

Then the male alien at the head of the table stood, hesitantly. He couldn't meet my eyes yet talked strong and sure, like a doctor at a check-up. "Kindle, what are you talking about?"

"I'm the new dummy. I think. I don't know."

I could see him searching for words. "Dummy? Like a puppet?" he said slowly like he was checking for a concussion.

My heart felt like it was swimming in choppy water. Choppy, frigid waters with sharks. This wasn't a test. These aliens had no idea what was going on. "What's going on? Is this the conference room?"

Before I could continue, there was a commotion outside.

"I'm sure, Mr. Ventriloquist. It's her." It was the alien who had booked before, opening the door. And behind him was an alien so familiar, but I couldn't place it. He had short blond hair and wore a luxurious golden suit.

The Ventriloquist gasped and stumbled against the doorframe, clutching his chest. He was shaking so hard, his teeth rattled as he spoke: "Kindle? Kindle, is that you?"

"I don't understand." But then I did. My mind broke open like a dam, and in rushed memories I'd buried a long time ago.

I'm sitting on a rug in a squat living room with a fireplace crackling in one corner and the couch cushions pressed up behind my back. Outside it is snowing hard, and I am scared of it. The snow burns my family. I sit on a red rug with yellow squares, picking at a loose string. I like the way the pattern feels running through my fingers. It reminds me of sewing lessons Vince was going through. One day I was going to follow in Mother's footsteps. On one side of me is Poppy but she's too young to listen to whatever I was. She is facing the couch, watching my father's mint doll collection shine from the wall.

I look away from Poppy and to the figure in the rocking chair. It's Father. He is reading from a book with colorful pictures of children, mountains, and birds. I know this because he occasionally turns the book toward Vince and me. Vince doesn't look at the pictures. He plugs his ears and closes his eyes, demanding that he imagine the picture for himself and that pictures are cheating. I'm not upset about this.

I look at Father again as he reads, using funny voices. Mother stands. She is always prim and proper. She mummers Father's name. It is not his real name. Nobody knows it. Not even his coworkers. Only Mother docs. Everyone else just calls him the Ventriloquist. And as for my mother; she's the Puppeteer.

Chapter 17

I couldn't breathe. I held a hand to my chest like Father had. Too much stimulus was pouring out of my head. The memories kept coming, flowing, and reattaching themselves to empty neurons. They couldn't hide in the shadows anymore. This is what I remembered:

I am an alien. My species doesn't have a name. We come from the planet Mocot where everyone has the ability to control voices or bodies. Our planet is dying, as we have used up nearly all our natural energy sources.

My parents created a way to solve it. My mother was an experimental scientist obsessed with humans and my father was an ambitious businessman. Together they found a new source, one hidden in caves of a faraway planet called Aroramere. It looks like a golden substance that, when mixed with other chemicals, creates an energy source ten times more powerful than anything on our original planet.

The only problem is my species comes from a very hot planet. Our bodies are not used to the cold so snow and ice burn like acid on our skin. My parents, to combat that, started abducting an alien species called humans who had no problem with the cold. My mother had already been experimenting, making jig dolls and shadow puppets, but my father took it to another level by helping her create more advanced puppets like marionettes, rods, and dummies. These new human experiments became the miners.

My parents then moved to the icy planet to become overseers of Aroramere and the humans. They started a family to help control the puppets. I have dozens of more siblings who work in the control rooms. I never got close to any of them except Vince and Poppy because the rest grew up before I was born.

Vince and I have the power to control bodies like my mother. Meanwhile, my little sister Poppy can control voices like my father.

The worst fact is that I loved my family. I loved being an alien. I thrived when it came to transforming humans into puppets.

One thing I didn't remember was why I left if I loved it so much.

***

Back in the conference room, I covered my eyes and fell to my knees. I just wanted to be left alone. I wanted the world to stop. I wanted to close whatever book this was, I wanted to pause the movie. No, the world couldn't be doing this to me. But it was. I had been so ignorant not to see it. It was why my memories of my home had been stronger back on Aroramere. Because I literally was home. I had never been abducted twice.

My father grabbed me in his arms, and I cried so hard as he lifted me off the ground. I was so emotionally drained that I couldn't do anything but hang my arms around his neck so I wouldn't fall.

When he put me down, and while the room was clapping, I studied him. Instead of this menacing figure of shadows, he was, well, my father. The guy who taught you how to ride a bike. He taught me to read and write. He got me the best toys.

But how could he be *this*? How could he abduct innocent teenagers and force them into slave labor, to make his conference calls for him?

My head exploded again as another wave hit.

The hooded alien never had Vince prisoner because he *was* Vince. That's how he knew I'd be in the Studio when I went to repair the marionette Lin broke. I used to love that room. I used to love turning humans into puppets. It was my passion—combining sewing and doctoring. He had also pulled me away from our mother in the

215

ballroom so she wouldn't see me and told me to escape.

But why? Didn't he want me back?

"Vince," I whispered as if it could summon him. For him to wrap his arms around me and take me to the fantasy land he had always promised.

"Vince! Yes!" My father said like I was a child speaking her first words. "He's your brother."

"I…I know," I managed.

He beamed down at me. "That's great!" Then his face slipped into a second of guilt. But he recovered it. A trait that seemed to go hand-in-hand with my childhood. "How much do you remember?"

I wanted to test him by saying "everything", but I couldn't hurt him now. Not when he just got his daughter back.

"A lot. It stops…well, I don't remember running away. Or why I did." I wanted to see the other faces in the room, but he was wrapping an arm around me in such a way that I couldn't. Not even his.

"That's all right. It was an accident."

Was it? How come I could remember the first flavor of lollipop I ever tried was cherry, but couldn't remember running away to Earth? This isn't how memories should work.

"Now," my father continued, "I'm going to wrap this meeting up very quickly, I promise. For now, why don't you see your brother Vince?" he said like I'd forget him again. "He's waiting inside the spaceship. Then, I promise, we can ask each other questions until you're sick of my voice. Like how you got here."

I nodded.

"And to see your mother."

Mother. I could remember her in full detail from her long blond hair to the way she talked–sweet and delicate like her voice was going to float away without her. I remembered her teaching me to sew. I remember sitting at the kitchen table, learning my times tables and how to give CPR.

A chill spread through me. I missed her so much. I wanted to crawl into her rare embrace. I wanted to go back to when I was a kid, and you didn't question why Mother made humans do my chores so I could learn algebra.

But Vince was where I needed to be right then.

The family spaceship was there, sitting on the vast expanse of white powder. I tried to remember the moon's name, but it was lost on my overstimulated brain.

The spaceship was a round oval, big enough to fit about seven people with a dome over the top. A classic UFO. As I got closer, a shadowy figure inside ducked.

"Vince!" I shouted. "Vince, it's me."

No reply.

"I know who you are. I know who I am. You're my brother."

A door slid open, and he jumped out, wearing his brown hoodie. He quickly flicked off the hood, and I felt like I'd fallen out of the sky and hit the ground hard. He was so grown up. He wasn't the teenager I had left.

Well, technically he was eighteen, but he looked so much like my father. He had short white hair that stood up like he'd been electrocuted, and a hardened face which I wondered was my fault or not. But split across it was a smile and a whoop of joy.

We ran at each other and met in the middle with such force that he almost knocked me flat on my back. I gasped at the strength he hugged me with. He wasn't the nerdy older brother I remembered. It was almost like he'd come back from war.

I was crying on his shoulder. He pulled me back, his face adorned with a slight scowl. "You shouldn't have come back, Kindle. Now you're right back where you started."

My mouth fell. "What? I didn't. I was abducted! I didn't have a choice."

"You could have run from the hook. You could have gone inside a building."

"Vince, I was in the middle of the ocean!"

He snorted, but in a way I recognized as joy. "You? The ocean?"

I smiled, remembering we couldn't swim. "It's a long story. But yeah, I can swim now."

Vince was grinning and we both burst into laughter. "Nice, Kindle, nice."

I gave one last burst of laughter. "I missed you."

"No, you didn't. You didn't remember me or Poppy."

Oof. I dropped back at that sucker punch. Poppy. My little sister. The girl who spent ninety-nine percent of her life in the garden our parents had built her.

"She's thirteen now. It was hard without you being here. She really looked up to you."

"I'm sorry."

"No, no. What I said came out wrong, Kindle. You did what was best, especially after the fight you had with Mother and Father." His face darkened.

"Fight?" This didn't produce anything. I'd had lots of fights with my parents growing up. That's what teenagers did.

Vince looked up at where Father was practically skipping over to us. The perfect picture of happiness that made my heart soar.

"Not here," Vince whispered.

I frowned but matched his tone. "What's with all the mystery? I'm back."

He just shook his head. "You don't remember what happened."

Father took a deep breath, letting it out in a smile and shiny eyes. "Well, the gang's all here. How are you two getting along?"

"She's already being a dork," Vince said.

I rolled my eyes and Father laughed.

"Oh, won't your mother be surprised," he said.

Vince turned to the ship. "Let's just go, okay, Father?"

"Yeah, that's fine." Then Father put a hand around my shoulders. "I'm so sorry, poppet. If I had known…I never meant to use you as a dummy. How did you get this far without anyone noticing?"

I swallowed, thinking of Vince. But something told me not to rat him out. So instead I shrugged before remembering my father hated when we didn't use our words. "I don't know."

Father shook his head. "I suppose it doesn't matter now that you're here."

"Exactly," Vince said. "Now come on. I'm sure Kindle's still confused."

I nodded, finally telling the truth.

"I'll turn you into a human later, but I'll have to find the right tools first. Your mother and I haven't done this before."

Again, I just nodded, too exhausted to do anything else.

The family spaceship was exactly like I remembered it—exactly like the dummies' except bigger and with a softer couch Vince was leading me to.

I wanted to tease him that I knew how a spaceship worked, but he looked so worried with his hand hovering over my arm that I let him.

While we were getting situated, Father buckled himself into the driver's seat. This driver's seat was toward the front of the spaceship and consisted of a single egg-shaped chair and a control board wrapping around like a school desk.

"So," Father said, "what's the human planet like?"

Vince shot me a "be careful" look, and to be honest, it scared me a bit. Why wouldn't he just accept I'm safe now?

I regarded his wishes anyway. "Well, um, it's strange. Lots of oceans, and it's huge. In some places, there's only snow and nothing else."

Father shivered. "How horrible. Hopefully, you weren't in a place like that."

"No, I was in a tropical place called Florida. Lots of birds and water. I was adopted by a nice woman named Tiffany and her daughter Mora."

"Is Mora a teenager?"

My stomach sank. But it shouldn't have. Just because I came home, and he was my father didn't mean he wouldn't change his ways of abducting people. "N-No."

"What a bummer. You could have seen her again."

"Can we stop talking? I'm kind of tired." I turned to the window and put my head on the armrest.

"You're going to break your chin that way," Father said. "But, yeah, we can take a break."

"Good."

The stars made a lump in my heart. Lewis had shown me these same stars not too long ago. And just like on Earth, I never thought I'd be among them like this. And what about Lewis? How was I going to tell him I wasn't...exactly...human? Would he still accept me? Could we still kiss like we did back in the cave? My heart grew fuzzy at the idea. I had to find a way to get to him. But how?

I repeated these questions until I drifted off. I awoke to an awful rumbling noise and my father trying to shout over it.

"What?" I sat up from where I'd been slumped over on the seats. Outside was the same sky-blue room I'd met Adam and Lottie in. Where were they now?

"I said that your mother and sister are inside. All they know is I have a surprise. Vince is already inside."

Some brother. "They're going to be disappointed it's not food."

Father laughed, but then went stern, a trick I never learned to master. "Hey, let's keep this whole planet Florida and humans thing away from Poppy. It might be too much for her."

What? I wanted to argue. Poppy loved Earth. She always adored it when we pulled up a human who had been trying to hold onto grass or wildflowers. Those plants always went to a special portion of her garden. And what did he mean by "too much"? I mean, I knew she had anxiety and was naturally a skittery child, but I guess she wasn't a child anymore. Had I done this? Had my leaving broken her this much?

"Is it my fault?" I said mournfully, lifting my head to meet Father's gaze.

"No, poppet," he said with a faint smile. "It's just who she is. Let her focus on one thing at a time."

I nodded. One thing at a time. We could both do that.

Together we walked through the blue room. I now recognized it as a place to put the ships when the weather got chilly. The dog that wasn't here, I recognized as my father's dog, Voice. She usually joined Father for company when he went on long conference trips. Father worked as the trade-man and manager for the gold energy source.

We stopped at a wall with a door. I didn't recognize this door.

"You stay here," Father whispered. I'm going inside to talk to your mother and sister first." He grinned. "Then you come in when I call for you."

I agreed, and he left with the same happy walk he had had when leaving his office.

My stomach bunched up. This was *the Puppeteer*. How many empty nights had I filled with visions of getting my revenge? Of turning her into a giant marionette puppet we could all control? I wanted her to suffer, but now she was my mother. The one I had mourned in a car crash four years ago.

"Come on in, my surprise," my father downright sang.

I had never felt anxiety like this. She was the Puppeteer, and I was just going to walk into her arms?

Apparently so for I barely made it into the kitchen before she grabbed me into a hug. I managed to pull back to get a look at her. Blond hair, teary gray eyes. She wore a dress and had the softest face. It was a kind face. A sad face. The face of a mother.

I winced as more memories barged in, but now it wasn't one memory, it was thousands. We used to make cookies on the weekends. We would play dress-up together. I had wanted to be just like her.

"Oh, Kindle, baby." She cupped my face in her hands. "You're home now. Oh, I can't believe you were a puppet here and I didn't even know." She pulled back for her shoulders and head to drop. "It's my fault. I abducted you. I didn't know it was you. I just needed one more puppet. And what an amazing coincidence I managed to get my non-human daughter. Oh! Forgive me, Kindle, I'm a horrible mother."

"If you hadn't abducted her," Father said softly, "she wouldn't be here now."

"I know, darling, but it's just—" Mother sat on the kitchen table which still had five chairs after all this time.

Father came over to her, and opened his mouth, but shook his head instead.

I watched Mother. She looked so frail like she couldn't even stand on her own. Some of the marionettes were like that after long days. It *kind of* made me happy. To see her unable to move and my father unable to speak. This was what I had dreamed of for months, so why was I only *kind of* happy? I was literally right beside the Puppeteer. But just because she was related to me didn't mean I could just ask her to release the puppets. No, she was far too dangerous to reckon with when it came to her work. I'd have to do this myself. But first I'd have to blend in. And that wouldn't be hard. This was where I belonged, and I wanted every bit of it. Did that make me such a bad guy?

Mother jerked back with a huge intake of breath which seemed to unlock the two of them.

"Now," Father said, "she was telling me about the human planet Florida."

"Earth," I corrected. "That's what it's called. And those other pup—"

Mother laughed loudly at Father's flushed face, cutting me off. But it still made me realize that they were still very much in love after all that happened.

"Of course it is," Mother said. "Earth! You should know that, dear."

Father made a dramatic defeat. "Now, I'm sure you want to see your sister."

I nodded. Poppy. I could ask Mother another time. She would always be here. But Poppy, I couldn't lose her again.

Mother blinked and gave him a curious look before studying me. "I think it would be best if you didn't mention Earth."

Father started saying that he already told me that while I was asking why.

"Oh," Mother said, twirling a strand of blond hair. "It's just not good for her mental health."

Which is what Father had said. Either they discussed this story ahead of time or it was real. But even though it's awful, I didn't think Poppy's mental health was that bad.

Mother said she was in her garden, so we set off for a trapdoor in the middle of the hallway.

Poppy loved to garden. She hadn't been old enough to be assigned a job like controlling the puppets or turning the humans into marionettes like Vince and me.

My old job…How I had loved it. The sewing, the creation of new life forms. I loved making the controllers and rearranging anatomy. Is that why I knew my way around the Studio when Lewis was there? Is that how I even knew how to reach the Studio in the first place? Is that why I was obsessed with making puppets on Earth?

The Puppeteer opened the trapdoor, calling Poppy's name. Thumping noises and Poppy appeared. With squinted eyes, she blinked a few times. They widened when she turned toward me.

Beside me, our parents were beaming, but Poppy was different. Her lips were pulled into a frown as she swept a leaf from her hair. She had a dullness in her eyes that reminded me of the puppets I called "sheep."

What had they done to her?

Chapter 18

"Poppy, it's me." I stepped forward like I was approaching an injured animal. "It's me, Kindle. Your sister."

I heard Mother tsk like I wasn't in earshot. "She knows who you are."

Something inside Poppy's eyes clicked and she reached for my forearm. "Kindle!" Her eyes welled up. "Why'd you leave us? Why'd you run away? Nobody will tell me."

"Poppy," Mother said as my stomach fell, "it doesn't matter why she's back. She's here."

My sister smiled. She almost looked okay again, but I couldn't forget the "sheep" look she had had before. "You're right, Mother. She's back."

"Come on, gang," Father said. "Let's have dinner."

"Dinner?" It felt so strange in my head. "Will I be able to eat?"

Poppy took a step back. "Are you sick?"

"What?"

Mother turned to Father with a pinched look. "Will she be able to drink her tea?"

He frowned and patted her shoulder. "Not tonight, but I'll try to find a way. Tomorrow Vince and I will…"

Poppy looked as confused as I felt.

Father glanced at her tilted head. "We'll figure something out."

As we walked through the house again, Poppy was bursting with questions again. I already knew from my Earth days it was easy to feel guilty about something you didn't even remember, but it didn't hurt less when Poppy interrogated me as to why I left. Anger rose in me. Why hadn't I been here for her? Why had I left? Why did I lose my memories? As I tried to find words to justify actions I didn't remember, Mother put a hand on my shoulder.

It was gentle, but her nails dug in. Was this a "don't tell her about Earth" threat? Or an "I'm glad you're back, poppet" hug? She had never been one for hugs. I glanced back at her, mouth drying. Her face was all motherly but her actions were what made me think carefully. She had hurt people. Would she hurt me? Was it too late for Poppy? Or was this all trauma?

"I don't know," I said to both Poppy's questions and my own. I turned to my sister. "I don't remember."

Poppy beamed like I'd seen the puppets do when they talked about the Puppeteer. "That's okay. I don't remember a lot of things either."

Ahead, almost to the kitchen, Father stumbled on air. He turned to shoot me a look. A look that told me to be quiet. I nodded back. I'd be quiet, but just for Poppy. And medical or not, Poppy had something wrong with her.

When we girls caught up to Father, Vince was already at the table, a book in his hands. Mother bopped his book and told him no reading at the table. I smiled a little as he scowled. A debate that had been going on as long as Vince could read.

Vince perked up as I sat next to him while Poppy rushed for my other side. For once it didn't feel fake. This really was my family. I wasn't a puppet spy, but rather a family member. A sister. A daughter.

Everyone else filled up their plates with mushroom casserole, sweet potatoes, and a side salad. They also took turns vanishing into the kitchen to get tea. At one point I was alone with Vince who was already inhaling his meal.

"I'm glad the rods don't have to serve us anymore," I said.

He choked on a forkful of lettuce. He managed to recover without the tea he had in a transparent sports bottle. "We can't talk about puppets or the abductions. Not with Poppy here."

"Why?"

He put a hand to his throat and made a motion of choking. "Father." He tossed me a stern look when Poppy came back out. I stared at the golden tablecloth as she slid her chair back. I had thought, out of anyone, Vince wouldn't speak riddles with me.

Poppy grinned at Vince when she was sitting. "You and your sports bottle. Someone might think you work out."

I laughed. She wasn't that savage before.

Vince tossed his head back. "You know what? I might just buy one for Kindle."

Poppy snorted. "Not on my watch. Those things are so ugly. Not like my little teacup." She lifted a teacup shaped like a pink rose.

"That's nice," I said to her, getting a glare from Vince.

Vince turned away and tensed up when Mother and Father came back.

Mother set a yellow teacup with painted stitches on it in front of me. *My* cup. "Just in case you feel like it later." She smiled softly and sat across from me.

Father sighed and sat in the remaining chair.

"I don't think I feel like it," I said. Although mushroom casserole was my favorite, the desire to eat anything felt like the desire to eat carpet.

"Are you sure?" Poppy said. "You always said to feed a cold *and* a fever."

At this point, I had to put my foot down. Whatever they didn't want Poppy to know, I was telling. It was wrong for her to be treated like this. "It's because I'm–" Before I could say "a puppet" my throat grew thinner. Something that felt like a hand, slithered up and out. "*...fine, Poppy,*" Father made me finish in my own voice.

Poppy nodded, but I glared at Father. Vince raised his eyebrows while still staring down at his plate.

Mother nudged Father, but he just gave her another stare I couldn't interpret.

Mother took my pretty little teacup away and started to head for the kitchen. She stopped. "You can drink this later. We'll just reheat it."

Ew. That sounded worse than regular hot tea.

When Mother vanished, Vince picked up his bottle and chugged the tea in one sitting. That was new. He couldn't stand the stuff as a kid.

When he finished, he flipped the bottle over and slammed it down like he was taking shots.

Poppy frowned. "You're so weird, Vince."

Vince wiped his mouth. "Says you."

"What's that supposed to mean? Father, what does that mean?"

"Nothing, poppet, nothing." Father glared at Vince who stood up with an empty plate, shoving the chair back with an ear-splintering screech.

Vince had slammed the plate into the sink and was storming out when he ran into Mother.

I flashed back to when she made everyone get on their knees back in the ballroom. I stood up, trembling.

"Are you leaving, already?" she said, calmly.

Vince bobbed his head as he stormed for the door.

"Well, at least play some video games," Mother said.

Vince spun around. "Those are Poppy's games. Let her do your dirty work for you!" He slammed the door behind him, making the teacups displayed on the walls rattle.

"Don't listen to him, poppet." Father patted Poppy's blond head. "It's just a phase." He looked at Mother. "He just needs more tea. It soothes, you know?" That last sentence felt directed at me.

The rest of dinner passed in silence. When everyone else had scraped their plates, Father suggested we all play a game and led us into a giant living room. It was covered head to toe with Earth toys from all decades. Even the couch was designed after a deck of cards. It was designed to look like the living room I had first cleaned when I had pretended to be a rod. I got the idea that the living room the rods worked on was the original, but why build a whole new house and lock it away from the rods?

Vince was in the corner by a large bookcase shaped like a jack-in-the-box. He was thumbing book pages even after Father cleared his throat.

"Vince?" he finally said in the softest voice. "Would you like to play charades with the others? I have work to do, and you would make even teams."

"Charades? Let me guess: Mother's idea? Of course it was." His bitter tone disturbed me. Last time I checked, we didn't talk to family like that. Except that our parents are criminals. I wanted to sit down. This back-and-forth debate on Mother and Father's goodness made me dizzy. Why couldn't they just be my parents?

"That's because Mother always wins," Poppy said. "I call her on my team!"

I shrugged at Vince. "Guess we're teammates."

"I guess," Vince said, smiling a bit.

Since I drew the shortest stick, I went last. Poppy was a bee, Mother was a dog, and Vince was a wolf. It was a bonus round when I came up, meaning anyone could shout out what I was.

I stood in front of the couch, right in front of Mother. "Do I have to be an animal?"

"No," she said. "Usually, we pick easy things for the first round."

Oh God, there were more rounds? "Okay. Um, category is an occupation."

"Doctor!" Vince blurted, grinning.

I put my hands on my hips. "Do you really think I'm that predictable?"

"Yes. Did I get it?"

"No. Now shush."

I closed my eyes. I was going to be a miner. A puppet miner. A marionette. Everyone had to know what that was. It was a triggering nightmare to even pretend I was back in the Dollhouse. But I wanted to see the look in Mother's eyes. I hated to realize it, but I wanted to know what side of her was more dominant. My sweet Mother, or the hateful Puppeteer.

In my mind, instead of being in that living room, I was in the deepest, darkest, dustiest mine. I was holding an axe that left blisters in my calloused hands. It was heavy and bulky, and my shoulders were aching. And someone, one of my older siblings, was controlling me with their powers.

I startled myself out of the darkness of my closed eyelids.

Mother, eyes wide, was glancing at Poppy with a look of unease. Poppy was deep in thought, hand wrapped around her chin. And Vince was squirming. I slowed down.

Before I could say anything, Poppy blurted out: "It's a drummer! Like with bongos or something."

Mother put on a fake surprised face. "Oh, that's it, isn't it, Kindle?"

"No—" My throat closed as Father took over my voice and made me say: "Just kidding. Yeah, it's a drummer."

"Yes!" Poppy jumped up. "We won round one!"

"Dessert's ready," Father called from what sounded like deeper into the house. But I knew he had been here. Right outside the door frame, watching me. As much as my parents loved me, they couldn't let me slip.

Vince and Mother left like they'd never eaten dessert before, but Poppy stayed behind to make a tally on a whiteboard under her and Mother's names. I grabbed her forearm as she capped the marker.

We stared into each other's eyes. Hers portraying worry, and hopefully mine betraying nothing. I remembered her questions from before. Why had I run away? Why couldn't I remember? Why would nobody tell me? One thing I knew for sure, I wouldn't leave Poppy or Vince ever again. They were my siblings. And they were innocent.

Poppy seemed to recognize who I was and smiled. "Hey, Mother and Father will still let you get a cookie even if you didn't eat dinner. I'll make sure of it."

It took me a second to realize what she was talking about. "No, no. It's fine. I was just going to ask you if you knew what a miner was."

She frowned. "Like, the one that digs up rocks?"

"No, I mean the other kind. The puppet kind?"

"Oh, is this some kind of toy?"

"No, I mean a puppet is a toy, but I mean the real kind."

"Real kind?" Poppy shook her head. "You're not making sense."

I had to fight to keep my cool unless Father heard me. "I mean the puppets that are alive! Down in the mines?"

Poppy stepped back to the board. "Kindle, you're scaring me. Puppets aren't alive. They're toys."

I dropped her arm, my body flooding with a sickening realization. Poppy didn't know. She didn't know that Mother and Father abducted people. She didn't know about her abilities. She didn't know her house was flooded with medical experiments. She didn't know people were suffering right outside these very walls.

It explained why we had two houses. One for the rods to clean and keep. Because of course, Mother wouldn't get rid of them. One, she was a neat freak. And two, she needed to be in control of something. Even if what the rods cleaned were for her and Father's eyes only.

It also explained why every time Vince or I tried to say something, Father got us. He and Mother had to have something to do with Poppy, but what? It had to be some other kind of drug. Something they were sneaking her. But how? Poppy was the most superstitious person I knew. No way would she take pills randomly without checking them a million times.

Whatever it was, as a puppet, I couldn't eat or drink, leaving me immune. I just had to stay a puppet for as long as possible. Or at least until I figured out who to trust.

Chapter 19

After three more gruesome yet tamer rounds of charades, I slept on the living room couch. And the meaning of "slept" hadn't changed a bit. I could hardly remember what it felt like to sleep, to dream, to wake up several hours later. Instead, I had to suffer.

At some point in my misery, Mother came in and apologized for turning my bedroom into a spare room for random crap. She said I couldn't sleep in Poppy's room either because she couldn't sleep without someone else in the room.

Baloney, I wanted to spit. *We used to have sleepovers all the time. Our bedrooms were one wall away. And paper-thin walls at that. Don't tell these lies, Mother.*

But I let her. The only thing I really believed was that she missed me. And she gave me a heated blanket in return.

Later, Father tried to convince me to let him perform an operation to turn me back to my normal alien self. Or at least the best he could do given his knowledge and the tools he had. He said mother was better at this stuff.

I denied his offer. Told him it wasn't best to operate at night. Told him morning would work better. And he, knowing nothing about puppet making since that was Mother's specialty—blindly obliged.

When he left, I curled up into a small ball like I did that first night as a marionette. I was just as scared, confused, and alienated as back then.

As the hours passed, I let myself wander in and out of my memories. It was almost like dreaming. I decided I had two sets of memories. One consisted of my happy childhood with Mother and Father, while the other was my life on Earth and getting abducted by the Puppeteer. Somewhere, hidden in the middle of that, was an event that determined who my parents really were. Even as a young child, I knew about the puppets and what my family did. It was just how things worked. I didn't question it, I didn't revolt. But at some point, I must have. What else would have pushed me away from here? Did I leave to save myself or save my parents? Obviously, Mother and Father didn't have any hard feelings. If they weren't the reason I ran away, then what was?

I recognized the arrival of morning by the clatter in the kitchen, giving me a headache. Vince, on the other hand, was in the dining room with a fresh cup of coffee so black it reminded me of

Lewis's hair. I had thought about him last night as well. My stomach hurt from so much worrying. The last thing we'd done was argue. The last thing he knew was I became a dummy. What was he doing? Was he waiting for me to come back? Not to mention if he continued with the escape plan without me, I'd be in the crossfire…as well as my family.

"How was the couch?"

I jumped but didn't miss a beat. "Awesome. You should try it."

Vince chuckled into the black abyss of his coffee. "I'm good."

"I didn't realize Mother let us drink coffee."

"Not until we drink our tea."

"Right. The sports bottle." His transparent sports bottle was upside down on the kitchen table just like he'd done the night before.

"*Right*," he said, squinting his eyes.

I frowned. God, how I hated this secrecy. "Is there someplace we can talk in private?" It was his turn to frown, his eyes lost in concentration. "It generally concerns me how hard you have to think about this."

He huffed. "You should be concerned. But I know just the place. Just let me put some more milk in this first."

As he hurried to the kitchen, I flopped down in his seat to get some headache relief. On his placemat was his sports bottle. I flipped it upright, only for it to refill with tea. I glanced around. With nobody here but Vince making a mess in the kitchen, I unscrewed the lid.

I gasped to see the bottle still full. It was like one of those magic bottles that came with the antique baby dolls Father collected. If you tilted the bottle at a certain angle, it looked like the liquid was being drunk. When completely upside down, it appeared empty, but nothing had come out. As long as Vince kept it upside down, Mother and Father were clueless.

Before I screwed the lid back on, I took a whiff of the tea and saw stars. My numbing head lurched forward, but I caught myself before getting a concussion on the table.

How clever. The poison Mother and Father were using on Poppy was in the tea all along. And Poppy loved tea. Yet Vince knew.

"Good morning, Kindle," Mother said, strolling into the kitchen.

My mouth dropped. Thankfully, the bottle was still upside down.

"What's wrong?" Mother asked.

"Nothing." My heart wouldn't stop pounding.

"Oh, well your father has to go to work again, but I'll be taking the day off." She clasped her hands together, beaming. "Oh, it's so nice to be a family again."

My stomach sank. "Yeah."

"I have to send your father off now. I'll see you later," Mother said. "You too, Vince."

Vince was standing in the kitchen doorway, arms crossed. His scowl looked out of place against Mother's radiant smile. "What's Poppy doing today?"

Mother waved her hand. "Gardening."

His eyebrows raised. "No video games?"

"Day off." She quickly glanced over at me and tripped on her next words. "All those video games are bad for you. An Earth invention, I believe?"

"Uh, I guess," I stammered, too caught up that this was the second time Vince had a strong distaste towards Poppy playing video games. And that just wasn't like him.

Mother smiled at us and patted Vince on the shoulder. "You should drink more tea, Vince. It's good for you."

"Uff," strangled from my lips, but neither Mother nor Vince noticed in their infinitive stare down.

Mother smiled at him, one still full of love. Before she had left the room completely, she turned back. "Kindle, poppet, if you want to visit Poppy, just give me a shout."

My mouth dried. "That sounds like you lock her up."

Mother laughed. "Oh, she's still getting used to you."

"What does that even mean?" A quivering heat rose from my soles as I almost flung the bottle across the room if Vince hadn't grabbed my hand first. He squeezed my fingers, telling me to stop. I wish I could tell him not then. The anger was too consuming. "You act like she's stupid or something!" I shouted. "She's not this fragile. She never was."

Mother looked at the floor, jaw set. "Please, Kindle, don't talk about Poppy like that. You've been gone for so long; how would you know?"

Those last words, despite the steady tone, had the same effect as Father's powers.

Mother nodded, soaking in her own satisfaction. Then she left us.

I caught Vince's stunned gaze and tried to tug out of his grip. Tears slipped out. "I don't understand anything," I whispered.

"I know," he said, nudging my shoulder. "Come, on. Let's go." With his sports bottle in hand, Vince led me out of the room.

"Now, don't tell Mother I know this place exists," Vince said as we turned into the hallway leading to the laundry room and guest bathroom. It was kind of funny having a "guest" anything. We never had guests. In fact, Vince, Poppy, and I were homeschooled and never saw another of our kind. We had never even gone outside.

I closed in on Vince. "I already assumed everything you're showing me is a secret to Mother."

"Good," was all he mustered as his attention was now on a wooden buffet.

"So," I continued. "This house. It's not the one I grew up in. And it's not the one I worked in as a rod. When did this happen?"

"Once you…left," Vince said, his eyes darting, reminding me there were still things he hadn't said. Hopefully, this secret place would these secrets to blossom. "We have two houses. The house you worked in as a rod is the house we grew up in, but after you left Mother and Father built this almost exact replica, but I guess you noticed enough to know it isn't the same."

"But why? What's the point? Why not let the rods in here?"

Vince hung his head slightly. "Poppy. It's all for Poppy."

"What does—?"

Vince cut me off with an open palm directed at me. "Not now."

The buffet Vince was rooting through was all over both houses. I never had the chance to snoop through them, with having to keep my disguise and all, but I guessed they had to be empty. This one, however, held a small flashlight that Vince hurriedly cranked a few times before a steady beam blasted along the opposite corridor wall, reflecting greasy smudges and previously hidden dust particles. Vince continued down the hall, the light bobbing until it hit an "X" made of a shiny material.

When Vince handed me the flashlight, the "X" disappeared.

"Clever," I mumbled.

If he heard me, he didn't answer. He was grabbing at the "X" until he wedged something loose A *thunk* echoed down the hall. A hot and scratchy wind of fear held my throat like Father was controlling it. So much for being sneaky. Vince twisted the now protruding "X" like a doorknob and swung a portion of the wall open.

He motioned for me to squeeze in, so I did. The tiny room made my stomach fall. It was identical to the room the rods slept in. Maybe the males, maybe the females, but it was still here with its horrible white beds and empty dusty walls like an abandoned mental hospital. An empty fireplace took up the back wall.

"No!" I said much louder than a whisper. I backed up, but Vince put a strong palm against my back, pressing on my infraspinatus muscle. "It's okay, Kindle. It hasn't been used in years."

"Do you even know what this is?" I strangled out but regretted it as soon as his face dropped.

"Of course I do." He said, calmly, but I could see the pain in his eyes. "Like I said, Mother and Father made the houses nearly identical. They've forgotten about this place." He eyed the dust. "Obviously." He sat on a bed. The springs cried in pain. He patted beside him, but I shook my head. That wasn't the only thing shaking. I wanted to scream just from being in here.

"So," I started, feeling like the walls were going to jump out at any second. "I found out why you love that sports bottle so much. Pretty smart. Not a drop touches your lips."

Vince smirked. "Ah, so you've figured it out. I was waiting."

"What about Poppy? Why doesn't she just stop drinking the tea like you? It's obvious something's wrong with her. She doesn't even know about the puppets."

"It's a brainwashing medication made from the golden stuff the marionettes mine. It's more than just an energy source, Kindle. It's a chemical that can be used to hurt or heal depending on the creator's intent. And it's in our tea. Mother and Father brainwashed her on purpose."

At this, I actually sat beside him. My legs could no longer hold me. I could have mined the substance used to poison my own sister. She could be drinking my handiwork right now for breakfast.

"But as for your question…There's no hope in just stopping for Poppy. She's too far gone. Thankfully I snagged a small sample of the golden substance. I've been working to see if I can use it to against the poison."

"Like a vaccine!" I said.

"More or less. I'm going to finish it soon. He rubbed the back of his neck. "I sure wished you were here. You were always better with this medical stuff."

"Thanks," I said.

"You don't have to."

"No. I do. This isn't just a thanks for the compliment. This is for, well, everything. I wouldn't be here without you."

"I wish you hadn't come back."

"I know." We both stared at our swinging feet for a moment before I spoke again. "Is this why I don't remember? Because I took the golden substance?"

"Yeah." Vince sighed. "You took it and left. But that's all I know."

"No. That's all you're telling me."

He turned away. "Same difference."

"Vince…"

"If you can manage to stay a dummy—the puppet kind—"

I crossed my arms. "I didn't need a clarification."

Vince smiled faintly. "If you can stay a puppet for a little while longer to avoid drinking the tea, then we can figure out how to escape with Poppy."

"E-Escape?" My jaw dropped. "But what about—"

He looked at me like I'd lost my head.

"Vince! The aliens! We have to rescue the puppets. All of them. We have to—" My voice dribbled away when I saw his pained face. I slid back along the bed just in case he was actually going to vomit. "What?"

"No. We can't."

"But they're people too! They're alive!"

Vince continued to shake his head harder with each of my words. "No, no, no. I've got everything planned. I've got enough for me, you, and Poppy. We can throw everything to the wind. I've set up an escape pod. We can leave in maybe a week if all goes right."

Tears burned along my eyelids. The last thing I expected to feel after getting my brother back was lost, lonely, and confused. Right when I was reaching for the blinds, someone beat me to it. I'm in the dark again but this time Lewis wasn't there to hold my hand and filter the sunlight in with his witty ways.

Lewis! Oh God! Another gut punch. The last time I had seen him was our fight. He would never know. He probably thought I was dead or on another planet. Which was worse at this point?

"No, Vince. There are people I need to save. I know someone who can help us."

"That alien. That human," Vince said. "I've seen you talking to him a few times. What's his name?"

"Lewis. His name's Lewis. He's so smart. So brave! He knows this place. He's been so helpful, and I know he can help." My words stammered out, the fear of losing Lewis scrambling my mind. "He's a broken marionette, so Mother can't control him. Trust me, Vince. He's worth it."

"Wow," Vince said. "You're so in love with this guy."

My face flushed. "What?"

"You're so readable, Kindle."

"Well, you've never seen a girl you haven't been related to!"

"Oh!" he said, holding his stomach. "That was mean." Then he fell over laughing, and soon I was joining him. So this was what family felt like.

After we finished wiping the last tears from our eyes, I looked him dead in the eyes. "So, why don't you want to save the puppets? It doesn't seem like you."

Vince sighed, but it was different this time. I knew he wasn't going to hold back. "It's not that I don't want to. I would love to. But we can't. I'll save your friend, but this is too dangerous."

"I don't get it!"

"It has something to do with why you left."

"Is it really that bad?"

"I'll take it to my grave."

"Please, Vince. Why can't you tell me?"

He stood up fast. "Because I'm your older brother! I should have protected you. I should have been there. I should have known."

And when I finally looked at my brother, I knew this wasn't the same scrawny bookworm I'd left years ago. He had seen things. Things that change you. But in the end, I knew he'd come around. He had to. Or at least I hoped.

Chapter 20

Three more days ticked on like the time bomb I was. Everyone acted like we were one happy family again. However, if it wasn't for Poppy, we probably wouldn't. The air was static with tension, and I was more than glad to give my parents the cold shoulder, especially when they mentioned the operation to turn me fully alien again. They were getting more desperate with their plan. Step one was to shrug when I asked where my pillow was. The same for the TV remote. I spent many nights alone on the couch, questioning my madness, but I pushed on.

Step two was to kick me off the couch and put me in my old "bedroom". And "bedroom" was an ugly word. When Mother creaked open the door, any hope of spending the night on a blanket was dashed. They literally shoved a bunch of boxes around to make a pit of cold, hard, wooden floor.

"Well," Mother had said when I gestured angrily to the floor, "since you really don't need to sleep, you don't need all those pillows and throw blankets do you now? You're charitable, poppet. It's going to your siblings to keep them warmer. You don't want your siblings to suffer, do you?"

What a funny thing for you to say, I thought. *When you care so little for the freezing puppets in the Dollhouse.*

I was very close to saying the last bit out loud but bit my tongue like a champ. How badly I wanted to detonate. To accuse her of everything. But as Vince had told me earlier that day: "What good would that do? You're only telling her things she already knows."

Fine. He did have a point. So, I bit my tongue and only communicated to Mother and Father with nasty glares. I had plenty of practice giving them to Mora when Tiffany was around.

Now, on the third day, Mother and Father pulled the ultimate rug.

It started with wailing. Poppy's wailing. I was wandering the halls, looking for Vince when I heard it. Poppy found me before I found her, and her tears didn't mask the anger in her eyes.

My stomach felt like an anchor had been thrown in the middle. Sinking, sinking, sinking.

"How could you?" Poppy jammed a finger at me.

"What?" I didn't really want to fight first thing in the morning, but there I was. "I didn't do anything." The truth was, I had been avoiding Poppy. Awful, but every time I saw her, I saw another puppet. Not one of the body or voice, but one of the mind. When you don't know anything, everything makes perfect sense. I wanted her to know that, but then she'd start questioning, and that was the worst part. I could see she was struggling to keep up with reality. People talking behind her back, and everything seeming to have another meaning. It hurt to watch. I often wondered if this was why Mother and Father locked her in the garden so often. Because it hurt them too.

I highly doubted that.

"Don't act like you don't know," Poppy continued. "You told Mother and Father that the garden was dangerous for me. Just. Like. Everything. Else. Is."

"I never said that."

"You really think Mother and Father would lie to me?"

I snorted.

Poppy fell to her knees in the middle of the hallway, hands to her face, and wails echoing.

God. What a jerk I was.

I kneeled beside her like Vince would have me. This was my little sister and all I've done is ignore her. I would bet a pretty penny Mother and Father told her I was dead or never coming back. Now here I am, and everything's changing.

"What's going on?" I asked gently, awkwardly rubbing her head.

"You wouldn't understand."

"I'll try."

Her breathing was shaky and shy. "I think there might be something wrong with me."

If only she knew.

I kept a stern face and nodded. "Like what?"

Her voice was a mere whisper of a breath. "I think I'm dying."

My face betrayed me. Cheeks sucked in and mouth agape. I was back in the tunnel with Lewis, finding out he was made of wood. I was with him in the other house, helping him take steady steps. I was in the Studio so mad my blood hurt.

"Wh–why do you say that?" I stammered.

"Because Mother and Father are hiding something from me. I know they talk about me. They get upset when Vince criticizes them, and he always seems worried about me. He spends a lot more time reading medical books than fiction. Every time I can't do something it's because it's 'bad for my health.' Plus, Mother and Father let me do whatever I want. Video games all day and a huge garden? Doesn't that sound strange to you?"

Video games. Why did that keep coming up? "Oh, Poppy, you're not dying. They just don't want you to run away like me."

"Are you sure?" She sucked in a breath. "I guess you know more than me. It's just…I don't know." She tilted her head back to look at me. "Why did you leave?"

I slowly shook my head. "I don't remember."

"Did you miss us?"

"I…I didn't remember anyone. I had amnesia. It was just luck Father stumbled upon me."

The fog, the sleepiness, in her eyes cleared. "Oh. That makes so much sense."

"Are we done?" I asked. Something Tiffany always said to Mora.

Poppy nodded. "Can you talk to Mother and Father and tell them that's not what you meant? That I can have my garden back?"

"I'll try." But I wasn't sure how to go about doing that. Just like my blankets and couch, they would only give Poppy her garden back if I agreed to the operation. And that would never happen.

"It's cold in here," Poppy suddenly said.

A single shudder went down my body. I hadn't noticed until then, but I was clutching my upper arms, trying to keep warm. I couldn't break out in goosebumps like humans, something I had always wondered about back on Earth, but I knew by the dull ache in my organs the temperature was dropping. It reminded me of the snow and that reminded me of Lewis.

Where are you, Lewis? If I could be drawn to you like a magnet, I would. I need you. I'm sorry I got mad. It wasn't professional of me. But now I might never tell you about that kiss in the cave, and that my being mad didn't change a thing about it. I would relive that moment over and over…

"Kindle? Kindle?" Vince's worried shouts echoed.

"I'm here!" I stood. "With Poppy."

"Why's it getting so cold?" Poppy shuddered as Vince turned down the hallway.

"I don't know," Vince said slowly but his eyes told me what I already knew. Mother and Father. The blankets and the garden weren't enough. If I couldn't starve, I'd just have to freeze. Exposure on Earth probably made me more suitable for the cold, but not Vince and Poppy. They were already rubbing their noses and blowing on their fingers.

"We have to make a fire," I said, not seeing a fireplace in any of the halls.

Poppy shook her head. "We don't have a fireplace."

But there was a fireplace. In the secret room Vince had shown me. And poor Poppy didn't know it even existed. "No. We do."

"Kindle, no," Vince said.

I knew what he was thinking: Not there. What would happen to Poppy if she found an abandoned room filled with hospital beds? Questions we couldn't answer, that's what. But we needed to be more honest around Poppy. She had proven to me she knew a lot more than we had thought.

"She can handle it, Vince." I kept my gaze on his eyes, pummeling every word into him.

"I–"

"We're going to freeze!"

Vince didn't say anything. Just grunted and ran the other way.

I reached back for Poppy's hand and yanked her along, the whole time, thinking Mother would round the corner and grab us. And that jumpy feeling didn't leave until Vince was sliding the door shut behind us.

I heaved a chest-rattling sigh and leaned back on the brick wall. My breath spiraled around my face. The back of my neck was still prickled like Mother was tracing it with her powers. But unless Mother was right outside the door, she wouldn't be able to control us or find us. No, this old rods' bedroom was far out of her reach and mind.

Poppy's hand fell out of my grip like the way a dead bird falls out of the sky. I half expected it to hit the ground with a thump. But it didn't. It curled around her mouth, scraping at her upper lip. She was pale, but not because of the room's dropping temperature.

"What is this place?" she said so softly I felt huge in comparison.

I glanced at Vince for his lying expertise, but he was fiddling with the firewood.

Vince cursed and slammed a log down. "My-my fingers are so numb I can't get anything done!"

"I'll do it," I offered, grateful for any excuse to leave Poppy.

"Wait!" Poppy grabbed my hand. "What is this place? Please, Kindle, I *need* to know."

"Does it seem familiar?"

"No," Poppy grunted as she struggled, her mental capacity making her shake.

Vince pushed my arm away from her. "Your turn with the fire, if you can."

"Tell Poppy the truth." I let every word harden.

His nod was more of a quick jolt that could have easily been a shiver.

There was a stack of familiar-looking firewood to the right of the furnace and a pack of matches above. Could matches expire? I shook one out, ignoring the several scattered around my feet that Vince had nicked the heads off of. I went to strike it, but the firewood was all wrong. As I made the square base, Vince and Poppy were gasping and whimpering. Like they were running out of air. Like it hurt to breathe.

My teeth were chattering as I finally struck the match and tossed it in the kindling. The flame was slow, but when it hit, it *hit*. I sighed, leaning back on my heels so my toes wouldn't touch the concrete floor. Vince and Poppy gathered around, looking halfway to death. I'm sure Poppy had lots of questions about why I was able to withstand the cold. But there was no proper way I could tell her I had built up years of Earth's winters.

Vince scooted dangerously close to the flame, pushing me toward the cold firewood stack. To pass away the silence, the cold, and the fact that Mother and Father had gone berserk, I tossed a small scrap of wood from hand to hand.

"It's got numbers on it," Poppy said, probably just to break the silence. Lots of things in here probably had numbers on it. I glanced up to show I wasn't ignoring her. She pointed at the piece of wood in my hand. I flipped the wood over.

"Q32."

"That's Lewis' number!" I screeched. No, no it wasn't. I tried to calm down, but my head was swimming. He was Q33.

It hit me then why the wood looked and felt so familiar. This was puppet wood. Marionette wood. Controller wood. I remembered Lewis turning to wood. This had to be what happened to dead puppets. They turned to wood. Like the cave we found. But what could have caused so many puppets to die? And why did the dead ones have the escape plan tattooed on?

Vince grabbed my shoulders, nearly knocking me over. "Oh no, she's remembering."

"Remembering what?" Poppy and I said, but my brain was already spitting things out like gunfire. Mother and Father. Setting a fire. Puppets screaming and running.

I tried to remember more. To try and glue the pieces together, but nothing came. I started to shake my head like a captured animal. Like I was going to start foaming from the mouth at any second. Nothing would come. But I had those memories. They were somewhere. I just couldn't reach them. But I had been so close.

I stood up so fast I saw black. I stumbled about, squawking when I hit a sharp corner of a bed with my hip. Only one thought circulated.

I need to get to Lewis.

With everything I had, I rammed into the wall. I was shot back with pain and adrenaline running up my arms and shoulder.

Lewis. He's in danger.

I ran out of the room, barely hearing Vince and Poppy's cries of terror. I slammed into the wall. From what Vince had told me, it was around here that the two houses connected. Our sick happy family on one side, and the puppets on the other.

Lewis!

The wall started to crumble.

I'm coming!

I made a crack.

The splinters stung and my shoulders ached. I leaned back to ram again, if I tried hard enough, I could hear the rods screaming. I went for the wall again, only to stop suddenly.

But I didn't stop my rage storm. Mother did. She stood at the end of the hallway, wrapped up in several layers and her hair a mess. Her hands were out like she was holding a marionette.

I willed myself to move. Like how all the heroes in Mora's movies could overcome evil with the power of thought, but I couldn't. I screamed and cried out in my head as Father came too.

I couldn't even cry as Mary and Woody, twins older than Vince, came around the corner pulling a stretcher. They were wrapped in multiple clothing layers as well. As they lifted me up, I saw the wall to Vince's secret hope. It was shut. Vince had said he'd always protect me, but where was he now?

Protecting Poppy from something she didn't even know was here, that's where.

Mother made me close my eyes and cross my arms like I was in a coffin.

Fear washed over me like waves. No, like slaps to the face.

I was lost in the chamber of my mind as someone rolled me down the hallways. I tried to keep track, but the stretcher was spinning to keep me disorientated.

I thought I was smart, but they were smarter.

We finally stopped, leaving me slightly motion-sick. The air felt musty and unused.

"Mary, poppet," Father said, "help your brother with the hook."

Hook? That meant I was in the Studio. I slipped out a moan, but Father caught me quickly.

"Oh, darling," Mother said, "let her speak. I want to see what she knows."

Father didn't at first, but then let me go. With the pressure off my throat, I screamed.

"Mother?" Mary said, voice wobbling over my scream.

"It's fine," snapped Mother. She grabbed at my mouth, almost sewing my bottom and top lip with her pointed nails. My whole face felt numb.

She whipped her fingers back like she just realized she hated touching people.

"I know you burned them," I shouted before anyone could do anything. "The first group of puppets. All of them." I didn't know all of it, but I knew that. Those puppets in the caves…they were real people burned and hidden away by my parents. It all made sense.

Father chuckled. "Do you know why?"

"Because you're monsters," I spat.

"Because of you."

Words chilled in my throat.

"You see," Father said in the same soft voice he used for reading us children's books, "when you were small, maybe twelve, you wanted to go see what your siblings did in the control rooms, so you snuck in there when your mother and I weren't watching. That happened to be the day one of the puppets had an accident. One of your siblings made a mistake, plunging one young puppet off the side of the mountain. He broke."

Lewis. I tried to cuss Father out, but either he or Woody caught me before the first syllable.

"You were so upset by this for weeks, poppet. Nothing we could do would convince you it was fine. You just couldn't get over it. You made it your mission to 'uncover the truth' about the puppets. You became rather good at it, I must admit. You were quite the spy. But one day we discovered you had slipped up and left a note behind. It told of a rebellion you were communicating with through new puppets sent to the Dollhouse. You left them your plan by tattooing words on their skulls. Which is rather clever I must say. Regardless, we decided not to leave for vacation that day and stayed home. The puppets attacked, but we were ready. We started to stop them, in, er, gruesome ways involving fire. You freaked out, took our brainwashing potion, and decided to run away. We tried to stop you, but you wouldn't. You left us for Earth."

It was like I'd been punched in the stomach several times. All of it was true. I was their kindle. "Why?"

"Oh, poppet," Mother said. "We had no choice. We had to burn them and hide them in a cave or else someone else might try to rebel. And we can't lose more laborers."

Something pricked my arm. Dizziness came over me. Every time I breathed in, I saw stars dance on my eyelids. I struggled to think. "What's happening?"

"You won't remember a thing. Not the puppets, not the abduction." Mother said. "It'll be like you never left."

"We don't want to do this to you, Kindle," Father said. "All we want is our happy family back."

I couldn't remember what we were talking about. Only one thing: telling Lewis the plan. The plan I had gotten from the puppets in the cave. Lewis was going to initiate it soon, and then everyone would burn just like before. Then the world was gone. It was like nothing existed before. The only thing I could concentrate on was waking up in my loving parents' arms.

Chapter 21

In the living room, Poppy waved me over to the television. The screen was filled with different characters and her cursor was hovering over a girl with long brown hair. They looked strange.

That's because they're humans! The marionettes!

I shook my head to shoo the voice in my head away. I had passed out in the hallways yesterday and Mother had given me some kind of medicine with a side effect of voices. She seemed concerned about them, but I felt fine. This would pass in time. Besides, Mother knew everything. She would never do anything to harm me.

You were brainwashed! It's the tea! They gave you an IV full of it! Don't drink it!

"Is this that new videogame Father built?" I put my hot tea on a coaster shaped like a pansy. I still didn't like the taste, but Mother said it was the only way to get rid of the voices. Especially stupid ones that told me not to get better.

"Yep." Poppy handed me a controller that looked like a marionette controller. "It's this cool mining game where you have to control someone to some caves."

I lifted the controller. "Why does it look like this? Rather odd, don't you think?"

Poppy rolled her head back at Father's antique toy collection. "Father built it, so of course he'd make it puppet-themed."

"True. What a strange hobby. Now what character do I pick?"

"Whoever you want. I usually pick a different character every time. They don't have names, just numbers."

"Cool." I moved my controller, which was easier than it looked, to a random girl with short black hair. "I'll just pick her."

"Cool. There used to be a girl that reminded me of you. I used to play her a lot but haven't seen her in a while." Poppy hit play.

The waiting screen loaded up, but the loading bar didn't inch past seventy-five percent.

Poppy sighed. "Just a few more minutes until eight. That's when the game starts."

"Wow. Father went all out on this."

Poppy said something, but the voices were too loud.

Wake up, me! This isn't who you are! The plan is about to start. Death! Destruction! They'll storm this place and kill you too. And then Mother will get angry and kill all the puppets again.

"Shut up!" I covered my ears. The world swirled.

Poppy's eyes widened. "Well, I mean, if you want me to…"

"No, not you." I sighed. "I've been hearing voices ever since I took that medicine."

"Oh. Is it that golden liquid? The one that tastes like vinegar and dirt? Yeah, I got that too after I passed out once at the dinner table. Mother said voices were a side effect. Actually, I got it not too soon after you left."

I shook my head. Everyone was saying I had run away, but I remembered zip about that. I wanted to ask her more about it, but the videogame was starting.

Don't play! You're controlling the puppets! This is sick. Stop it!

I frowned and gripped the controller tighter. Voices weren't going to ruin my fun.

The game started out with me in a mansion. My character was facing a door at the back of a line. A green light flashed across the screen. Poppy, player one, lifted her controller and started to tilt it in a way that would make a normal puppet move. I followed her. We had to work together in rhythm, I had to move the character exactly like the other characters were. Their movements didn't look like a computer, but rather like other players. Giggling, we moved through the jungles until we reached a mine. There Poppy said the objective was to mine this golden substance. You couldn't win or lose. Just like an idle clicker.

As we swung the axes in perfect rhythm, it hit me that the voice in my head sounded a whole lot like me.

Poppy burst out laughing. "Do you remember a few days ago, Kindle? When you tried to convince me that puppets came to life?"

I snickered. "No. Did I really say that?"

"Totally."

We both laughed.

The game took a long time, hours actually. Poppy taught me to hit the auto-pilot button if we needed to pause. About three hours in, Father came in with four fishing rods. "You girls want to go fishing? Vince is coming."

"Vince's coming?" Poppy pushed auto-pilot. "He never comes."

"I think he's just excited Kindle's back." He smiled at me, and I smiled back. It was so good to be home from wherever I was before.

Father led us through the house with me in the back. I didn't get far when Vince jumped out in front of me.

"We need to talk.," he blurted.

"You scared me!"

He grabbed my arm and pulled me around a corner. Ever since I'd fainted, Vince had been treating me like an idiot. He was mean, snappy, and talked like I knew what he was talking about. If anything, he was the one that hit his head.

"Crap. They got you good. Do you remember anything about the day before yesterday?"

I scowled. "You know I don't." I waited for the voice in my head to peep up again, but nothing. Good.

His face looked like a water balloon about to burst. "I'm so sorry, Kindle. I was protecting Poppy, but I should have come after you."

"Get away from me!" I screeched. "You're not the brother I remember."

He didn't even look hurt as he loosened his grip. Instead, he smirked at the direction Father went. "You have no idea."

My lips tightened. "Can you let me go now?"

"Don't you find that odd? That you can't remember anything?"

"Vince Kerr!" Mother was standing behind him, hands on hips. "Don't harass your sister. She's very sick. Where's your father? He should be watching you."

Vince shot me a pleading look, but I didn't know what I could do or what he wanted me to do for that matter.

"Go to your room, Vince. You're not allowed to go fishing today." Mother held out her arms and, to my surprise, Vince actually walked away. Sure, he was yelling at Mother, calling her unfair, but he actually walked away. At the end, he shouted something bizarre: "His name was Lewis! And you loved him!"

When he left, Mother tsked and patted my shoulder. "Don't listen to him. He'll get better soon. He might just have to take the medicine you are."

I nodded. I still wouldn't tell her about the voices. Or how happy the name "Lewis" made my face. No, I was scientific. Rational. These voices were just fake. They meant nothing. I didn't need her to worry about me anymore. Besides, my parents would never poison me. They loved me.

Poppy was calling for me to hurry, so I ran to her voice. At the very end of the house, a place I didn't remember very well, was an opened door. Through it, I could see grass and hear birds. Strange that it wasn't underground like the garden.

In the center was a massive pond. The water was dark with little yellow algae like the nighttime sky. How deep was it?

Father was over at a series of bushes, batting at them like he was pressing buttons. Poppy just ignored him, playing around with her fishing rod with the biggest hook I'd ever seen. It had to be at least the size of her face. Goodness, what kind of fish were in there?

I thought I heard mechanical hissing as Father stepped back from the bushes, but it was just the medicine again.

You're going fishing for humans! You're going to abduct people. Wake up!

I swallowed. "So, what are we going fishing for?"

"Human fish," Poppy said.

"Human? That's such a funny word. I think I sort of remember it."

Father's neck tensed, but I could sense him eyeballing me like I'd sworn. Meanwhile, Poppy was ecstatic.

"Really? Did you hear that, Father?"

Father's face smoothed out. "Yeah. Good for you, Kindle. See? I told you that medicine would help."

Poppy cast an imaginary fishing rod into the lake. "Come on, Father, you're holding us up."

I grinned "Yeah, Father."

"Oh, don't get too excited, you two," he said. "I haven't caught anything in a while."

"Except that yellow one you caught a while back," Poppy said.

That was you! This is the Studio! The tea's making you think you're outside!

He shifted from foot to foot. "Yeah…that one." I threw my hook in the water, and for a brief second as that happened, I was transported somewhere else.

It was a night with a thousand stars in the sky, but they looked so…wrong. I was floating overhead like one of them. The ocean. The smell of salt, the shuffling of feet on sand, the lapping of waves. Wandering around were two figures. One small, one big. They looked normal, but once again, something was wrong.

"When will she come home, Mama?" the young girl said.

The older woman sighed. "I don't know, Mora. Now go find your shoes before it gets too dark."

Mora sped off to the right. She was clacking the sand off little, pink flip-flops when something glinted in the sky. A giant hook. Mora didn't see. She was holding a familiar-looking doll. She hugged it to her chest. Tears were streaming off her chin. "Please, God, let her come back."

The hook was coming down further. Lights flickered and car alarms in the parking lot went off. Mora looked up, jaw dropping. The hook was a few feet from her now. She reached up and touched the silver. "Are you an angel?"

No, that's Mora! I have to save her!

Something overcame me. Anger. Hot, blinding white anger. I threw my rod away and tackled Father. He stumbled sideways, shouting. His rod fell to the shore, and he pitched forward.

I sat up from the grass, hands and knees feeling like they'd been through a shredder. What was that?

"Help! Poppy!" Father was hanging from the shore in the water, but more like he was clinging to a cliff as he dangled straight down. "I can't hang on!"

Poppy was there in a blink, grabbing his hands and pulling. "Kindle, help me!"

My head felt like someone had blown my brains out. Still, I managed to grab his arm. Although heavy, we pulled until he could knee his way out. Red-faced, he rolled off the mud and sand

and onto the grass, one hand over his eyes and one on his chest.

"Father!" His heartbeat was like a hummingbird under my fingers. "Are you all right? I'm so sorry. I got scared by a tug and tripped." I don't know why I felt compelled to lie like that. I just knew I didn't want him to know about the visions. I turned away, face heating up.

Father sat up, blinking a few times, looking utterly dazed. "I think we're done fishing for the day."

The rest of the day passed quickly. Poppy and I spent more time on the videogame, and she showed me her room which she had been moving stuff around in to make room for my bed. I didn't have a bed yet. I would just have to sleep on the floor in a sleeping bag.

As I walked out of the bathroom after changing into pajamas, Poppy threw one of her five thousand pillows at me. I barely caught it.

"This is going to be fun." Poppy bounced on the bed with her knees. "Just like a sleepover."

I tossed the pillow back at her. "Yeah. I guess so." Who was Mora? Why did they look so weird? Why did Father get so mad when I said human sounded familiar?

"Except we'll both be asleep before eleven." Poppy clapped and the lights shut off.

I managed to grin even if she couldn't see it. Slowly, I snuggled down into my floral-print sleeping bag. Poppy's room looked like a slice out of the garden, and even her closet was no different. The room went dark, but I didn't dare close my eyes. I kept seeing those *things*. That little girl, if I could call it that, reaching out for the hook. Surely another side effect? But it felt so real. I mean, fish didn't look like that. Not so like us.

I pulled my head out of the sleeping bag. "Poppy?"

The bed creaked as she rolled over. "Hmm?"

I stared at the ceiling with fake stars. "When I was fishing, I got this sort of vision. There were these *things* that looked like us and one of them was talking to the sky and a giant fishing hook came from it."

"From the sky?"

"Yeah."

When Poppy stayed quiet for a few seconds, I wondered if she was holding back a laugh. "What did these things look like?"

I shivered. "Like us, except different somehow."

"Ooh, maybe they were aliens."

I rolled my eyes. "Aliens aren't real, Poppy."

"Got any better ideas?"

"A hallucination from the medicine."

"How boring. Well, goodnight."

"Goodnight." I pulled the sleeping bag over my head. What an idiot I looked like to Poppy. It *had* to be another side effect.

I closed my eyes but, for some reason, I kept thinking this was one of the first times I'd slept in forever. It was almost scary to drift off. Instead, I thought about what Vince had said. I loved some guy named "Lewis?" My face heated at that. Why would he say that? Did it really happen? No. I would have remembered it. Unless I hit my head hard enough…No.

A vision came to me. A boy on a horse looking like a knight. He had thick, curly black hair that looped down his forehead. And green eyes that made me feel weightless. And that smile! Where was he? Where was this boy? Why did I remember him so well?

As I rolled over onto my stomach, it hit me. He *was* real. It didn't make sense. It wasn't scientific. It wasn't plausible, but he was real. Lewis Bryant. We'd kissed in a cave. Why? I mean, I didn't mind it, but where was he?

He's in danger!

Danger?

I glanced over at Poppy to see if she heard it too. No. It was just a voice. Mother told me not to listen to the voices, but what if Lewis was in danger? My stomach boiled, and as I rolled onto my back, I knew it to be true.

I bolted up in bed. Poppy hadn't moved, just a breathing lump under her floral comforters. Heart pounding, I slowly unzipped the sleeping bag. Every second I crept to the door, a blind panic threatened to consume me and leave me dizzy. Timid shouts of fright burst and fizzled out in my mouth like fireworks. Through the door, I made my way down the house until I was in a hallway. One wall looked like a truck had crashed into it. Somehow this seemed familiar.

That's right. You ran into this wall. You were trying to save Lewis.

"Lewis?" I whispered, throat raw and eyesight mixed with tears.

I cleared my throat. "Lewis?"

No. Louder.

"Lewis!" The blind panic took over me now. I had no idea who this guy was except that I needed him. And forget about being scientific and sound. "Lewis! Lewis! Lewis, Are you real?"

A hush came over the hall that left my skin cold. My stomach heaved and I slapped a hand to clutch my jaw and mouth. I bolted across the house to the nearest bathroom. I barely had time to get on my knees when I spat out a golden, glittery liquid. My body shuddered as tears spilled out. After several deep breaths, I got to my feet with the sturdiness of a jig doll.

What was wrong with me?

Grabbing my arms, I shuffled out and back to Poppy's room. Amazingly she was still asleep. Getting into my sleeping bag, I went to join her.

I woke up around one with Poppy leaving the room, whispering about getting water. She left the door open. I was about to get up and close it when the door suddenly slammed shut. Some backpacked figure was making its way toward me.

Through the dark, I could barely make out the shape.

Lewis!

He blocked out my shout by slapping a hand over my mouth. The other hand grabbed my hands like a bouquet of flowers.

"Listen," he said. "I don't know if you recognize me, or what they did to you, but we have to stay quiet."

I nodded my head furiously. I know you! I know you! Well, at least I knew his name.

"Listen. I'm going to remove my hand, but you can't say anything." He paused to reflect on something. "And if you don't remember me, well, don't scream or it will be the last thing you do." He let go of my mouth.

I had so many things to say. Why was he real? Who did what to me?

"Now follow me." His voice was tough and emotionless. "There are eyes everywhere." He glanced from side to side before looking back at me with a face of regret. "Now I'm going to get you out of here. To leave this place."

"Leave!" I shrieked.

His eyes widened. "Shush!"

But I couldn't. "This is my family! You can't make me leave."

Lewis covered my mouth. "Dang. They brainwashed you or something," he whispered.

Then he stepped back, bringing me with him into the hall light. My heart fell. I almost threw up again. This wasn't Lewis. I didn't know what *it* was. It had thick, yellow strings attached to its knees and wrists that led up to a wooden marionette controller strapped to his back. He didn't even look like my species. It looked…alien.

"Get away from me!" I shouted, shoving it back. I snatched Poppy's over-fluffed pillow and hit the creature in the face. "Father! Someone, help!"

I tried to bolt past the thing, but it hooked its arms around my torso. He seemed just as surprised with its strength as I was.

"I'm sorry, I'm sorry," it said as we waddled into the hallway, me hanging from his arms, "but you have to come with me. We have to go back to the Dollhouse."

It dropped me, and unprepared, I fell to the floor like a stone. From its backpack, it yanked out a pickaxe and waved it in front of me like a wand.

"Time to go. And don't ask any questions or we'll be here all day. I can tell there's something not right with you."

I nodded; throat dry.

"Come on." The creature twisted my upper arm. "Everything's already in action. We're just getting a head start."

God, the escape plan.

It dragged me through the house to the hallway which now had a large hole in it. On the other side was another house just like ours. There were slight differences. The creature pulled me, saying how sorry it was, all the way to the…laundry room?

It scanned a card against a keypad which turned blue, and my captor flung open the door. But this wasn't the laundry room. Instead of washing machines, it was filled with mini UFOs with "escape pods" overhead, and it was heading for one.

"We're not getting in," the marionette said. "I just need to grab an antidote in here that I saw earlier."

The pod's door swung open. It was so small that it only had a driver's seat and a passenger seat in the back. Everything was either black or white. In a small rack on the left side were bottles of a golden liquid. A label underneath read "antidote."

"Kindle?" Poppy's voice echoed down the hallway. "What is this place? Why is there a second house?"

The marionette and I froze as Poppy's scared voice grew louder.

I looked at the marionette, at the way it held the pickaxe. No. I wouldn't let it hurt Poppy too. With a quick shove, the marionette was on his back like a beetle in the UFO. I jumped in after and pulled a lever labeled "launch." The air turned into a liquid as we blasted off. I flew backward into a chair. With my last few conscious seconds, I saw the marionette coming closer.

Chapter 22

Everything hurt when I came to. I wasn't curled up anymore but thrown across the spacecraft and onto a cushy sofa. My nose tickled with dust and dirt. Using my arms, I pushed myself into a sitting position, head swaying with neon dots.

I was still in the UFO. The smell of sun-dried mud and grass came from the half-parted doors. Outside the windshield was nothing but brown with specks of grass. It must have landed face-first.

Hopefully, this meant a habitable planet.

Sucking in a shuddering breath, I got up on wobbly feet. But, oh God, my head. The sunlight was way too bright. I gingerly curled my fingers around my temples. But it was pulsing, alive with every memory I ever had. From on Earth, from being a puppet, from my childhood, and finally to being brainwashed.

"Oh no. It was you." I stumbled toward the doors. "Lewis? Lewis, where are you?"

I grabbed the doors and pried them apart until my fingertips burned. We had landed in some kind of cornfield. If we were on Earth, that is. It was also sort of cold, but not enough to bother me. Perhaps because the sun was going down. Or it could be coming up.

"Kindle?"

"Lewis!" His voice was coming from the left. Through semi-crushed stalks, I could make out a dirt road. No sign of Lewis, though.

I thought about calling his name again when he appeared down the path.

My heart flew to my mouth, sucker-punching me in the jaw along the way. Was it wrong I'd forgotten he was a marionette when I wasn't?

I laughed. Then my legs were moving. But, get it, I was moving them. Not Mother, not my siblings, not even Vince. And nobody would control me any longer. He scooped up his controller to run at me.

We collided in the middle harder than we should have. He knocked me off my feet and landed half on top of me, half next to me. I wasn't sure if we were crying or laughing. Maybe a bit of both.

"Oh, Lewis," I said. "I didn't think I'd see you again."

He offered his hand and pulled us both onto our knees. "Aw, but you tried. I knew it was you who made that hole. I heard you calling my name."

Hole? God, he meant the crack I'd made in the hallway. "Is that how you got through?"

"Yep." He tilted his head back, so the sun made his face golden. "Was I right? Did you make it?"

"Um…yeah…but how did you get past my—" I stopped before I could say "parents." Me being an alien would be the last thing to leave my lips.

But Lewis didn't miss a beat. "What's wrong? We're not still mad at each other, are we?"

"Oh no. That was a huge overstatement. Forget it."

"Okay. I was just checking."

"But how did you find me?" Did he know?

"I knew you were a dummy, I overheard that much and managed to sneak out after the other two aliens. I should have stayed to see if you were all right, but instead, I went to the Dollhouse, like a coward."

"No, no! It's what I would have wanted you to do."

"But I could have saved you faster."

"No, you saved me in the nick of time. Now, continue."

"All right. So, when all the other marionettes woke up, I told them that you were kidnapped. Me and some other rods spent the next few days looking through the house for you, but nobody knew where the dummies went. That was until I saw the hole in the wall. Later that night I snuck out. And it was so weird. You were in this whole different house. I snooped around before finding the room you were in. There was another alien, so I waited for her to leave before I grabbed you." He chuckled. "You fight like a bronco, know that? Then I took you to a pod when I realized you were poisoned or something. Were you? Um, never mind. I know we're on Earth, by the way. Kansas to be exact."

"What? How do you know?"

As he rattled on about how he put in the longitude and latitude of his house, I was sweating it. I. Was. An. Alien. Well, at least an alien to humans. And not just any alien. I was the Puppeteer's daughter. Not to mention the escape plan which would literally kill everyone if my parents found out. But to tell him I would have to admit to being non-human.

A bead of sweat rolled down the nape of my neck, followed by another. "Lewis," I interrupted. "Lewis, there's something I've got to tell you."

"Huh?"

"I'm…not like you." His face fell. "No. Let me restart." My voice was swimming. Please don't let me cry. "I'm an alien."

He said nothing as I buried my face into my arms, heaving sobs. Then he wrapped me in a bear hug. I was sitting with my back pressed against his chest. He rested his chin on my head. After sputtering a few times, he finally spoke:

"I know, Kindle."

He was holding back tears, but my head still dampened where his chin touched my hair.

Everything settled into place like fresh snow.

I let out a sigh of relief, a small one so he wouldn't be tempted to let go. "How?" My voice was still shaky.

"When the Puppeteer took me to the Pit, I noticed how much she looked like you. I started putting the pieces together. I experienced the snow you did, but it didn't burn. I started thinking about how the house kept triggering your memories. Plus, when I questioned Lin, he said you knew a lot of stuff on the quiz that I didn't even know. So, um, yeah. That's how I figured it out."

"Oh." That was not what I wanted to say. Not at all. But it was all that could come out. What I really wanted to ask was if being an alien changed anything between us. If it made kissing him weird.

Instead, I managed: "Did you hate yourself?"

"Hate myself?" He adjusted himself. Or maybe he was squirming under the truth.

"Do you regret–" *kissing an alien?* "–knowing me?"

"Kindle! No...I was just surprised I got one before you did."

I grinned. "I'm glad you feel that way."

We moved so we were back to facing each other. The dirt was staining my knees, and for the first time, I realized I was still in Poppy's flowery two-piece pajamas. Above, birds chirped. This had better be Earth.

"So, what happened to you?" Lewis finally said.

And so I told him everything. I told him about how glad my parents were to see me–and honestly how happy I was to have a family. I told him about how the corruption sank in. I told him about Vince and Poppy. I told him about the operation and what the golden stuff was. Then with a big breath–to put the poisonous cherry on top–I told him about the previous revolution. About how everyone had died.

I had the horrible thought of asking him if he hated me now as he buried his face in his hands. But I had more questions. "Lewis?" He didn't react. "Hey, how did you give me my memories back?"

A gun went off with a noise like the sky had split in half.

My screaming was drowned out by the ringing in my ears.

"Not so fun being the victim now, is it, alien?" a male voice said.

"No!" I screeched, an inch away from total hysteria as I turned to find my attacker.

"Dominique!" Lewis shouted with as much anger as there was surprise. "Stop it. She's with me."

Dominique? A marionette looking like an older version of Lewis stepped out of the stalks.

"That's what they want you to think, dude. It's the gold stuff. They sprayed it in Dollhouse. Makes you worship them like kings. They killed everyone. I was the only survivor!"

"She fixed me! I wouldn't be alive without her."

"I'll give you three seconds to prove it." Nobody had to say the gun was on me for my spine to curl up.

"Look at my controller. It doesn't match yours. See? It's fixed. She fixed it."

"It looks a lot like mine," Dominique said.

And of course it was. It's not like I had a special flair to my work.

But I wished I did more than ever for my eyes had met a gun. I couldn't tell you what type or what kind; all I knew was it was going to hurt.

Lewis screamed as Dominique swung the gun around, but it wasn't at me. It was at Lewis.

"No!" I flung my hands out.

Dominique spun around and threw the gun. Or, rather, I made him turn around and lose the weapon with my powers.

I avoided Lewis and stared right at Dominique. It was a trick. He wanted me to use my powers? Or prove my loyalty to Lewis? Either way, there was something not right with Dominique.

"Fine," Dominique said, strangely calm despite being frozen all twisted up. "You can let me go. I was just making sure you were on Lewis' side."

"You're sick," I spat, but let him have control of his body again. That was the first time I'd used my body-controlling power since I left Mother and Father. I had tried to use them on Mother and Father to stop them from killing the puppets, but I hadn't been strong enough.

And now that was going to happen again if we didn't think of a plan soon.

"I can't believe it's really you," Dominique was saying, eyes watering. "I thought you were…dead."

Lewis swallowed; his voice scratchy. "I thought *you* were dead."

The two rushed together and hugged. Both were crying softly repeating words of confirmation that the other was really there.

"How long has it been?" Lewis managed to ask when they pulled apart.

"Four years."

"Four years," Lewis whispered. "How did you escape?"

"A UFO like yours. I was the only one. But it's destroyed now. Jesus, how are you alive? Where were you?"

"I fell off the mountain and lived in this crater."

"For four years?" Dominique exclaimed.

"Yeah, but Kindle saved me."

"I can't imagine…" Dominique shook his head. I had no idea if he was talking about Lewis' time in the crater or about me saving him.

As the two talked more, recounting our adventure, I looked up at the sky. So this was Kansas.

"Come on, alien girl," Dominique said. "We can continue talking later." He had already started toward a dumpy red car, but at least Lewis was still standing at the end of the cornfield, waiting.

"Kindle," Lewis called.

I jogged up to him. "Where are we going?"

"Like I said, we didn't land too far from my house," he said. "Remember? Longitude? Latitude?"

"I don't even want to know why you memorized that."

I thought that." He looked at Dominique in what could only be described as awe. It was the same way I felt when I found Vince and Poppy again. "I thought that he would be here. It was the only place I could turn to. And of course, Mom and Dad."

Dominique stopped, keys jingling lifelessly at his side. "They moved."

"What? Mom and Dad?"

"Somewhere down south. I've been in contact, and they visit sometimes."

"Sometimes?"

Dominique turned toward Lewis. "We were abducted off their front lawn. Plus, we're not exactly human anymore." Dominique rattled the keys in the lock harder, swearing faintly. "Stupid piece of..."

"But...still!" Lewis' voice cracked and he glanced at me for a split second. The lostness in his eyes could have carried me into space.

"They'll come back for you," Dominique said. "Maybe."

"Can I call them?"

"Whatever. They left me here when I came back as...this." He gestured in disgust to his body. "And they frickin' blamed me for it. Every time they looked at me, they just saw the son they lost and the one they could never speak of. So shut up and let me get these keys in."

This seemed to return Lewis back to his proper state even if he did stay a bit back from Dominique. Oh well. More Lewis for me.

He looked off at his brother, like Lewis was floating between the two of us not sure where to go. "I'm sorry my brother's being a colossal jerk."

Honestly, I'd hate myself too if I were in his shoes. With all my memories back, I knew what I had done from all angles. The fire. The death. But it wasn't my fault. It was my parents. And now it was going to be their fault all over again.

"Lewis, the revolution. You didn't start it, did you?"

"Of course I did." Then I think it dawned on him. Slamming a fist on the back of Dominique's car, he swore. "How did your parents find out the first time? Maybe we still have a chance. I mean, these are different people, right?"

Dominique looked like if he hadn't stuffed his rifle in the trunk, he'd be aiming it at me. "What's going on?"

"We need to go back," I offered. "Back to my parents."

"Screw that," Dominique said. "My brother's staying here and so are you. I can't let someone like you get out of my sight."

There was no use pretending that was a compliment, so I swung back to Lewis, red dirt flying. "We have to fix the pod."

"The spaceship?" Dominique said. "Ha!"

I ignored him. "We need tools."

"And you know how to fix this?" Lewis said, eyes only on me.

For a second I thought he meant the whole situation, but, no, he meant the pod.

"I–No." No use pretending now. "But can't Dominique?" And yes, I'd act as if Dominique wasn't there. If he wasn't going to address me properly then neither was I.

"What?" Dominique said.

"But you said," I said to Lewis, "that he worked with NASA."

"NASA and frickin' UFOs aren't the same thing!" Dominique huffed.

"We have to try, Dominique," Lewis said. "This sucks all right, but we have to save those other puppets."

"And my siblings," I added.

Dominique rubbed his eyes. For the first time, I really got to see how much he and Lewis were alike. Same curly black hair, same thoughtful eyes hiding a brain running a million miles per hour. Same way they shuffled when indecisive. And I could only hope I could make Dominique as good as his little brother.

"Fine." Dominique said, no more, no less. But I guess we didn't need reasons as long as he was on our side. At least he wasn't cussing me out, calling me "alien." "You two stay here. I'll run home and grab tools."

I was ready to argue again, but Lewis grabbed my hand.

He'll be back, his fingers running up my wrist said.

I nodded. Dominique swung open the driver's seat and chucked his controller in. I wondered if he did it dramatically just because I was here, or if it was worse on Earth's gravity. Either way, he had no problem blaring some hybrid of country-rap and blasting off, spitting rusty clouds in our faces.

I step back to the crops, coughing, brushing the dust off. "I'm sorry this happened," I said, as we started back toward the escape pod. "I can't believe I did it twice."

"The good thing is it hasn't started yet," Lewis said.

"What?"

"It was going to start early tomorrow. Unfortunately, we can't tell if time is the same here as it is on the alien planet.

"I don't think I like Kansas so far," I grumbled, bringing my arms up to my shoulders.

"Maybe Dominique will bring a coat."

I highly doubted that.

"Hey," he said. "That question you asked me…about how you got your memories. Well, this is going to sound shady, but I found a bottle on the pod. It was this golden liquid that said 'vaccine'. I shouldn't have, but I was freaking out. I wasn't even sure if you were breathing, but when I gave you it, you started shaking, started talking nonsense. Saying that there were too many memories. Then we crashed."

Crashed.

We were at the escape pod. Lewis crouched by the pod like he was posing on social media with a caught fish.

The pod was wrecked. God, how close we'd been to getting hurt. It was stuck in the Earth facedown like I'd suspected. No windows were cracked, but there seemed to be a small trail of white smoke coming from somewhere inside. The doors were still cracked open, and leaves and dirt had skittered inside. I hoped the temperature wouldn't drop anymore. I had no idea how well the pod worked in temperatures that weren't mine–excuse me, *alien*.

Grinning, Lewis kicked a tiny yellow flower in much to my glare. "At least it wasn't a rental."

I just stared at him, the coldness chipping away at my smile.

"Oh, cheer up," he said. "Dominique will know what to do."

"I hope so."

And as if he heard me, there was a crackling honk coming from back at the road.

"I got it," Lewis said, jogging back down the path we'd taken. I started to go after him, not sure if we should leave him with some trigger-happy maniac, but I had no idea which way to go, and getting lost would just waste more time we didn't have.

When they came trotting back with supplies bundled in their arms, I hoped the bitterness from the cold had met my eyes which were focused on Dominique. I couldn't help but shudder for a different reason. They looked so much like the marionettes en route to a mining site–tools in hand with silent dead looks. I wondered what had happened between them.

Dominique kneeled by the pod before dropping inside. I kept repeating to myself that the pod was broken, and he wasn't going to blast into the thermosphere without me. Eventually, he popped out, looked at Lewis, and said: "Okay, I can do this. Got a few questions though."

I jumped when I realized he was talking to me. "Yeah, sure." It more came out as one word: "Yeahsure."

I sat back on my heels and let Dominique work. I tried not to watch Dominique too much–I hated how people watched me work. He asked a few questions, and Lewis would occasionally sit by me, but mainly it was just me alone, drifting aimlessly through my thoughts, which was never fun. I kept thinking about Mora and Tiffany. They were here. I was technically "back." I felt right under their noses compared to the vacuum of space between us before.

Lost in my thoughts, I didn't hear Lewis come up behind me and put a hand on my shoulder. "Are you all right? You seem a bit cold."

I didn't know how to answer that. We'd been out here for maybe thirty minutes of hellish chill. How was he still standing there without his teeth clacking together?

"I can't leave." As much as I wanted to, Dominique was here. "I don't trust"—I nodded at Dominique–"with the spaceship."

"I trust him," Lewis said. "Besides, you don't want to get sick before this flight, do you?"

Crap. As a puppet, I couldn't get sick. I'd almost forgotten I wasn't invincible anymore.

"Ok. Let's go back."

"Hey, Dominique, we're going back to the house, Kindle's cold." Frozen was more like it.

He just waved us away. I wondered if it was his idea in the first place. But why would he want me to leave?

No. Stop it, Kindle. Don't get paranoid. Stay smart. Stay sharp.

I stood, legs like ice shards. I shouldn't have stayed out so long. The walk back felt much longer than the first time, but eventually, we got into the car; Lewis in the driver's seat and me shotgun. I shuddered as he turned the key, bringing the rusty thing to life. I decided not to ask when he learned to drive.

"Wait, what about Dominique?" I couldn't believe I'd just stuck up for the jerk. But if he knew how to fix it, surely that meant he could fly it. He had escaped Aroramere after all.

"He'll be fine. He can walk. I mean, it's not that far."

A little flame inside me–my last cause of warmth–hoped he was lying.

As the car heated up, I started to lose that flame. I mean, Dominique was helping me. And without him, none of this would be possible.

I looked at the sky where the sun was beginning to dip down. Somewhere up there was my family. And somewhere up there were rooms of angry puppets ready to attack.

Chapter 23

A white, vinyl house appeared in range. Or what was probably once white. Now it was stained shades of brown like a chocolate cake. It had a similar wrap-around porch and a roof with maroon shingles. Lewis parked on the grass next to a ramp leading to the front door. When the headlights snapped off, I could see Lewis' reflection in the window. He was hanging his head at what must have been the farm. Overgrown and empty fences for miles and a shoddy barn as the cherry on top.

"I'm sorry," I said because I couldn't think of anything else. It seemed like Dominique didn't have the same fondness for the farm as Lewis did.

"I hope they're okay," Lewis said, looking beyond me and out toward the barn.

"Yeah." I put my arms around my shoulder. Without the car on, the chill was creeping through the windows.

Lewis swung open his front door like ripping off a bandage. The inside was better kept than the outside. Not clean, but decent. It looked like I expected a farmhouse to look. Wide open spaces and animal décor scattered around the place. What really caught my eye though was a nearly empty room. The only decoration was a desk and computer pushed against a wall. The wall held a huge corkboard with different maps of space. There were phone numbers and drawings of the hooks that had abducted us. A few items, like a pickaxe and bucket, were resting on a rickety chair piled high with books. I couldn't read the spines, but one dictionary-sized book was propped on the desk and titled "The History of Aliens." The front cover wasn't of my species. It was green with large black eyes and two antennas. Its mouth was full of forked teeth and a serpent tongue.

I chuckled. I should have. Dominique had stayed here somewhat because of the fallout with his parents, but mostly because he was looking for his little brother. He probably thought it was my fault. Had his parents given up on Lewis?

The poisonous thought that at least mine hadn't slithered through my brain.

Footsteps pounded down the stairs. Lewis was standing at the bottom staring at a phone in his hands like it was going to bite him. "You probably know how to use this better than I do." He sadly met my eyes. "You want to call your guardian? Uh, Tiffany?"

"No." I squirmed. "I mean I want to. It's just…"

"It's hard." He swallowed. "I want to call my parents but…What do I tell them? Hey, your sons were really abducted by aliens and your oldest isn't a nutjob?"

"Yeah. Tell Tiffany I was an alien? She'd rather I have run off with some dude."

He chuckled. "I guess you kind of did." Our eyes met and my face flushed. "I missed you, Kindle. A horse isn't much company."

I smiled. "I wouldn't think so." I wrapped my arms around his shoulders, and he grabbed my sides. "I don't know what's going to happen next, but I'm glad you're here."

"Me too."

He pulled me closer, and I grabbed his face. Together, our lips met, and the world seemed to slow.

A large bang rattled the house. Pictures and trinkets fell from the walls. A cuckoo clock started chiming off hour. We dove apart, covering our heads. I could hear the rip of windows shattering. When the rumbling stopped, I barely had time to pull my head out of my arms when Dominique flung open the front door. He was covered in a rainbow of dirt, grass, and red dust.

"Are you okay?" Dominique shouted.

"What the heck was that?" Lewis shouted, uncovering his ears.

Dominique ran to his computer, his controller knocking over a stack of books.

"It's another one," he said, reaching behind the desk to pull out a rifle. "It fell from the sky. Landed with a huge impact not too far from where you guys landed."

"Another what?" Lewis said.

But I already knew. Another UFO. Another escape pod.

"Stop, Dominique!" I rushed over to him. "That's my brother."

Dominique snorted. He was heading towards the front door he had left flung open. "And how do you know it's not the Puppeteer?"

"Because that's what brothers do."

At least that made him stop. He and Lewis made quick eye contact. "No. I don't care if he's your brother. Remember who your parents are."

That hurt more than I thought it would. "I trust him with my life. Give me fifteen minutes. I'll scream if anything goes wrong. Just let me make sure he's not hurt. I won't try anything funny. Promise."

"Dominique," Lewis said quietly.

Dominique thought for the longest time. "Fine, but you better be a loud screamer."

I would have busted down the door if wasn't already open. It was still cold, but my adrenaline kept me warm, and the air was still burnt from the crash. It smelled like singed hair.

The crash wasn't hard to spot. Across the street, trees had been bent forward like they'd been pushed. The orange clouds above had a hole in the middle like an eye peering down.

I crossed the road, jumping over large branches and fresh potholes.

Not too far in the woods was a UFO identical to the one Lewis and I took. The door was opened and some of the paint on the sides had been peeled back, yet it looked better than ours had. Maybe even flyable.

I stumbled over a thrown rock. "Vince? Vince?" I peered in. Nobody.

Suddenly my head snapped upwards, and my arms twisted around my back. I screamed.

Grass crunched behind me. "Kindle!" Vince stopped controlling me.

I grunted, falling against the UFO.

"I thought you were a human."

I pulled myself back up. "Listen, Vince, none of that matters. What's going on back home?"

"Chaos."

I wished I was still on the ground. "It's too late. The rebellion has started."

"Rebellion? What rebellion?"

I hadn't told him. Why didn't I tell him?

I shook my head. "I'll explain later, but first you need to follow me."

"No," Vince practically laughed. "I'm not staying here another minute. I need Poppy."

"Poppy! Is she alright?"

Vince hung his head. "She's real bad, Kindle. They upped the dosage. Her mind's pretty much dead. It's like she's barely there."

He kicked at the dirt. "I *am* going back for her. I shouldn't have left. I'm a failure."

I put my hand on his shoulder. "You're saving me right now. And we can leave to find Poppy soon, but first, we have to get out of here. Poppy's in more trouble than you know. So is everyone else. All the puppets."

His shoulder muscles tensed up. "What? Why?"

"It's a long story. Here, it's getting cold; let's go somewhere warm. Lewis, my friend, his brother lives just across the way."

Vince turned in the direction I was pointing. "Is it safe?"

"The brother, Dominique hates aliens, but I think he trusts me."

Vince gave me a look of disgust. "You think he trusts you? Kindle, no."

"He's going to be worried and come looking for me. With a gun."

Vince looked sick. "Fine. But it better be as warm as you say it is. Oh, and did you find the antidote, the vaccine, I left in the pod?"

"I remember everything, don't I? Yeah, Lewis must have given me it in the pod. Why did you leave it there?"

"For you. I made Poppy chase you into a pod. I hoped this would work. Thankfully I didn't keep too much in there. An overdose quickly becomes fatal."

"Oh."

"I know. Now tell me about the danger Poppy's in."

I shook my head. There was too much to explain. "When we get there."

Dominique swung open the door when we got close, the gun still in his arms. Lewis was lurking behind him.

"I told you," I said. "This is my brother, Vince."

"Uh, hi," Vince said, eyeing the gun warily. It occurred to me then that Vince had never talked to anyone outside the family before. "Um, Earth is nice."

Dominique frowned but stepped aside to let us in. "Are there going to be more of you?"

"No, it's just him," I said.

"And we need to leave now," Vince said. "My sister's in trouble."

"Poppy?" Lewis said.

Vince looked at him strangely. "How did you know that? No, you must be Lewis, my sister's friend."

"That's right."

"Then thanks."

"Eh, she's saved my life. I think we're even now."

"I wouldn't expect anything less." Vince turned to me. "So, what's this rebellion you're talking about?"

Explaining the apocalypse that was happening back in space was the hardest and most mortifying thing I had to do. I told everyone how the escape plan Lewis and I had found on the beach was actually an escape plan I had used years ago that resulted in everyone except Lewis and Dominique burning to death. Dominique swore and stormed off in anger.

Meanwhile, Vince had a mile-long stare and his voice matched. "This is terrible." Suddenly he slammed his hands on the kitchen table we were gathered around. "Do you know what happened last time? Everyone. Died." He turned away. "No, this can't be happening. I'm not rescuing anyone from this mess. Not again. I'm getting Poppy and leaving. That's all." He kicked over his chair before storming off too.

I turned around and ran after him. I found him by the front door, face hidden in the crook of his elbow. I didn't need a better look to know he was crying. Despite turning away from me, I saw the way his shoulders bounced and heard him gasping for air.

Although we weren't a touchy family, I wrapped my arms around his shoulders. "I'm so sorry, Vince. Please, tell me."

He shook his head, causing his chest to rattle harder.

"Vince…I know I screwed up, but I want to make things right this time. Please, Vince—"

He shook his head, causing his shoulders to rattle harder. "We were only kids," he said so quietly I almost missed it. "I was barely a teenager when Mother and Father found out about your rebellion. I didn't even know. I—I had to watch it. I was stuck in a stone room, a tiny room, and the air and walls were getting hotter. No matter how hard I plugged my ears, all I could hear were the screams of burning puppets, burning people. Nobody was spared. They couldn't help themselves. They literally walked straight into the flames through Mother while Father choked the rest. Then at the end, you were gone, and Poppy didn't remember anything. I was all alone surrounded by parents who pretended it didn't happen. They hid questions with smiles and whispered threats. I watched as they rebuilt their empire." A tiny sob escaped. "And I didn't know where you were. If you were dead or alive."

Vince looked gutted like he'd just thrown up. I stepped back. He'd been the toughest one out of us. My personal rock, yet all this time he was fighting this. No wonder he wanted to leave home so bad.

"I…I don't know what to say, Vince."

"That's why you're right. I can't do this again. We have to do something. We have to stop the Puppeteer and the Ventriloquist."

I gasped. I had never heard Vince call our parents that before. But I understood. They could no longer be Mother and Father. They were the Puppeteer and the Ventriloquist. And this rebellion might just be the hardest thing I'd ever do. It might just kill me.

We did end up making a plan that night and re-tweaking it the next morning for an idea Dominique came up with. Since he still couldn't sleep from the controller, he had spent the most time reviewing the plan. In the end, our plan went like this:

First, Vince would repair the pods. Dominique had taken pictures of his work, but Vince said he'd done it all wrong. Heated words were exchanged before Dominique finally let Vince fix it.

Second, Vince and I would take one pod while Lewis and Dominque took the other. We would head back to Aroramere.

And third, we'd stop the Puppeteer and the Ventriloquist. Somehow. Something with the gold liquid Vince had brought.

And lastly, take every puppet back with the use of the remaining escape UFOs.

Chapter 24

Vince leaned back in his seat. I sat next to him, my shaking legs and occasionally bumping into his. If he noticed, he didn't say anything.

I had quickly learned that "driving" the UFO was nothing more than pushing a few buttons on a screen and letting it go.

I pressed down on my knees to stop some of the shaking while he continued to stare at the radar that showed Lewis and Dominique's spaceship as a blip, blasting through empty space with us. Dominique had been mad that I was the one who came up with the previous plan that nearly killed him years ago. But Lewis finally redirected his brother's anger at the Puppeteer and Ventriloquist instead.

Vince cleared his throat and looked at me. "Do you remember how to use your powers?"

Up to the point where I used it on Dominique, I hadn't attempted anything unless controlling the sock snake in the caves counted and runaway

Galaxy back on the beach. But I didn't know what I was doing then. My power is a genetic connector wrapping me and the Puppeteer together, and I wanted nothing to do with her.

"I do, but I never want to again."

Vince sputtered. "Why not? How do you expect to get through the plan or life without it? What if you need to use it?"

"It ties us to our parents."

"And so does our blond hair and gray eyes. Whatcha going to do? Chop it off and dye it?"

"Why not? You dyed your hair white."

Vince just sighed and shook his head.

We both turned to stare at a different half of the tiny ship. My blood boiled. How could Vince be this ignorant? Our species' powers were too strong. They weren't right. They weren't ethical. I itched to tell my ignorant brother this. To shake him until the truth slapped him across the face. We had to lose everything to start anew.

The screen Vince had used to punch in the coordinates was blinking. With whooshing noises, the pod slowed into Aroramere's atmosphere. Smoke rose from various spots in our house and an avalanche covered the front. Thankfully we weren't heading in that direction. Instead, we swung around to the back with the Ventriloquist's launchpad.

By this time, I had calmed down. No. That was a lie. I was still exploding on the inside, but I must have looked otherwise, for Vince gave me a small smile. I smiled back.

"I don't remember this place too well," Dominique said when we were on the ground. "So, what's first?"

"You and Lewis will try to round up as many uncontrolled puppets as possible," Vince said. "Get them to stop. Meanwhile, Kindle and I will find our parents and hope they haven't gone too far."

Too far. He didn't mean distance.

I tilted my head back as a breeze picked up, scattering a smoky smell this way. Might be too late for that.

"What?" Lewis said.

"Don't argue," Vince snapped back, but I think he was grateful someone challenged him. I would have been. At least then it wouldn't be all in his hands.

"But–"

"Shut up! Listen, Kindle and I have powers. You don't."

"Then I'm definitely not letting you guys go in alone." Lewis turned to me. "Kindle, don't do this."

But there was no way I wasn't doing this. I knew he wanted me to stay in his arms–but I wouldn't let Vince go in alone. As impossible as he was, he was still my older brother. One of the only good family I had left.

I reached over and squeezed his hand to scare away that thought. "I'll be fine."

"I need you to be."

"I'll be *fine*," I said harder, but I knew Lewis wasn't buying it.

I expected Vince to interject himself at any second, but he and Dominique had given us space to talk. My whole body had butterflies like I was going to have a heart attack. Kissing Lewis before hadn't felt like this. Before we knew we had each other. But this was war.

"Kindle," Lewis said. "I love you."

I sniffed. "I love you too."

He kissed me like it would glue us together at the lips.

I pulled away. "You know that won't make me stay."

He smiled. "It was worth a try."

I looked back to my brother rolling his eyes. "Shut up, loner. Let's go."

I led us toward the blue room, the room I had first woken up to after being turned into a dummy. It was untouched, just a long room of blue. Not even Voice, Father's dog, was there. As I unlocked the door to the house, the deepening pit in my stomach told me something was off, but the air was getting too bitter with smoke to argue.

I crept into the family dining room with Vince breathing down my neck. The puppets had already been through. Everything from the wall décor to the table was smashed. A salad was scattered across the floor like green confetti. The smell of a raspberry vinaigrette was strong.

Were they eating when the rebellion happened? Were they scared? Did they feel vulnerable? Powerless? Was Poppy with them? And if so, where was she now? Probably scared out of a mind she didn't own.

Leaving Vince behind, I peered into the kitchen. The fridge had been pushed aside to reveal the pit. At least someone got out. Would the Puppeteer and the Ventriloquist really recruit old failures? No. They wouldn't stoop that low.

Vince shouted in pain. I swung around, arms outstretched. Vince was crumpled on the ground, holding his head. Ashley stood behind him with what looked like an axe with the blade removed, ready for swing number two.

"No, stop!" I shouted a split-second before using my power to make her freeze.

"What the–? Who's got me?"

I stepped closer. Her face flushed with relief before recoiling. "What? How are you doing that?"

"Don't freak out," I said even though she couldn't if she wanted to, "but I'm not exactly…human."

"What?" Her eyes did what her body wanted to–shudder. "No. How could you do this to us? You…you lead us into this!"

Vince groaned as he got up. "We're trying to help you, rod."

"You okay?" I asked.

"Dang. Yeah. I mean, yes." He removed his hand to study his hand. "An acquaintance of yours?"

"She's the head rod. Or she was until Lin took over."

"Who? Another boyfriend of yours?"

I made a face. "Jesus, no." I turned to Ashley who was attempting to hold her breath until she fainted. "Stop that." She didn't. "Stop that before I have to slap you. And I really don't want to do that." Luckily, she abandoned her little charade before I finished that sentence. "This is my brother, Vince. He's on our side. We're trying to stop our…our parents."

"Okay. Fine. Just let me go," Ashley said.

I let her go. My hands were already cramping. Vince moved his hands in case she ran again, but all Ashley did was flinch.

"So…why didn't you tell us you were an alien?"

I wanted to say she was the alien but was sick of that back and forth.

"I didn't know. Not until I vanished. I was sort of kidnapped by the Ventriloquist. My father."

"But you're still a dummy, right?" There was a tinge to her voice. Like she wanted me to say no.

"No. But I'm not sure how he did it."

"What's…what's it like?"

"Being an alien?" Vince snorted.

"No…" Ashley's voice softened. "Being free." The word "free" struggled out, making her face contort.

I wanted to say that I still wasn't free. Not with the Puppeteer and the Ventriloquist still around. But that wouldn't help. I had to stop being a Negative Nancy if I wanted her to fight for me.

"It feels…great," I finally settled on.

She nodded. "So, what now? Where's Lewis? Is he all right?"

"Fine. He saved me."

"He said he would."

My face heated, and my cheeks twitched for a smile I didn't have time for.

"What were you doing here?" Vince said. "Where's the Puppeteer?"

"She's here in this weird second house. It must be where she lives…but I suppose you know that. It's the hole Lewis went through to find you. We've already knocked it down. But that's when things went wrong." She buried her face in her hands. "God, Kindle, she knew we were coming. I don't know how."

I swallowed. She didn't, but she wouldn't let that show. "Let's go, Vince." I turned back to Ashley. "Go find the other puppets. They're evacuating. I don't know where though." We should have really talked this through.

"Good luck," Ashley said.

A loud bang echoed. It took down the paintings.

My head felt eclectic, and my breathing was gone as the room shook, letting the last few wall décor fall. I tried to focus on everything at once, but everything was scattered. The walls, the furniture, the smell of smoke. Ashley took off running, clutching her headless axe and Vince was gripping my upper arm, nearly breaking bones.

The numbness inside of me broke when Vince jerked me away from the wall. "We have to go." Although his posture was steel, his eyes quivered.

If I could melt through the walls and take him with me, I would have, but he was stronger than I could ever be as he tugged me along, still with a viper grip.

Tripping over my feet, my ears rang from the explosion. Any second there could be another, and we were running straight for it.

It wasn't long before I was right. We were in the living room–a dark splash against the blinding white hallways. The Ventriloquist was pressed against the back wall, his toy collection scattered across the floor. He had the couch in front of him for protection. Or at least previous protection. He had the upper hand, literally. His hands were raised and about a dozen dummies were on the floor, grabbing at their throats. I remembered the way it felt–struggling, red, suffocating–as Vince let go of my hand. I spun back into insecurity.

"Father!" Vince shouted.

The Ventriloquist turned his head only a few inches. "Vince? Kindle? Go! Get out of here!"

"No, Father." I froze. Holy crap, did I actually say something? I wanted Father to turn against me. To use his powers on me so I could slink back into the corner and let Vince take over.

By the look on his face, my tone had gotten through. I had just told him to get lost and he wasn't going to take it.

A dummy flung a grenade-like thing at him. It hit the shelf above and a white powder rained down. The Ventriloquist screamed a scream no child should hear their father scream. My heart leaped back into my throat as blisters formed against his neck. Snow. They were throwing snowballs. Just like the plan said.

The dummy wound back another snowball, but this time at Vince. I screamed. My heart ballooned. The Ventriloquist was still cowering, holding his blistering face and neck. But then a blur pushed him out of the way and took the snowball to the back instead. I flinched, turning away at Vince's startled cry. When I glanced back, Lewis was blocking Vince with his body. I bit my tongue at Lewis' disobedience, but whatever. I had to get Vince out of there before they had time to get more snowballs which I couldn't help but notice was getting slushy. Still, cold water would hurt as well.

I grabbed Vince by his jacket's hood making him gag. Vince pinwheeled back as Lewis and I yanked him again. The puppet, who I now recognized as Adam the dummy, scampered back to the small table, still clutching the snow in a way that made me shudder. His face suddenly turned red, and he fell forward, crashing into the others. Father had his hands outstretched and was twisting and turning.

Vince reached out his hands, but Father flinched. Lottie had a snowball, her eyes on Adam.

I was controlling Vince now as I moved for the doorway. We should never have come in. We were too weak. The Ventriloquist was too powerful.

When Lewis, Vince, and I were far away from the violence, I dropped Vince's hood. His teeth were gritted.

"What was that for? I had him. I had Father."

It was refreshing to hear him say "Father" instead of "the Ventriloquist," to know I wasn't the only one ping-ponging.

"No, you didn't!" I shouted. "He didn't even flinch, not to mention you were about to be creamed with snow."

"It wouldn't have hurt that bad. I could have taken it."

I wanted to kick him in the shin and ask him how bad that hurt, but I shook my anger out. "We need to give Mother and Father the brainwashing liquid. The gold stuff the Puppeteer slipped in our tea." I nodded at my bag.

"Isn't the Ventriloquist still too powerful?" Lewis asked.

I turned to him. "You. I can't believe you came. You were supposed to be with Dominique getting puppets away from my parents."

"Dominique can handle that. I was standing around doing nothing. And, besides, I knew it was only time before you two hotheads got into trouble."

While I was trying to come up with something in response, Vince shook his head. "Thanks for coming, but it's going to be dangerous from here on."

"I'm fine," Lewis stated, voice like steel. The back of his shirt where his control was was soaked. "You'll need me."

"Yes, but what we also need is a sibling that can control voices. A powerful one." My mind broke out a list of siblings with that rare ability. "Pippa, Etta…uh…"

Vince got to his feet amidst my rambling. "Poppy."

"Poppy?" I shrieked.

"She's the strongest voice controller out of them all. That's why our parents went through all that trouble to protect her. She's a weapon."

"But…but she's brainwashed!"

Vince poked the bag with the golden liquid in it. "But with this, we can fix her. It worked on you, didn't it?"

I crossed my arms. "All right. Where do you think Poppy is?"

Vince was already taking great strides down the hallway, which was slowly turning into a run. "Where do you think she is, thin head?"

The garden.

Vince stopped hard at the hallway that branched off toward the spot Father had taken us fishing. His shout was like a gunshot. I ducked, heart racing.

"Stop!" Vince was running forward again like he'd never stopped in the first place.

Now that he was out of the way I could see rows and rows of marionettes lined up like they were marching in a parade. Behind them were mine carts filled with rods who were holding the sides like Mora used to do when Tiffany took us grocery shopping. They kicked and screamed, but their grip was too tight. The puppets were being marched to the hole Father had nearly fallen through. The hole that led to Earth.

There was only one person evil enough to do this.

Mother.

"Vince!" I ran into the crowd.

Between the gaps puppets I caught glimpses of her.

Vince came to me, his body language like he was on extra shots of caffeine. "She's marching them toward the pit. The place where you went fishing. It isn't a pond."

"It's space," I could barely say.

Vince nodded so hard his neck might have snapped. "We've got to get Poppy now."

My heart beat toxins into my blood. "Do we have time?"

Vince pushed past me. "Not much."

As Vince led Lewis and me to the garden, "not much" kept pounding through my veins. How much was not much? How much was not enough?

I never got an answer as Vince popped open the hatch to the garden with ease. He slid down the ladder and I followed. If I had thought the garden was a safe haven, I was wrong.

Flowers were tossed aside, and the ground was ripped up like giant claw marks. There wasn't a single space that screamed of the beauty the garden had before. Surely Mother and Father wouldn't do this?

Every hair stood as hissing came from the other side of the garden. From a large mound of dirt rose that stupid sock snake.

How? How did it get here? No. I wasn't this dumb. This had Father written all over it. Trying to protect his precious daughter from who he truly was. Even if it meant killing her. But where was his precious daughter?

"What is that thing?" Vince was pointing at the sock snake. My swirling mind had abandoned that long ago.

"Some kind of sock puppet snake. I saw it before when I was a marionette."

Vince's mouth was still hanging with questions, but he shook his head. "There's Poppy!"

"What about the–?"

Vince ripped the bag off my shoulder, the leather burning my skin. He ran zigzags away from the snake–like that would help. I could barely breathe. He had left me to die.

Vince spun around, waving his arms toward the snake. "Cover me, stupid!"

Okay. He didn't know anything about me. Cover him? Like he thought I was a superhero?

Powers didn't mean anything. He thought we were so powerful compared to humans, but that didn't mean anything.

A chill spread over me at the thought of Vince turning back and seeing me still standing there, so I started speed-walking but found myself running, legs fully extended for the sock puppet. It hadn't noticed Vince, but it had noticed me as it reared up.

Screaming, I held my hands out like I was holding a marionette controller for the snake. It hesitated only a second before breaking free. Dang, how did I control this before? Where was its nervous system? Where did the strings go? Wasn't it just one big spine?

"Get back, Lewis. I've got this."

"What can I do?"

"Get to safety."

He gave me a look. "I'm not leaving you."

"Fine, then help Lewis. You made the antidote work once. You can do it again."

Lewis nodded and ran after Vince. Although I didn't think Vince needed help or that Lewis could but couldn't let him near this murderous creature.

This snake…it's just a spine. You don't need a four-string controller. You just need two.

Holding my hands out, I imagined two strings. One in the front and one in the back. I imagined each string as a separate nerve. Feeling full control, I slammed the snake down. Then again, and again, and again until it fell still.

I dropped the fake controller and stumbled to my knees then my back. My arms ached so much I couldn't lift them. All I could do was stare at a ceiling painted the wrong shade of "Earth-sky blue."

If someone had told me a year back that I would be doing magic, I would have laughed in their face. Now I was laughing at a poorly painted sky after defeating a sock puppet.

With that last thought, I sat back up. Vince and Lewis were heading this way. Poppy rode on Lewis' controller while Vince trailed with one hand holding up Poppy's head which wavered like a drunk's. We met somewhere in the middle of the garden where Vince practically flung Poppy at me. I caught her ragdoll body by the collarbone, then under the armpits.

"Next time," I huffed, "you get the controlling part. That hurt."

Vince caught Poppy's other arm to dish me without batting an eye. "You're just rusty. You were actually quite powerful before you left."

I snorted as we began our one-two walk back to the ladder. There, Lewis pushed a bench for Poppy to be on. Stretched out, she started showing signs of consciousness—moaning and tossing.

"Poppy?" I kneeled beside her, remembering when we were kids, and a skinned knee was the end of the world. "Poppy, you need to wake up, so we can see if you're concussed." Vince was shaking his head, but I wanted to see for myself. I was the better doctor out of the two of us.

"I am awake!" Poppy blurted. She sat up and wobbled. Good. No concussion. "Woah. I'm really awake. Where am I? And who are you?" Her head bobbed toward Lewis.

"The garden." Vince squatted down to our level. "Listen, I gave you some medicine. You're going to get a lot of strange memories fast. Memories about Mother and Father that you don't want, and frankly we don't have time to explain. We need your help to–"

I was going to tell him this was too much for her when Poppy spoke.

"Stop them," she whispered. She looked ill. "I may not know what's going on, but I know it's them. The last time they ripped up the garden was to execute all those puppets." Poppy put her face in her hands and moaned. "All those humans. Oh, all these memories. They hurt. I want them to end."

"You're not going to be able to stop the memories," I said, "but you can stop Mother and Father."

Poppy nodded. "Everyone always said I was gifted for a reason, and I guess that reason's now. Take me to them, Kindle."

I was about to tell her to rest and take it easy when Vince started doing the opposite, herding her toward the ladder. I guess "not much" time was officially up.

We hurried back to the room where Mother and Father were marching the puppets towards the hole. They screamed and yelled while Mother and Father were braced against the back wall, talking as if over a meal. I grit my teeth. Soon, though, this would be all over. Once we gave them the liquid, they would remember none of this. They would just be normal parents.

But first, we had to force the stuff down their throats.

I turned to grab Lewis' hand. "You stay here, Lewis. I'm serious."

He opened his mouth but closed it. "Yeah. You're right. I trust you."

Vince stepped forward first, looking like the hero the puppets wanted me to be. Poppy followed, glancing back at me, calling me to hurt the people I loved. Yes, I *had* loved my parents at one point even if they did make selfish choices, even if they thought everything had a rewind button. And maybe I still did.

Vince called their names and Poppy turned away from me.

"Poppy!" Father yipped, his neck had blisters blooming like flowers. "Go back, poppet. This is a dream."

"Forget it, Father!" Poppy yelled. "I'm not naive anymore. I can see what you've done. Kindle was right all along way before any of this. You take these poor humans and—Ack!"

Father had his hands out and Poppy was clutching her throat.

Vince swore. "You help Poppy with Father; I'll see if I can get Mother on her knees so I can feed her the antidote."

He charged for Mother who was probably stunned by his dirty mouth. She held out her arms cautiously like she was expecting a hug from a snake. Vince wasn't. He punched her in the stomach. God, how great that must have felt. It was an all-out brawl with Mother fighting to get off her knees as Vince forced her limbs downward and Father was choking the ground as Poppy got the upper hand. But Vince wasn't going to hold Mother by himself and give her the antidote.

I tried to run, but my limbs stayed in place, but out of fear and panic. It was my time. My time to pick a side. My parents, or the puppets? I had once told Lewis I was a sheepdog and the puppets were my flock, and I still felt that rage. I pushed through the parade of puppets until I was beside Vince. I held my hands out and forced Mother onto her stomach.

"Hold it!" Vince shouted; his powers still focused on Mother. "This is going to hurt."

For a second, I thought he was talking to Mother and Father, but he wasn't. As soon as he let go of his hold on Mother, lightning shot through my arms. There was a bubble growing between Mother and me. It was growing and I couldn't push it back.

My arms were stretching. Vince finally got the bottle and started for Mother.

"No!" I gasped. "Get Father!"

From the corner of my spotty eyesight, Poppy and Father were engaged in a choking battle. Their hands outstretched, using their magic to clog each other's windpipe.

I didn't see Vince leave, but suddenly I heard Father sputtering as Vince poured the antidote down his throat. I was dizzy in the head as Mother tried to get on her knees.

"Kindle!"

My name? I strained my ears back. It was the only thing I could physically do without losing my magical grip on Mother.

"Kindle! Kindle! Kindle!"

Lewis. He was starting a chant. Then Ashley. Even Lin. Then the whole room. Screaming, I held on. I held on through the pain that had captured my whole body. I held on through the fatigue and the will to die. Vince was in front of me with the antidote toward Mother, but I couldn't even keep my eyes open anymore. If I let my grip go then it was the end. At least it had been a nice ride.

"Now!" Vince shouted. The connection between Mother and I broke. I slumped back into Poppy's arms. Mother and Father were on the ground.

"Rest, Kindle," she said. "It's over now."

Tears spilled without my control. "It is?"

Poppy was crying too. "Mother and Father will wake up without remembering anything. We'll have to start over, but we'll be better."

Better. The word felt like a roaring fire on a cold day. It felt like Earth. It felt like my siblings. It felt like Lewis. It felt like home at last.

As I stayed wrapped in Poppy's arms, I saw Vince sneak over to my parents. He watched their pale faces, his lips turned up in disgust.

"How…?" I staggered. "How much did you give them?" They didn't look right. They didn't look.

No. Don't think it. Don't think that word.

…alive.

"Enough," Vince said, eyes like steel. "They won't be kidnapping anyone ever again."

"Because they forgot," Poppy said.

I tipped my head back to see her biting her bottom lip. I couldn't tell if she knew or not. Maybe it was for the better that she didn't. I met Vince's eyes and nodded.

He did what needed to be done.

No more. No less.

"Now, let's get to those escape pods!" Lewis cried, swinging a fist into the air.

Epilogue

I wrapped a second towel around my bathing suit and exposed skin. Miami's salty air and gull cries brought through the laughter of Vince and Poppy. They had never seen the ocean and so far, it seemed to be a big hit. I opened my eyes as sand squeaked nearby. Tiffany was busy racing some of the teens down the beach, teaching them how to run now that they weren't puppets, getting them back into shape. Vince waved a flag at the finish line through pages of a book. He seemed to really like Earth fantasy. I wasn't sure what had happened to Lin or Ashley when they got back. Further down the beach, Poppy was planting seagrass on the dunes with Galaxy who stared at the plant hungrily. Voice, my father's dog, ran back and forth between Adam and Lottie.

The last few months were hard. All the puppet people, including the shadow puppets and jig dolls, were flown back to Earth. It was a beautiful reunion not only with nature again but with family. Every last puppet was reunited with family all across the globe. Thousands of teenagers had come back from space.

Lewis and Dominique were still up in Kansas but were working on moving down here with their parents so Lewis would be closer to me. It was a happy reunion–him and his parents. They were so loving and welcoming, obsessing over Lewis and Dominique now that they knew the latter was telling the truth. And of course, he still came down here to see me. We were still going strong even if he got a lot of hate for it. Eventually, he wanted to move to Florida to be closer to me. And bring Galaxy of course. Galaxy had been one of the first to be transformed back by me, and Lewis and Dominique were helping her get on her feet. Thankfully, Dominique had moved on from hating my kind.

As for Mother and Father…nobody talked about them. And after a while, when I looked at Vince's eyes, I could see warmth in them again. We never spoke directly about it, but I would always make sure to pay extra attention to him. As for Poppy, I wasn't sure if she knew, but I had my suspicions. This made Vince and I swear to tell her the whole truth if she asked one day. We weren't going to be like the Puppeteer and the Ventriloquist because we were a real family. A rough family. A tough family. The three of us. As for the rest of my siblings, we never heard back after we left. They had moved back to our home planet. Well, not my home planet. For me, Earth was enough.

<u>Author's Note</u>

Thank you for reading *Puppet People.* If you enjoyed it, remember to leave a review. Reviews let other people find my book to enjoy as well.

If you want another adventure, try my first book *The Door in My Hand* which is about a famous teen daredevil who finds a door growing in her hand and must find a way to stop a monster from stepping through.